THE JUSTICE CHRONICLES

BY

ERIN WILSON

I dedicate this book to my parents who taught me the love of books and reading. And to my beautiful Joycelyn for her encouragement and support

PARALLEL JUSTICE

ONE

California desert 1890

The first bullet buzzed his head like an angry
bee, followed by the report of the rifle. When the
second shot kicked up sand in front of him, Evan was
already digging his spurs and heading for the hills to
his right. He leaned low over the horse's neck and
looked back over his shoulder. The sight of the Indian
warriors charging after him was strangely, a
magnificent picture. Riding four across, with long,
black hair flowing out behind them, the buck warriors
had a presence of fierce power unleashed. Their
images shimmering in the desert heat made them
almost dreamlike or nightmarish. Evan looked ahead
to the low, rock covered ridge, his fearful eyes
desperately searching for escape.

He was lucky to have something to ride
toward. The past few days in the desert had not
surrendered much shelter. Sweltering hot days and
bone chilling cold nights had been his only
companions. With nothing to see for miles around but
scrub, rocks and cactus, Death Valley was aptly
named.

He could hear the rifle shots, but didn't have too much fear of the bullets. To aim straight from a galloping horse at four hundred yards was difficult at best, but anyone can get lucky. He looked again over his shoulder to see they had not gained much ground. Evan was thankful he had not pushed his horse too much in the past few days. He was going to need every bit of energy it had.

The horse started up the hill, which slowed him considerably. It wasn't much of a hill really, more like a giant mole tunnel, running through the middle of the valley. It was fifty feet up to its highest point and covered with low brush. There were lots of boulders thrown randomly around, like giant hail stones from a distant past.

Evan zigzagged the horse left and right toward the top and a group of large rocks which he hoped would give some cover. The bullets were hitting closer to home now as the savage barbers closed the gap. He reached the top and found it to be twenty feet flat across before dropping down the other side. From the bottom of that side, he saw the desert continue on forever. He circled around behind a rock big enough to hide himself and his horse. There was another large boulder sitting perpendicular to his rock, so his instant fort had the appearance of the letter L. He grabbed his rifle and jumped off his horse. He scrambled up and

4

threw himself down on top of the rock, expecting to find his assailants charging up the hillside. Instead, he saw they had pulled up a hundred yards away, sitting and watching. They appeared to be having an argument, most likely, about what course of action to take. Of course they knew what was beyond this hill, nothing. Their horses were used to the desert. If he tried to keep running, they would eventually catch him or knock him out of the saddle with a lucky shot. More likely, though, his horse would just run out of life and they could walk right up and kill him at their leisure. The only question would be how to divide one scalp between the four of them. That option didn't seem particularly appealing to Evan, so he dug in and prepared to finish this one way or the other.

The sun was dropping on the western horizon and it was becoming harder to make out any detail, but the coming dusk did nothing to quench the heat rising from the valley floor. The temporary relief of the cold night air was still a couple hours away. He fired a couple shots in their general direction, hoping they might think better of attacking him and go home, but he knew different.

He watched as they moved off east and cut back to the base of the hill. In the final seconds of daylight, he saw them dismount and begin to make camp. There was a good and bad side to this. The good being that most Indians didn't like doing much at night as they believed that's when evil spirits were roaming about. The bad, was it meant they were in for the long haul and would probably be around when the sun came up in the morning. There were also four of them, so they could take turns watching him, while he would have to keep an all-night vigil for himself.

He slipped off his perch and went to the horse for his spyglass and some beef jerky. He patted the horse on the neck.

"Sorry old friend, I'm going to have to leave you saddled and ready to go tonight."

He reached into his saddle bag for a handful of oats and held it up for the horse to eat. Unwinding the strap of a canteen from his saddle horn, he poured some into his hand for the horse, before tilting some for himself.

He untied his blanket from the back of the saddle, climbed back up onto his rock and looked through his spyglass to the Indian encampment. In the darkness, he could make out their small fire and thought about how cold the coming night would be. Evan could only make out three figures in the dark. He swept his vision to the left and came spyglass to spyglass with their lookout. The Indian was actually grinning at him. Evan shuddered. The brave had war

6

paint streaked down one cheek to offset the ragged scar on the other, like two bloody rivers flowing from his eyes.

Evan gathered his blanket around him as best he could and settled in for the long vigil. As he lay there, his mind drifted back to where this journey had begun. Deep in thought, tears began to well in his eyes.

TWO

The McLaughlin family moved out west in the spring of 1874. Theirs was a family of merchants and when news arrived that Angus McLaughlin had died of a heart attack while sweeping the front stoop of his general store, his only living brother, James, being the optimistic son, decided this was a sign that it was time to give his own family a new start. He struck a deal with his neighbor for his own small store, sold or gave away most of the families meager belongings, and with a couple trunks full of clothes and personal items, boarded a train heading west. His usually composed and steady wife looked back on their small South Carolina home with more than a little trepidation. Their energetic, five year old daughter, Mary, however, could hardly contain her excitement. If it were possible, her emerald green eyes were sparkling even more than usual, as she had her head mashed against the train window, watching an all new world pass by.

They arrived in Nevada City, a small, quaint, little town nestled near the base of the eastern Sierra Nevada mountain range. While Mrs. McLaughlin went about cleaning and making Angus's house their own home, James reopened the store and the family settled in to their new surroundings. The town welcomed them with open arms and it wasn't long till

Mary's infectious happiness and free spirit made her the darling of everyone she met.

The first time Mary met Evan Longview, she was six years old. He came into her father's store one Saturday morning to pick up supplies with his father. He was three years older than Mary with shaggy black hair and dark eyes hinting of mischief. He was tall for his age and even then you could see he was going to be a handsome man.

When he walked by her sitting on a barrel, eating a stick of candy, he tipped his dusty hat to her, smiled and said, "hello, ma'am." She giggled shyly, jumped off the barrel and ran to the back of the store.

It wasn't till another year passed that Evan and Mary became regular friends, their encounters being limited to an occasional passing in the store with the usual smiles and giggles. When Mary turned seven, her mother convinced her father that she needed to get educated. Seeing the restless nature of his beautiful daughter, he easily agreed and Mary began going to school.

****

The Longview family had been in Nevada City for a while now. Grandpa George Longview had been one of the earlier sheep herders that came from New

Mexico to supply sheep to the hungry miners heading for the California gold rush. When he had died in 1866, his young son and wife moved into the main house with their new baby son, Evan, and took over the family business.

Floyd Longview was not an overly ambitious man, and so was content to make a decent life for his family. There was always a need for good sheep wool and meat, and so through a couple draughts, some heavy winters and a few bouts with rustlers, the Longview's tightened their belts, worked hard and survived. Longview *did* understand the desire for his son have a better life, and so when Evan turned 10, Floyd worked even harder and sent his son off to school each day.

Most of the girls and some of the boys, whose parents allowed it, shared the single room school house at the edge of town. As their ages varied, most of the students sat in groups of children close to their own age. Even within his own age group, young Evan Longview chose to sit separate by himself. On the first day of school, Mary spotted Evan sitting across the room and waved frantically till she got his attention. He smiled shyly and gave a little wave back. During the first recess, Mary found Evan sitting under the shade of a large pine tree.

"What are you doing?"

"Just thinking."

"About what?"

"What work I'm missing at home."

"You'd rather be working at home?"

"You ask a lot of questions."

"Well, you don't say very much."

When the bell rang to end recess, Mary gave Evan a quick wave and turned to run back to the school. After the first day, Mary would often sit with Evan during the recess, sometimes talking, sometimes just sitting quietly. At the lunch break, Evan would go back to his tree and eat the sparse lunch he brought every day. Mary would usually run down the street to her father's store and eat lunch with him on the front step or play with the other kids until the bell rang for class.

For the next few years life held pretty steady. Though it remained a peaceful place to live, the sleepy little ranch town began to grow, especially when a rich gentleman from back east bought a large ranch west of town. He also bought one of the hotels in town and began to renovate it into a dance hall and gambling establishment.

Francis Johnston came west to Nevada, after an altercation with a local police constable in St Louis. Seems the constable didn't like Johnston groping his sister, a waitress in a popular, drinking establishment. In the ensuing scuffle, after beating the policeman to within an inch of his life, Francis finished him off by stomping on his neck, breaking it and killing the young man. Despite the family money and standing in the community, Johnston's father figured it might be a good time for him to head west and start his own empire elsewhere. So with his young wife and nine year old son in tow, Francis caught the next train out of town. They ultimately settled in the sleepy community of Nevada City and began to buy, bully and take, a huge section of the county, becoming one of the largest land owners west of the Rockies.

It was clear from the beginning that Lucias Johnston was as mean and cruel as his father. On his first day at school, he managed to anger the teacher, scare most of the girls and alienate himself from all but a few of the boys. The ones that followed him about mostly felt it better to stay on his good side than to go against him. At twelve years old, he had thin, dirty looking hair, a large mole on his nose and a

12

mouth that even when he was smiling gave him a dark, sinister look.

One day, during the lunch time, Lucias snuck up on some unsuspecting girls and took away the ball they were playing catch with. As most of them cowered away in fear, one girl, Mary McLaughlin, stood in front of him.

"Give us back our ball!" she demanded.

"Whoa, what's this? Aren't you a feisty one, and pretty also"

Mary lunged forward to grab at the ball, "give it back."

Lucias put his hand on Mary's head and held her away, laughing out loud, "come on little one, let's dance." He quickly pulled his hand away and Mary fell forward, sprawling awkwardly on the ground. Lucias stood over her, laughing.

Suddenly, he felt a presence behind him. He turned to find Evan Longview standing over him, "why don't you pick on someone your own size?"

Looking up at the older, taller boy, Lucias didn't back down. "Why don't you mind your own business?"

"She is my business." Evan snarled and took another step closer.

Lucias looked into the taller boys eyes. Not being afraid, but like most bullies, sensing when he is at a disadvantage, Lucias gave Evan a nasty smile and turned to walk away, throwing the ball back over his shoulder.

Evan leaned down to help Mary to her feet. Throwing her arms around him, she giggled, "my hero."

"You should stay clear of him."

Mary looked up into his face, "why… I have you to watch over me?"

Evan looked down at Mary for a second, a small smile beginning to turn up his lips. The bell rang for class and the moment was broken. They turned and walked together to the classroom.

When Mary turned thirteen, her mother decided she needed to get a little more sophistication and smoothing of the edges. So with much crying and many tears, Mary was put on a train and sent back to Charleston, South Carolina. A few years with a wealthy Aunt would help to make her a polished, grown up woman.

As soon as Mary left town, Evan took a horse and rode up into the mountain, tears streaming from his cheeks.

When Evan turned seventeen, he stopped going to school and began taking on most of the heavy work around the family ranch. He was repairing a broken fence post out in the pasture, when he heard the loud clanging of the porch bell. It was usually used to call for dinner, but as it was only midafternoon, Evan stood and looked questioningly back towards the house. He could see his mom standing on the front porch, waving a towel above her head to get his attention. Sensing something was wrong, Evan dropped his tools and began running to the house. As he got within range, he could hear his mother saying something about his father.

He was out of breath as he reached the porch, "What's wrong…. Where's pa?"

She turned and led the way into the house. "He's in the living room, lying on the couch. I was in the kitchen when he came staggering in from the barn. He just collapsed, muttering something about feeling weak. I checked and he has a very hot fever, Evan."

Floyd Longview was sprawled out on the couch with his eyes closed and his breathing ragged.

There was saliva at the sides of his mouth. Evan felt the cold hand of fear wash over his body.

"Evan, go to town and get the doctor... hurry!"

Evan hesitated for a second, still staring at his stricken father, and then turned and bolted out the door. He sprinted to the barn and grabbed one of their two horses. He didn't bother with a bridle or saddle; he just jumped on and rode the two miles to town as fast as the horse would go.

When he got to town, though, he couldn't reach the doctor. There was a small crowd of people blocking his front office door. Mrs. Golden, from the diner next door, saw his distraught face and said the doctor was really busy with three patients who had come to his office in various states of illness.

"My pa is really sick also... he needs the doc!"

But the doctor never did make it to Evan's home. He too succumbed to the mysterious virus that swept through the quiet, little town. No one really ever knew what happened or what caused the sickness. It might have been a contagious, passing cowpoke or something that just blew in off the eastern plain. In the end, it claimed more than twenty people from town and the surrounding valley, including Evan's father and mother. It also took James McLaughlin, the store keeper.

To live and survive in the west, you needed toughness and strength, so after a period of mourning, the town began to gather its spirits back and looked to the future once again. Mrs. McLaughlin was determined to keep her husband's work alive, and so wrote to her sister to send Mary home. She was needed.

Evan also, after time, went back to work. Mending fences, tending to his sheep and working to make the house he now inherited his home.

One Saturday morning, while in town to pick up supplies for the ranch, Evan came out the front door of the store and almost knocked over a young lady making her way up the stairs. She had on a beautiful flowered dress that perfectly complimented her fiery red hair and green eyes.

"Excuse me…. I didn't see….Mary?"

"Hello Evan."

THREE

Nevada City 1887

A magnificent sunset was beginning to show itself on the western horizon. And though the reddish, purple clouds were a splendor to see, they also seemed to carry a subtle warning of ominous events to follow. The main street was surprisingly quiet, except for the festively lit Grand Hotel in the middle of the block. A few well dressed, stragglers made their way in through the front doors. The music of celebration wafted out as they entered the open door.

Inside, the main ballroom was decorated with banners and flowers. A small band of musicians was working away in the corner. Most of the town had turned out for this wedding. Evan Longview and Mary Mclaughlin had been seeing each other since their school days. They were well liked, and seemed to have a solid, happy future in front of them. There were a few couples dancing, but most of the people were standing in small groups around the room, awaiting the arrival of the newlyweds.

A few local ladies gossiped conspiratorially in one corner.

"It's about time these two got married. They've been sweethearts since grade school"

"He's such a nice boy. They make quite the handsome couple. He just dotes on her. I heard he spread flowers all along the road to his farmhouse."

"Really! How sweet. Well I hope she can cook. Good cooking is how you keep your man happy and at home, that and a little fun in the dark...."

Their husbands were smoking cigars and speaking in another corner.

"He's a lucky lad, she's quite the filly"

"I hope she can cook. That is so important in a successful marriage."

"Good thing he's a hard worker. That ranch of his could be profitable, but it's going to take all the effort they can muster."

The music stopped, and conversation dropped to a low murmur as the Preacher stepped to front of the room.

"Thank you. Now, it is my great pleasure to introduce to you, Mr. and Mrs. Evan Longview."

Mary appeared, her high cheek bones and deep green eyes the perfect partners to her flaming, red hair, piled high on her head. She was an angel in a white, floor length gown, bringing tears to the eyes of her still beautiful mother, who wore the same dress on her wedding day.

Though it was an inch too short in the sleeves and leg cuffs, Evan was equally dashing in his only black suit. His straight black hair was touching his shoulders and his deep black eyes are swimming with joy as he walked arm in arm with the only woman he had ever loved.

They moved around the room greeting and thanking everyone for coming. The music started back up and soon Evan and Mary made their way to the center of the room for their first official dance as a married couple.

As they swung around the room, Evan was looking into Mary's eyes with so much love and wonder, he felt like his heart was going to burst. He wondered how it was possible for someone to be so happy.

More couples began to fill the dance floor. The music flowed throughout the room. A young man approached and asked to cut in, Evan smiled graciously, gave Mary a quick kiss on the cheek and stepped aside.

As they moved off with the music, Evan made his way to the side where he was accosted by a small group of men.

"Congratulations Evan, my friend," a visibly intoxicated Lucias Johnston blurted, "I guess the best man has finally won the hand of the local princess."

"Go home, Lucias, your drunk."

Lucias turned a vicious face, "It should be me, you know. I can give her whatever she wants. What have you got to offer, a lifetime of digging in the dirt, chasing sheep around the farm? I can give her a life of leisure, a bigger house. Nice clothes."

"I can give her love, Lucias. A warm home, a happy home, something you and your family are sorely lacking. Your family may own half the land around this town, but you can't own the people who live here or their hearts.

Evan turned to the other men with Lucias, "Take him out of here, before I have him thrown out."

Evan turned and walked away, Lucias glared at his back, muttering.

"This ain't over, you haven't won anything. Nobody turns their back on me! Watch your back Longview."

Lucias looked around the room and seeing Mary dancing, he strode to her and roughly cut in.

"Lucias!" Mary exclaimed

"It should have been me," Lucias hissed, "I could've taken care of you, given you anything you wanted."

Mary cried out, "Lucias, your hurting me."

Pulling her close, Lucias tried to kiss her. "It's not too late. Be with a real man."

Suddenly Lucias is pulled away and spun around. Evan punched him in the face. Lucias staggered back, bleeding from his lip. He glared at Evan, breathing heavily. The room became deathly quiet. He looked around like a caged, wild animal. He slowly took a deep breath. Turning to Evan and Mary, his face twisted into a snarling smirk. Glancing once more around the room, he whirled and stomped out of the room with his posse following behind. Holding Mary in his arms, Evan signaled for the band to start up again. Slowly the dance floor began to fill up as the conversation started up and the festive noise again rose, though now with a somewhat more strained feel.

****

The small ranch house was nestled near the base of a mountain that formed the south end of Evan's property. The twenty acres that made up the spread stretch out beyond the front porch like a George Innes painting. The darkness was complete except for the single light coming from a front window. Evan and Mary were holding each other close and dancing a slow dance to the rhythm of their own humming. The only other guests are their shadows in the flickering candlelight joining them in the dance. They are at home after a long day of wedding festivities.

"You were the most beautiful bride ever today," Evan whispered as he nestled his face into Mary's neck.

"And you were the most handsome groom," she purred back.

Evan pulled back, looked Mary in the eyes and leaned down to kiss her lips. "It's getting late….."

The heat began to rise in Mary's face, "I'll just go and get ready for bed…. Give me a few minutes before you come in, okay?"

Evan, also slightly flustered, "I'll just step outside for a quick bit of air."

Mary headed for the bedroom. Evan watched her go and then turned to go out the front door. As he stepped out onto the porch, his mind lost in the night to come, he didn't see the shadow on his right. He felt the sharp pain on his head as he was falling and succumbed to the darkness.

****

The throbbing pain in his head slowly came into Evan's consciousness as he began to stir awake. The night air caused a shiver and as he automatically reached to feel the location of the pain, he slowly remembered why he was sprawled out on his front porch. Lurching to his feet, he staggered to the door and rushed inside. "Mary!"

He saw the bedroom door ajar and rushed across the room. "Mary!"

Exploding through the door, he found Mary lying on the floor. "Mary, oh my God, oh my God."

Kneeling beside her crumpled body, he saw her neck at an awkward angle, she is dead. Her dress is up by her thighs and blood has dried, dripping down her leg.

Evan began to cry uncontrollably. "No, no, no. Not my Mary, no, no, no"

After a bit, he began to calm down, he stared at the body for a minute and then lifted his head and screamed skyward, "Lucias!"

****

Startled awake by his nightmare, Evan sat up, sweating in the cold morning air. It was dark, but the sun was barely peaking up on the horizon. Using his spyglass, he checked to see if the Indians are still in their camp. He grabbed his blanket and slid down the rock to his horse. He quickly packed up and stepped around the gift of horse manure his horse has generously left for the raiding Indians. He led the horse through the rocks and down to the desert floor. He mounted up, leaned over to talk in the horse's ear, "hope your rested buddy."

He shot off in a full gallop across the desert plain. After a few minutes, he glanced back and a look of relief passed over his face as he didn't see anyone following him. As he looked forward again, a laugh erupted out of him... just as his horse stepped into a gopher hole and went down, throwing Evan right over the top....where he disappeared into thin air.

FOUR

Nevada City - 1997

The bedroom looked like the room of a teenager. Pink curtains hung on the windows, and posters of Tina Turner and George Michael covered the flowered wallpaper. On the bed, nestled amongst the layers of stuffed dolls, Susan Aiello was giggling on the phone,

"...maybe there just aren't any more good men out there. I mean, look at my mom. After my dad died, it's like she just glommed onto the first guy she thought seemed stable. Sheez, I mean, Frank? Uck. If he's an example of what's available, seriously, we're going to die old maids.... besides, he scares me."

Susan paused to listen.

"..... Who? Toby Gentry, you gotta be kidding me! I wouldn't go near him with your body. Let's be real, he reminds me of my grandfather... and he's only, what, 24?"

Laughing, ".....I don't care if he has big feet"

A loud crash came from somewhere in the house. "Hey, there's something happening downstairs. I'll call you back, love you."

Susan moved out her door and down the hall to the stairway. She was a tall, statuesque beauty with curly brown hair and the smooth, cocoa skin tone that showed off her half Italian heritage. It was a large home with a, long sweeping staircase curving down to the left. An oversized crystal chandelier was hanging from the ceiling and Susan couldn't see below till she was halfway to the main floor. As she moved closer to the bottom step, she could hear loud voices coming from the study across from the bottom of the stairway. She recognized them as those of her mother and stepfather.

"You don't get it," Frank Johnston was yelling, "I don't give a shit if you're my wife. That little maid is half your age with twice as much imagination….. What do you think you're going to do with that?"

Susan pulled the door open and stepped into the room. She saw Frank taking a fire place poker away from her mother.

Frank stepped forward and smashed Susan's mother on the head with the poker. She collapsed to the floor.

Susan screams, "No!!"

Frank was bashing out of control and yelling at the inert body "You stupid, fat cow, what did you think? Don't you know who I am? I'm Frank Lucias Johnston and I own this town!"

Susan rushed across the room and tried to pull Frank from her mothers' lifeless body, but he threw her off against the wall, stunning her, and turned back to the body on the floor. Susan shook herself straight and ran from the room, out the front door. The long, graveled driveway lead to a well paved, country road. Susan ran to the end of the drive and desperately looked both ways for a car. A large SUV is almost upon her as she waved frantically to make it stop. Skidding to a stop a few feet away, the passenger window slid down and the driver looked over.

"What the hell are you doing, I could have killed you." Looking at Susan's face, the driver realized she was distressed. "Is something wrong?"

"Please help me. I think my stepfather just killed my mother. He was hitting her with a fire poker and there was blood everywhere... and he was going crazy." She stopped to gulp some air.

"Get in", the drive said, unlocking the door.

Susan yanked open the door, and jumped into the truck. As he pulled away, she asked, "Do you have a cell phone?".....

As the truck pulled away at the end of the driveway, Frank Johnston was leaning against the front doorway, breathing heavily. He has blood spattered all over his shirt and pants. There was an almost lustful, wolfish grin on his face as he watched the truck go down the street.

FIVE

Nevada City Sheriff's Office – 1887

An agitated Evan Longview was standing in front of the sheriff's desk. Evan had come to his office looking for justice.

"Now Evan, we looked around and we didn't find any evidence that Lucias Johnston was out at your place.

"Dammit Sheriff," Evan pleaded, "You *saw* him at the wedding. He's been after Mary since the day we started up together. He could never handle the fact that she would willingly want to be with someone like me instead of him and his money."

"That may be the case," replied the Sheriff, "but it isn't evidence of foul play. I'm sorry Evan, we'll keep looking, but there's really nothing I can do unless we find other evidence or a witness comes forward."

A frustrated Evan was starting to get heated up, "Ah, horsepucky, you know no one is going to come out against the Johnston's." A thought suddenly came to him, "Wait….your protecting them, aren't you? You're probably on old man Johnston's payroll."

"Now you hold on there, son," said the Sheriff, leaning forward in his chair, "you better be very careful what you say."

"No, now I see it, you're not going to raise a hand against that family… fine, never mind, I'll take care of it myself."

Evan wheeled around and started for the door.

The Sheriff called out after him, "Hey, now Evan, don't go and do anything stupid…."

****

Police Station-Detective Squad Room – 1997

Susan was sitting at a desk in a typical police room. The walls were painted an unoffending grey. The windows were blurry with a coating from years of cigarette smoke. The room was an open bullpen with ten desks in two lines of five and an open door to the Lieutenant's office at the end. Susan was dabbing her eyes with a tissue, trying to remain calm as she talked to Detective Ivarone.

"Ok, Miss…," Ivarone looked down at a note on his desk…"Aiello, we've dispatched a couple of cars to your house, uh.. Mr. Johnston's house, so tell me again what you saw."

Susan wiped her nose and dropped the tissue into the trash can next to the desk. "I already told the other officer. I heard some noise from my bedroom. As I came downstairs, I heard my mother and stepfather arguing in the study. When I opened the door, I saw Frank take the fire poker away from mother and begin to beat her with it. I tried to stop him, but he was out of control. He knocked me down and kept beating her." She began to sob again. "I was scared for my life, so I ran out the door and caught a ride from the first car that came by and we came straight here."

Ivarone handed her another tissue from the box on his desk. "Okay, okay, take it easy, take it easy. Did you hear what they were fighting about?"

Susan shrugged, "I don't know, he was yelling something about the maid, how she was younger than my mother…. maybe he was having an affair with her and my mother found out, … what does it matter? I saw him kill my mother, you have to go arrest him."

"Like I said, we've already sent a team to investigate." Ivarone stood up, "Okay, you wait right here, I'll get you something to drink. You want some water or soda or something?"

"No, thank you," Susan mumbled.

"Ok, we'll have to find some place for you to stay, till we sort this out."

Ivarone walked out of the room.

SIX

Johnston Ranch – 1887

The large ranch style house sat on the south side of a group of buildings surrounded by beautiful grass plain. It had a front porch that ran the length of the house. There was a swing to one side of the front door with a table and two chairs to the other side. The house was a bright white, like it had been newly painted. Off to the right, set further back, so the animal emanations didn't drift into the house, was a large barn. It too, looked to have been recently painted. Across from the house, completing the horseshoe shaped compound was a long, low roofed, bunk house with a single door facing the main house.

A horse and rider came flying into the yard and Evan jumped off his horse before it came to a complete stop. Standing defiantly in front of the porch, he yelled at the house.

"Lucias, you dirty, lowdown, piece of shit! I know it was you that killed my Mary. Come out here and face me!"

The front door opened and a tall, heavy, suntanned man stepped out onto the porch. He was dressed smartly in a long black jacket with a black tie. A large, bushy mustache dominated his face, almost covering his mouth. "What's all this commotion about, Mr. Longview?"

Evan could barely contain his anger, "Your boy, Lucias, raped and killed my Mary!" He swept an arm around, taking in the bunkhouse. "Him and a few of his piece of shit crew. They gang raped her and then broke her neck. Now where is he?"

"Those are some pretty harsh statements, son. You've got a lot of nerve coming out here and throwing around accusations like that. I don't believe you can afford the legal help you're going to need if you continue to pursue these outlandish and false charges."

Hearing all the commotion, a few men came out of the bunkhouse behind Evan.

"They're not false," said Evan defiantly, "He's always been jealous of me when it comes to Mary. He just couldn't stand to see me and her be happy. He had to ruin it. Now I aim to get my revenge, so send him out and let's finish this....or does he have to hide behind his father?"

Johnston gave a little smirk, "Why don't you go to the sheriff? It's his job to find the killer or killers."

"You know as well as I do, the sheriff doesn't do anything in this town without your say so... now, are you going to send Lucias out, or do I have to go in and get him?"

Evan took a step toward the porch. One of the men behind him drew a gun. Johnston looked over Evan's shoulder and nodded. The man stepped forward and cracked Evan on the back of his head, knocking him to the ground. The other men stepped in and began kicking and beating him.

"Don't kill him," Johnston said, "though I have every right, as he came on my property looking to cause my family harm." He looked down with disgust at the battered body, "but get him off my property. Throw him out like the trash he is."

The men picked up Evan and tossed him into a buckboard standing by the bunkhouse.

SEVEN

1997

Two city patrol cars, with their lights twirling and sirens blasting, sped through the quiet, exclusive neighborhood. As they approached the Johnston driveway, the radio squawked out at the officers.

"Car 34, please be advised, we just received a phone call reporting a break in and assault at the Johnston residence, proceed with caution."

"What the hell?" Officer Ron Kaminski slowed down to turn into the long driveway. "We're already here on a possible murder."

The two patrol cars started down the driveway leading to the Johnston residence. It was a large two story anomaly, looking like an old southern plantation house had been picked up and dropped into the middle of the Nevada desert set on one thousand acres of hills and desert shrubbery. Around back, it also has its' own lake, complete with boathouse and dock.

The patrol cars came to a stop fifty feet from the house. The officers slowly stepped out of their cars and drew their guns. Kaminski looked to the two patrolmen behind him and signaled for them to go around the back. As Kaminski and his partner approached the front door, it burst open and Frank Johnston rushed out. "Thank GOD you're here! My wife is dead….she's dead."

Not putting their guns down, the patrolmen moved slowly forward. "Mr. Johnston? Is there anyone else in the house?"

Johnston was wearing an expensive looking, red smoking jacket with black, crushed velvet lapels, black sweatpants with white stripes down the legs and his hair was wet, but combed neatly with a perfect part on the right side. There was a gold medallion the size of which would make a rapper jealous, draped around his neck, resting on a mat of black chest hair. He looked like a bad interpretation of a movie Italian mobster. "What? No, no, it's just me and my dead wife!

"Alright, alright, just calm down." Kaminski talked into his shoulder mike, turning to motion his partner toward the house, "Gonzo, Billy is coming in through the front, don't shoot him. Secure the back and come in. Don't touch anything. Just get a look around and watch where you walk." Turning back to Johnston, " Ok, tell me what happened."

Frank took a deep breathe, trying to relax. "Yeah, yeah…. I was upstairs taking a shower. I like long showers after a long day, you know what I mean. I think my daughter was in her room. She's actually my stepdaughter, came from her mom's first marriage. 25 and still living at home, kids these days… anyway, I'm in the shower and I guess my wife is downstairs cleaning up after dinner. I get out and I'm drying off. I stick my head out the door and yell for my wife to bring me my sweats. I forgot them in the bedroom and

38

I don't like to parade around the house in the buff with my daughter... err stepdaughter around, right?...anyway, I get no answer, so I wrap the towel and scoot for the bedroom. After I get dressed, I go downstairs. I called for my wife, but still get no answer. I didn't find her in the kitchen. When I get to the study, I find her lying on the floor with buckets of blood oozing out of her head." Starting to shake and breakdown, he continued. "I kneeled down next to her, but I can see she's dead. I picked up the fireplace poker lying next to here, not even thinking, cause I'm in shock, that it's probably the murder weapon."

"So you're saying she was murdered?"

"What the fuck? You think she bashed herself on the head ten times cause her roast got overcooked? What are you, a moron? Of course she was murdered!"

"Calm down, Mr. Johnston, I just meant, you're saying you didn't do it?"

Johnston's face mushrooms into a red balloon, "what the fuck you talkin' about? Of course I didn't do it!"

"Ok, ok.... You said your daughter was in the house when you got into the shower. Where was she when you got out?"

"I don't know," Frank was beginning to calm down a little, "I never saw her. Maybe she did it and ran off."

A car pulled up behind the patrol cars and two men in suits got out. Officer Kaminsky glanced at the new arrivals.

"Ok, I gotta ask you to wait here in the back of the patrol car. We are going to secure the scene and the detectives here," nodding at the two men approaching, "are probably going to have some questions."

He helped Frank fold himself into the back seat and closed the door. Detective Robbins peeled away from his partner and headed for the house. Robbins is a squat, square shouldered man, with close cropped, jet black hair and pale grey eyes that would be a distinguishing feature if he didn't have a birthmark just below his right eye, stealing all the attention. He will make the initial observations. His partner, Detective Krebs, the Jeff to Robbins Mutt, is taller and slimmer, with sandy blond hair that needs to be cut. His wireless glasses make him look more like a college professor than a homicide detective. He will get the statements from the responding officer and the witness/suspect. Robbins and Stocker have been partners for two years and fallen into this routine for most crime scenes. Robbins, with the more detailed observation skills, while Detective Krebs had the more genial, but pointed, personality, better suited for speaking with potential witnesses and suspects.

"What'ya got Ron?" asked Krebs as he approached Officer Kaminsky.

"A mess, that's what we got. Lady of the house is lying in the study with her head smashed in. Mr. Johnston, here," pointing to the patrol car, "claims he was upstairs in the shower and didn't hear a thing, came downstairs to find his wife dead and stepdaughter gone. And as you probably know, we got the stepdaughter down at the station saying she came downstairs to witness Mr. Johnston beating his wife."

"Why isn't he cuffed?" asked Krebs, glancing at the patrol car.

"Uh….I just thought because of who he was, you know, maybe…."

"Okay, but get him to the station and put him in lock up. We'll be back after we look this over."

"Yes sir, and also, sir? He claimed he picked up the probable murder weapon by accident, in his state of shock."

Kaminski headed toward his car, calling for his partner. Detective Krebs turned and looked at the house.

"Shit."

EIGHT

1887

The American flag was the only adornment on the wall, the United States Marshals office in Nevada being a place of serious business. It was a small, bleak, office, with two desks and two chairs. Standing behind the desk at the front of the room, the senior U.S. Marshal was just finishing swearing in a new recruit. "Welcome to the Marshals Service. Have a seat."

The new recruit looked around. He went to the other desk and got a chair. He set it down and sat facing the Marshal, and waited expectantly.

The Marshal studied his new recruit for a second. "Now Evan, I know why you joined the service, but let me tell you. We cannot allow you to use your badge to exact revenge on whomever you might feel is responsible for your wife's death. Revenge will not bring her back or ease your pain."

But that is exactly what Evan Longview was thinking. He had spent the last three weeks recovering from his beating at the hands of Johnston's stooges. He'd had plenty of time to mourn and think. His anger and sorrow had only continued to simmer within and both emotions remained near the surface of his persona, ready to erupt at the slightest provocation. He had come to the conclusion that no local help would be forthcoming and to get the justice he wanted, he would have to do it himself. He figured joining the Marshals service would at least give him some legal standing to investigate and dole out the justice he deserved. "No sir," he tried to give his best innocent look, "I only hope to use my energies in stopping other people from receiving the same fate as myself. If by chance I come across evidence of proof in my wife's rape and murder, then all for the better."

Over the next couple years.......

    ...The three men sitting around the campfire looked like they had been living out of doors for a few weeks and so they had. They were all similar in that they were in bad need of a shave and a bath. When they smiled, it was obvious they didn't have a dentist as a close acquaintance. Their clothes were filthy and worn with boots run way down at the heel. The only items you could find in decent shape would be the guns in their hostlers and the rifles lying near them. These were the tools of their trade, which was stealing, murder, rustling and whatever else they could do that required little education or conscience.

    "Did you see the look on that bank manager's face when I shot him?" asked Bill Chofsky, "that's what I like, to see their faces when they realize they're gonna die."

"I don't know," Ugly Tom Dunston replied, "my favorite time is when we're ridin' outta town all whoopin' and hollarin'. You can just see the fear oozing out of those chickenshit townfolk."

Like a ghost, Marshal Evan Longview appeared out of the shadows. "I'm with Bill there," he pointed at Chosfky with his shotgun, "the look before death is almost priceless."

The third, silent thief made a grab for the gun beside him. Evan blew him away. He quickly turned and put a second shot into Tom Dunston. Dropping the shotgun, he quickly pulled his pistol and aimed at Chosfky saying, "Oh don't look so surprised." He pulled the trigger and shot him dead in the heart....

****

...Terrence O'dowd has been a stagecoach driver for two years. He'd had many a partner riding shotgun, but never one as silent and sullen as the man sitting to his right today. His ever moving eyes seemed older than his youthful features, as they took in their constantly changing landscape. They had been on the road since first light this morning and hardly a word had passed between them. If it weren't for the rest stop and conversation with some of the passengers, O'dowd, normally an affable, talkative Irishman, might have been downright offended. Now after a short rest to eat lunch and water the horses, the afternoon sun was beginning to make him drowsy. Shaking his head to keep awake, he pulled on the reins a little to slow down the horses as a sharp bend approached on the trail. As the stage rounded the corner, the man riding shotgun sat up a little straighter, maybe sensing this would be a good place for an ambush. Sure enough, as they came around the bend, O'dowd was forced to pull hard and rein in the stagecoach to a stop as they were confronted by three men on horseback spread out across the road.

The robbers were all wearing long coats and big hats. They had bandanas pulled up to cover their faces. "Hello folks," the middle man greeted cheerfully. "Now we don't want any fuss, so if you would be so kind as to throw down that payroll box…"

Suddenly three gunshots rang out and all three robbers fell from their horses. Marshal Longview looked down, reloaded and holstered his pistol. "Let's go"…

****

…The Lucky Lady was like most saloons and gambling establishments. It was well lit and festive with a piano player pounding away on an out of tune piano in the back corner. The long bar ran almost the full length of the room on one side as you walked through the double doors from the street. There was a large mirror on the wall running parallel with the bar. The bar and gaming tables were full as was usual on a Saturday night. It was payday, and most of the cowboys and ranch hands from the surrounding area had come to blow off some steam or relax after a long week. The cigarette and cigar smoke was so thick, you could barely see the other end of the room. At a poker table up near the front, five men were involved in a serious game. The local hustler running the game was looking none too happy as a clean shaven, young gentleman in a dusty, suit was raking in yet another pot. "You are unreasonably lucky tonight, Marshal, maybe a little too lucky."

Marshal Evan Longview gave the man a quizzical raised eyebrow, "are you calling me a cheat, sir?"

"I don't know, maybe…."

A third older man put a restraining hand on the house gambler , "Now hold on there, Mal, the Marshal ain't done nothin' that I can see."

"The hell he ain't. If you didn't drink so much hooch, you old dog, you'd be able to see better. I know I saw him deal from the bottom of the deck."

Marshal Longview reached over and punched Mal in the face. Getting up, he moved quickly around the table and followed up with another punch. Mal went down and the Marshal jumped on him, pummeling him over and over until men pulled him away.

"Geez Marshal…"

Breathing heavily, Evan looked down at Mal, slowly looked around the room and stormed out the room

NINE

Marshal Office – 1890

Evan moved down the dusty street slowly as his horse ambled along at its' own leisurely pace. The morning had already been a long one. The grey clouds above went hand in hand with his hangover from too much whiskey the previous night. He was also feeling all of the hard miles he had ridden over the last couple days. He'd been sent to pick up a bank robber who had been shot while escaping and was sitting in the local jail till his wounded leg had healed enough to ride a horse. After two days on the trail with the dirty, foul mouthed and foul smelling thief, Evan had let loose at the Lucky Lady. Once again, though, all the whiskey, cards and distractions, could not keep his anger and pain from simmering just below the surface of his emotions.

Now, after being dredged up from a deep, snoring slumber, and summoned to the office, here he was, headache in hand, working his way through the morning, crowded street. The hustle and bustle of a town on the rise and going about its daily business pinged around in his head at every step. He was not unaware of the furtive looks and avoidance he was getting from the local townsfolk. His short temper and angry actions had become a bad habit and he was slowly losing friends and support to fear and resentment. After he dismounted and tied his horse at the rail, Evan stepped onto the porch and entered the Marshals office, steeling himself to face the coming storm.

"Good morning, Evan," the District Marshal belted out, starting another pounding in his head. "Come on in, have a seat, I have some news for you."

Evan moved into a nearby chair in front of the marshal's desk.

"I received a telegram today. It came out of Los Angeles in California. Seems a wandering cowhand was pretty drunk in a local bar when he started telling a tale of how he and his buddies had ganged up and raped a young lady in Nevada some time back. Apparently, he also mentioned that his boss's son at the time had finished up by breaking her neck."

The head pounding forgotten, Evan straightened up and could already feel the heat rising in his soul.

"An upstanding, law abiding patron," the Marshal continued, "overheard this conversation and ran to tell the local sheriff. The drunk was thrown in jail while the sheriff could verify the story. It came across our wire and I think this guy might have been involved in your wife's murder. The timing might be right but he stopped talking and won't even give his name. I have already wired to the sheriff to hold this man until we could identify him... Evan, you know the men who worked for Francis Johnston back then. I want you to ride to Los Angeles and identify the man if you can."

Evan was already on his feet and starting for the door.

"Evan...if, and only if....he is one of Johnston's hands, I want you to bring him back here to stand trial and testify against any other men in the group we can get out of him.....Evan!"

Evan stopped with his back to his boss, holding open the door.

"You have to do this right. If you bring him back all busted up, it is going to cause more trouble and I won't be able to back you up. You have to do this within the law, do you understand?"

With his back still to the Marshal, he paused a beat and then walked out, closing the door behind him. The Marshal looked after him with a look of worry and resignation.

Standing outside on the front step, Evan stopped to steady himself. He finally had a break that would lead him to the men who killed his beloved Mary and had crushed their dreams and hopes of a happy life together. The anger within was now boiling up uncontrollably, but he let it come. He wanted to feel the power and strength it gave him. He stepped into the saddle, turned and galloped down the street to the boarding house where he lived. He would pack and be on the way within the hour. "I'm coming for you, Lucias.... I'm coming for you!"

TEN

Southern California Desert – 1990

Man has always had a fascination with time travel or at the least, being *in* another time. Who can't say they haven't had thoughts of living in another period they find more romantic or interesting, going back to some point in their own lives to do over, or dreamed of the future with advanced machines and space travel? In the early 1900's, Albert Einstein's friend and mentor Hermann Minkowski showed, using mathematics, that space and time together would form a "fourth" dimension. The U.S. acted on this theory in 1943 with the Montauk Experiment. The government funded program included a project to make a ship, the USS Eldridge, undetectable to radar. It is alleged that this was accomplished with a dramatic side effect. Supposedly, the ship actually disappeared from time and space as we know it. Surviving sailors were discharged as "mentally unfit" and discredited. The whole affair was covered up and buried. The dream of actual time travel continues and man's ever evolving fascination with technology and machines makes the belief in its possibility a closer reality.

The early morning sun was just over the eastern horizon, but the heat was already making the sweat roll down his back. U.S. Marshal Jude Cavelot was standing apart from the activity of the odd group he had been sent to chaperone. He wiped his brow with a yellow handkerchief and he wondered, not for the first time, how he ended up with this duty. He watched as the young scientists before him moved about with pre-determined jobs. There were two open air tents set up for shade, refreshments and final prep work. The tents were needed, as there was no other cover in sight. It was just low scrub and miles of endless dirt. Vans and SUVs were lined up in the background. They had erected what looked like an upside down horseshoe shaped machine. It was bolted to a pedestal with a control panel, not unlike a music mixing board, standing alongside. There were video cameras on tripods set up on each side of the "horseshoe", with wires running down and over to the control board. It was programed to start the recording when the machine turned on.

Cavelot was not a handsome man, standing 5'10" and already with the early signs of the beer drinkers belly. He had a receding hairline and coupled with his high forehead, small close eyes and flat nose, he closely resembled the species of anthropoid so popularly believed to be man's origins. Cavelot wandered toward the machine where the oldest of the group was doing some final wiring at the control console.

"So, what you have you got here?"

Tom Davidson, the group leader, twisted a last cover in place and straightened up. He was taller than Cavelot and much thinner. He had the scrabble of two days beard growth in patches on his face. "You don't know?"

"Well,…it was kind of a last minute assignment for me. I was told to meet the group at your building, follow you to your destination, hang out and observe." Jude looked around at the bleak landscape, chuckling, "I guess I'm here to keep the media at bay and protect you from saboteurs."

"I suppose it won't matter if I tell you, you'll find out soon enough. What we're building here is a time continuum."

Jude looked over the machine with skepticism, "what's that, like a time machine?"

"Sort of," Davidson took a deep breath, with a look like he had done this explanation before, "a continuum is something that is continuous with no discernible breaks. What we're trying to do is connect two different time periods."

"So what happens next, you have a volunteer walk through this gadget?"

"As a matter of fact, that is exactly what is going to happen, and I'm the volunteer. We're setting the continuum to 1890, figuring there shouldn't be too much going on in the desert at this hour in that time period. This is only a trial run. I plan to step through, take some pictures of the sky and surroundings.... Just kind of see what's out there and step back. My assistants will wait five minutes and then reverse the continuum. Now, if you will excuse me, I need to see about some last minute details with my crew. "

As Davidson walked away, Jude is left to gaze wistfully through the machine. If he could only go back to another time, the things he would do differently. After one last glance, he turned to walk away and turned his ankle on a rock. Reaching out to steady himself, his hand landed heavily on the control board. He looked down, but couldn't be sure of what he pushed. He looked warily around to see if anyone was watching. "I'm sure they do a final check...damn vector heads anyway." He stepped away and went to sit in the shade of a tent.

Jude was twenty feet from the archway when a humming suddenly filled the air. Everyone turned to see something appear through the arch and land hard on the ground.... It was a man!

ELEVEN

It was ten seconds before anyone moved. The look on everyone's face ran the gamut from surprise and confusion to fear and awe. Davidson was the first to recover. He ran to the console board and gave it a quick look before shutting it down. He turned back to the stunned man on the ground before him.

Momentarily stunned, Evan Longview slowly got his senses back. He was lying on the ground. As the dust settled, he became aware of other people around him. He scrambled to his feet, pulled his pistol, and swung it wildly back and forth as he took in the odd scene around him. He was semi surrounded by six strangers in various get ups of dress. All, but one, were wearing pants that were cut off above the knees, but with socks and boots on, and he assumed these were not their under garments. Sensing he was not in immediate danger, he slowly looked around and observed one of this odd group was female. She was also wearing the strange short pants, with almost all of her legs showing and he quickly looked away in embarrassment. Evan could see a small jewel hanging from one man's ear. They were all wearing a hat of some kind. More like caps. The lady was wearing a bigger floppy hat with a wider brim.

The fifth man was older and wearing more traditional clothes. He had on blue jeans with cowboy boots and a white collared shirt. He had on a cap style hat with the words U.S. Marshal written across the front. He also has a U.S. Marshal's badge hanging from his belt, about four inches from where his hand rested on a pistol in its holster.

Stopping his gun to rest on the man Evan perceived to be the man in charge, he demanded, "Who are you? Where did you come from?"

Earring man held up his hand, "Easy now, dude… easy. We were here, man, you actually came to us."

Cavelot took a hesitant step forward. "You came through a window in time, sort of, which was programmed the wrong direction." He gave Davidson a guilty glance. Taking another step forward, he extended his hand, "My name is Jude Cavelot. I'm a U.S. Marshal. It's 1990, welcome to the future."

A stunned Evan slowly looked at his surroundings again. The expectant faces, the odd contraptions in the background. Finally, his search came to rest on the outstretched hand. He lowered his arm. As he twisted to put away his gun, Cavelot noticed for the first time, the badge pinned to the stranger's shirt.

Evan puts out his arm and gave Jude a strong, firm handshake, "Evan Longview, United States Marshal."

The two men locked eyes for a second, gripping hands. The moment passed and a smile broke out on Evan's face. "Well, I'll be, so you're what I'll look like in a….. hundred years."

The rest of the group began to gather around, questions flying from all directions.

"What were you doing?"

"Where is your horse?"

"Are you married?" Silence. Everyone turned to look at Emily Jepsen. "Well, he is kind of cute."

Tom Davidson held up his hand for quiet. "Yes, well, I'm sure Marshal Longview will answer all of our questions soon enough. He probably has a few of his own." Davidson took Evan's arm and guided him toward the tents. "Maybe you'd like some coffee and a chair. Tomas, grab an extra chair from the van, please."

As Tomas moved off, Evan stopped and stared at their vehicles. Everyone followed Evan's line of sight.

"Oh, those are our modern day wagons," Jude volunteered. "We still have horses, but those are called cars....actually, that's a utility vehicle and those three are called vans. Cars are smaller....well they come in lots of different sizes....shit, this isn't going to be easy."

Tomas set up an extra folding chair under one of the canopies. Jude stood by one of the corner poles. Evan eyed the canvas folding chair. He untied his holster strap from his leg and slid the holster around to the front of his waist. He looked around at everyone else to see what the correct action might be. He turned and dropped himself into the chair. It collapsed under his weight. He awkwardly scrambled onto all fours and quickly stood up to a few chuckles, only to find Emily standing right in front of him with a toothy smile and a cup of coffee.

"Sorry about that, those chairs are pieces of crap....oops, excuse me. Here you go. I'd offer you cream and sugar, but we don't have any."

An even more embarrassed Evan mumbled "Black will be fine, thank you, ma'am." Still feeling awkward and unsure of his situation, he took a sip of his coffee, wincing, he said, "think I'll just stand."

Davidson broke the tension. "Well, why don't we start by introducing our group. My name is Tom

Davidson and I am the leader of this merry band of scientists. The idea for and basic workings of the time continuum are my brainchild." Waving at one of the young men to his right, "this is Tomas Linkley, my right hand."

Tomas stepped forward to shake hands. He was another skinny man with a blotchy beard and piercing green eyes. His shoulder length hair looked like it just came out of the dryer, and though his hand is soft, his handshake is firm.

"Tomas is the mechanical genius who built the machine."

Sweeping his arm around the tent, Davidson introduced the rest of the crew.

"These fine young people are our hard working assistants, Yoshi, Peter and Emily, you kind of met. Besides being very bright and interested in what we are doing here, they come very cheaply as they are grad students from the local University."

Yoshi and Peter simply nodded, while Emily gave a slight curtsy and giggle. "Hello."

Evan again felt embarrassed by Emily's forward attitude and partial outfit, but managed a nod and a wave for everyone.

Davidson continued his story. "We are a small group with a government grant to build a time continuum. A window, if you will, to reach other periods of time, either past or present. We have succeeded; it seems, in at least one direction. Today was to be our maiden journey. I was to go back in time to 1890 to what we thought would have been an empty desert. Somehow the polarity was reversed and instead of me going back, you came forward. We are about 100 miles out from the city of Los Angeles and the year is 1990." He pauses to take a moment. "So…perhaps you would like to tell us your story?"

Evan looks around at the expectant faces. He looked down at his coffee, and not sure what to do with the odd tasting brew, he let the cup slip from his hand.

"Oops," Emily jumped to her feet, "don't worry, would you like another cup?"

"Uh…no thank you ma'am, that was different though."

"It was Hawaiian Nut, did you like it?"

"Umm…I don't think so, but maybe I just have to get used to it."

Focusing back to the entire group, he offered, "My name is Evan Longview. I am a United States Marshal. I was riding to Los Angeles to pick up a prisoner wanted for crimes in Nevada City. I was allowing my horse to stretch out his legs, but as we were galloping along, he suddenly went down and sent me flying over his head. After I landed and looked up, there you all were."

As Evan stopped talking, a strong wind picked up. Dust devils were beginning to pop up. Looking to the North, they saw a dark cloud moving their direction. Dust and sand began to blow all which way.

Jude stepped over and took Evan by the arm. "Com'n, let's get out of this." He started to lead Evan toward his truck.

Davidson called out after them, "Hey, where do you think you're going?"

Jude continued to lead Evan toward his truck. "I'm taking him back with me. He's a U.S. Marshal. My job was to observe and protect. Well, I've observed and now I'm going to protect. I'll keep Marshal Longview and the U.S. Marshal's office will decide what to do with him."

Davidson looked back at his equipment and at the oncoming sand storm. A look of frustration and disappointment came over his face. He dug a card from his pocket, and handed it to Evan. "Ok, take this card, it has my numbers on it. Call me later, please." He turned away, "damn, this sand is going to ruin everything." He started yelling orders to the crew, "We need to get the arch and console covered and get the tapes out of those video cameras!"

He ran to help pack up. Jude led Evan to a Chevy Suburban, pushed him toward the passenger door and ran around to the driver side. "Get in, hurry, and close the door."

Evan stood outside the door and looked it over. There was no door knob to turn or handle to pull. He gingerly put his fingers up under the lip of the plate and lifted up. The door opened. He jerked it open, hoped up into the seat and pulled the door shut behind him.

All was quiet

Jude put the key in the ignition and fired up the engine. Evan looked around for something to hold on to. Jude put the truck into gear and took off in a tight u-turn, speeding down the road. Evan was bracing himself with stiff legs and a terrified look on his face.

TWELVE

The suburban was racing across the desert floor. The scenery was passing by too fast for Evan to take much in. They settled into a smooth, continual flow, and he began to relax a little as the wonder of everything engulfed his senses. His eyes were darting back and forth between outside and inside. The desert was flying by, yet they seemed to be in relative calm within the vehicle.

"That sandstorm was going to cause havoc with the equipment back there," he remarked hesitantly. "uh…. how is this thing moving?"

Jude gave him a knowing smile. "This baby has a 350 hemi engine." He realized, again, that Evan had no idea what he was talking about. "Um…well, we have what they call motors now. They run on liquid fuel called gasoline, which comes from oil."

Still confused, Evan took this in as he continued to look out the window at the smattering of cars and trucks passing by going in the other direction.

Jude also was not sure what to say, "Pretty stuffy in here." He reached over and turned on the air conditioner. It began blowing cold air from the vents and Evan sat back quickly. "It's just air to keep us cool. I can also turn it to warm in the winter. Here check this out, your gonna love this." Jude turned on the radio. The Rolling Stone's HonkyTonk Woman came blaring from the speakers. Jude quickly turned it down to a lower level. "Sorry about that. This is a radio. It picks up signals from up in the sky and transmits them to this box. We can listen to any style of music or talk show we want. Go ahead, push these buttons here. See if you can find something you like."

Evan looked it over and slowly reached out a shaky hand. He pushed a button and immediately got a voice talking fast about something he couldn't comprehend. He pushed another button and this time got more music, a girl was talking in a singsong voice to some sort of rhythmic beat. He pushed another button and an obviously southern man was drawling along about the girl who just left him. Evan sat back and began to relax more. He had so many questions bouncing around his head, but didn't know what to ask, so he just sat, looked out the window and took it all in.

THIRTEEN

Southern California – 1990

It was a nice apartment, small, but uniquely furnished. In this area of West L.A., Venice Beach is considered very eclectic if not downright weird. The apartments and homes are crushed together so as to look like a cartoon neighborhood. The streets are barely wide enough for one parked car and one moving car. Parking is premium. The inhabitants, though, don't worry so much about the parking. They live in this area specifically for the idiosyncratic surroundings as well as the close proximity to the Pacific Ocean, the salt air giving all the buildings a worn but comfortable feel. Inside the apartment, the walls are decorated with artwork ranging from prints of past masters and contemporary artists to cultural figures acquired by someone who has traveled abroad extensively. Two women are sitting in the living room sipping glasses of white wine. Susan Aiello is curled up on the sofa with her feet tucked up under her in typical female comfort fashion. Her dark, piercing eyes smile with love and maybe a little too much wine, as she faces her friend. Tanetia Carver has been Susan's best friend since college. She is an African American beauty in her own right. Though standing only 5'5" tall, her trim but shapely figure, confident aura and aggressive demeanor help to make her appear taller and more formidable. This confidence serves her well in her profession as a lawyer championing for the poor and underprivileged.

Susan tilted her glass toward her best friend, "Thanks for taking me in Tanny, I just couldn't stay in Nevada"

"Oh puuph, you know you don't have to thank me, that's what best friends are for."

Tanetia gave her a quizzical look, "So… what are you going to do? I mean, do you have to testify against Frank?"

"Yes, the police locked him up that night based on my report. He was claiming some unknown intruder, but they couldn't find any evidence to that. My testimony is their whole case…" Susan paused to sip some wine. She looked at her friend with worried eyes. "I'm scared Tanetia. He has so much money and power. Somehow his lawyer got him out on bail. That's why I came out here. I just couldn't stay there and wait for the trial. The D.A. will send someone for me when the trial begins."

FOURTEEN

The SUV was quickly closing in on the majestic sight of downtown Los Angeles. For the last hour or so, Jude and Evan had been winding their way from the vast openness of the desert to the ever reaching sprawl of Southern California civilization. Now as they approached Los Angeles proper, Evan's head was on a swivel as all shapes of cars, trucks, buildings, freeways, signs and people seem to be everywhere. The sensory overload was happening again, only now at a much faster rate.

Evan waved out at the city, "I've never seen so many people at once. I mean, I've been to St Louis, but that's a small village compared to this....so many moving...things...so tall...."

"You ain't seen nothin' yet. Wait till we get into the actual city. There are over three million people in this city alone, and believe me, it's going to seem like they're all in one place."

Jude exited the freeway a short way from the downtown buildings. He wound his way through a neighborhood rolling down the back side of prosperity. The majority of people they see are of African or Hispanic heritage. Many of them just hanging out on the street or walking slowly toward a destination that seemed to be pushing them away.

"Back in your day, Los Angeles was probably 80-90% Mexicans. They're a smaller percentage now. As Southern California grew over time, many of the Mexicans moved with the jobs, though they still make up a huge percentage of the population in this area of the country."

"How do they build those buildings so high,…what keeps them from falling over in a wind storm?... Hey what was that!?"

A bicyclist goes racing by.

"Oh, that was a bicycle. Surely you've seen one of those?"

"Yes…yes, but it didn't look like that, and it certainly didn't go that fast. I saw a peddler once in Denver showing one for sale. It looked pretty wobbly and…what is that guy wearing?"

"Oh, those are bike clothes," Jude chuckled, "people who are serious about riding wear them because it supposedly makes them more streamlined and wind resistant."

Evan watched the biker for a second longer and then turned his eyes to other sights along the streets. "You all don't wear a lot of clothes around here."

"Nope, the southern California weather helps a lot, but times are definitely different now. You're going to be in for a lot of shocks. Women nowadays like to show off their curves. They don't hide them much. In fact, they don't hide much of anything. Of course, that's not always such a bad thing, if you know what I mean." Jude gave a little wink to Evan.

Turning into the parking lot of the U.S. Marshals office, LA Division, Jude found a spot to park between two other SUV's. They exited the vehicle and made their way toward the four story building that seemed tiny compared to the thirty story behemoths they had driven past. Even at only four stories, Evan looked up and began to feel a little nervous. There wasn't a cloud in the high blue sky and the temperature is its usual 78, yet Evan was beginning to perspire and show sweat stains on his shirt. There were people moving in and out of the doors as they approached. He marveled at the diversity of dress people were wearing. There were many in the same windbreaker with the "US Marshals" imprinted on the back, but just as many in a variety of pants, suits, ties, and even what looked like undershirts with some writing or pictures on them. The women were also dressed in a mixture of styles, some in pants, some in skirts that vary in length, but with none of them going much past their knees. There was even one young lady in very small shorts and a shirt that left her midriff exposed. Evan, again, could feel the embarrassment creeping up his neck.

Jude held the door for Evan and when he stepped inside he was immediately hit with the buzzing sound of voices and scuffling feet. In the middle of the room, there was a security desk with two men wearing blue blazers. They were there to filter and direct the traffic to the correct offices and elevators.

Jude stepped up beside Evan, "The Marshals offices are on the third and fourth floor. The other floors have a variety of businesses. Lawyers, real estate, insurance…there is even a little deli over there where we can get a quick snack."

Though strange sights are considered normal in Los Angeles, the men behind the desk gave an extra once over to Evan in his dusty western getup. Jude nodded to the blue blazers as he led Evan around the desk and toward the elevator doors against the back wall. "You're going to love this. This is called an elevator. We can use the stairs, but this will take us up to our floor with no effort on our part." Jude pushed the button with the up arrow. "We use the third and fourth floor, but all the work is done on the third floor. The high up, mucky mucks and decision makers have offices on the fourth floor, but they don't mingle with us lowly ground troops too much." Jude gave Evan one of his patented winks of good ole' boy camaraderie.

The elevator bell dinged and the door slid open in front of them. Jude took Evan by the elbow and gently led him into the elevator. It was an old building and the elevator was a small one. Evan was immediately overcome with a sense of fear. Jude pushed the three button and the doors began to close. Evan was on the verge of full panic but he struggled to keep steady. When the elevator jerked into motion, Evan quickly reached out and grabbed the hand rail along the wall. Jude was watching him with a slight smirk. "It's okay," Jude's smile grew, "even if it breaks, it is only three floors down."

Evan tightened his grip on the rail and watched the numbers above the door go up. When the elevator lurched to a stop and the door began to slide open, Evan was already moving to get out. He stood on the solid hall floor and worked to control his heart and breathing. Jude once again took his elbow and nudged him toward a door across the hall. "See, now wasn't that better that schlepping up three flights of stairs?"

The main bullpen work space of the U.S. Marshal's office was simple. There were glass partitioned cubicles lining each side, with an aisle down the middle leading to the Captains' office. The walls were the usual unremarkable beige with the only adornment being an American flag standing in one front corner and the California state flag in the other. When Jude and Evan entered, the sound of voices and movement came to a halt. Everyone was taking in Evan and his western wear. With his gun tied down in a leg hostler, and his dusty, worn hat, he looked straight off a movie set.

"It's okay everyone," Jude dead panned," he's one of us. He's been undercover down near El Cajon."

Jude led Evan down the aisle. Captain Harrison, hearing the silence, was standing in his office doorway, watching as they approached.

Jude and Evan stopped in front of Harrison and Jude announced, "Captain, this is United States Marshal Evan Longview, from Nevada City and 1890."

FIFTEEN

Captain Jerome Harrison had seen and experienced a lot in his life. He was not easily surprised. Born into a military family, he was exposed to many different places as his dad was transferred from base to base. Raised with two brothers, one older and one younger, he grew up with many different fronts. Admiration and fear for his older brother as Jerome was either following him around like a puppy dog, or running for his life when he stepped over the line. Warrior and tormentor to the younger one as he was either playing pranks on the youngest Harrison or defending him from local bullies. Machismo was a standard attitude in and around military families. After growing to a solid six foot two, Harrison followed his father into service and joined the Army straight out of high school. After two tours in Vietnam, and the horrors of that war, he came home to a broken family. His father had finally become too abusive to live with and his mother was now living in Nevada. His older brother was married and selling cars somewhere in Georgia, the younger brother, having just finished college, was looking for work as an accountant. Settling in near his mother, Harrison joined the local police force and served four years before making the jump to the Marshal's service. He worked from the Nevada office for ten years and when his mother passed away from cancer, he made the transfer to the

Los Angeles office, where he distinguished himself enough to have risen to his current position of Captain.

Harrison was looking hard at Jude, trying to detect any note of funny business. Slowly he turned his attention to the other man. Surveying his worn, dusty western look and noting a hardness in his eyes that went beyond the outward nervousness he was showing. He glanced over Evan's shoulder at the staring eyes behind them, "Let's go into my office," he said, as he turned and headed for his desk. He indicated the two chairs in front and Jude and Evan each sat down facing the Captain.

Harrison sat down, leaned back and crossed his arms. "Okay, what the hell is this all about?"

Jude glanced sideways at Evan and took a deep breath. "Like I said, this is Marshal Longview. He is from 1890."

Harrison quickly sat forward angrily and started to speak, "Now wait.."

Jude cut him off. "Look, you sent me out in the desert to babysit those science geeks. Well, they had this time machine gizmo and I guess it worked. They were preparing to get going, when it started humming and he," nodding toward Evan, "came flying out of nowhere and landed at our feet."

Harrison once again stared intently at Jude for few seconds. He turned his gaze to Evan, and asked, "What have *you* got to say?"

"Well sir," Evan began, "I guess that's about right. I was riding along when my horse must have stepped into a hole and threw me. When I landed and looked around, I found myself surrounded by the Marshal here and the....geeks."

Rubbing his temples, Harrison looked down at his desk, trying to gather his thoughts.

"Shit"

SIXTEEN

Frank Johnston's Home-Nevada City

Frank Johnston was sitting at his desk, with his gold plated telephone to his ear. His desk was a monstrous, ugly mass of oak that was too big for the room, leaving little space to get around the couch against the left wall. There are two overstuffed chairs sitting in front of the desk. The walls are adorned with surprisingly good quality prints of classic women in various repose, their curves and plumpness showing the desired sensuousness of a time past. A fireplace is located next to the couch with a portrait above it of a man looking vaguely like Johnston, dressed in a black suit of another century. The glass doors to the right offer a view of a spacious lawn ending at a white painted boat house and the manmade lake behind it. Johnston himself is dressed like the self-important man he envisions himself. Wearing an opened collared, black dress shirt, he has on the obligatory gold necklace and smoking jacket of the man of leisure, this one being purple with a dark blue lapel. His desk is empty except for the phone and computer on the left side and an obnoxious ashtray in the form of a naked lady on her back on the right, only adding even more to the tasteless effect.

Johnston was leaning back in his big swivel chair, smoke drifting from the fat, ugly cigar in his left hand. A phone in his right hand was pressed to his ear.

"Hello Stretch, long time....yeah, yeah. Listen, shithead, I got a situation here and you're going to fix it for me."

He listened for a minute, and then leaned forward over the desk as his neck started to become flush with anger. "You listen to me, numb nuts, you owe me, or did you already forget. I own you!" He paused to jam his cigar between the legs of the ashtray. "Now here's what I need. You follow the news? The D.A. is sending out a Marshal to bring back a witness, my stepdaughter. He'll be arriving 9:00 tonight. You make sure he never makes it to the wit, got it?"

The voice on the other end began to say something and Frank cut him off, yelling, "I don't fuckin' care how you do it! Just make sure he never picks her up and make sure she doesn't make it back here!"

He slammed the phone down and sat back in his chair. After a couple deep breaths, he leaned forward to pick up his cigar. Taking a lighter from his pocket, he relit the cigar and leaned back. He closed his eyes as he relaxed and blew a plume of smoke up to the ceiling.

SEVENTEEN

Jude's home was a small two bedroom bungalow on the west side of Los Angeles in Culver City, between Hollywood and the Pacific Ocean. The area was originally a nice clean family neighborhood, but as time and age set in, the families began migrating to other, newer parts of Southern California, leaving this neighborhood to the elderly who refused to move and lower income residents who cared less about appearances and more about scraping out an existence.

In a back bedroom, Evan was sitting in a chair, drinking a beer while Jude was going through drawers and the closet pulling out clothes.

Glancing around, Evan commented, "This is a nice place you got here. Do you live alone?"

"Thanks, I inherited it from my parents when my mom died, and yes, I live alone."

"Do you have a girl?"

Jude kept digging in the closet, "Nope, guess I haven't found the "one" yet."

Evan stared out the window with a sad expression on his face. "I did…found "the one". She was beautiful, fun, spirited…"

"Was?"

Still looking out the window, moisture appeared in Evan's eyes, "she was...murdered...on our wedding night."

"Oh man, I'm sorry. Did they ever catch the guy?"

Evan turned his gaze to Jude, the moisture replaced by smoldering anger, "Not yet, that's why I became a Marshal. I wanted to hunt them down and kill'em all!"

"Them?"

"She was raped before she was killed. There was more than one. I was on my way to pick up one of them in Los Angeles when I ended up here."

Jude turned to Evan, "you know who did it? Who was it?"

"A low down snake I knew all my life... Lucias Johnston"

"Aw shit"

A little later, Evan came out of the back room with wet hair and clean clothes Jude had supplied. They were a little big and short in the sleeves and pant length, but adequate nonetheless. Jude grabbed a couple more beers from the fridge and handed one to Evan.

"Boy, that shower is great. I could stand under that all night." He moved to the couch and sat down.

Sitting in an overstuffed chair, Jude said, "So, this Lucias guy, he sounds like a piece of work."

The anger quickly rose up in Evans face, "Oh he is...was. He's a sadistic, mean ornery bastard. Running roughshod over anyone who gets between him and what he wants, which is pretty much everything. His family owns most of the land and business in the area and they live like kings while treating everyone else around like servants."

Jude muttered under his breath, "I guess the bloodline hasn't changed much over time."

Looking around, Evan pointed to the big television in the corner.

"What's that?" he asked.

"Oh, you're going to love this. It's a TV." Jude thought about it for a second.

"Uh...let's see...um... you know those guys with cameras in your day, would take pictures for newspapers, or dead guys in coffins? Well it's kind of like that, only now they can take moving pictures of live events and then send them out into space where they bounce off another cool gadget called a satellite, which then sends it back down to earth to a gathering station, which then sends its own signal out to this box which puts the image back together again for you to watch, in real time, almost....whew!"

Evan was mesmerized by the images on the screen.

"Ok,...didn't understand a word of what you said...what are those guys doing, pretty funny clothes?"

Jude chuckles, "They're playing baseball. I guess it wasn't invented quite yet for you. It's a game...actually one of many games that entertain the people of the world. Wait till you see a football player. You know...some of these guys make millions of dollars a year? Just to play a game. And here we are trying to stop bad guys and protect people and we barely make enough money to live on."

"Well, I guess some things haven't changed that much," Evan observed with a chuckle.

"Look," Jude handed Evan the remote, "this button changes the screen... there are different shows to watch on each channel. This button turns it off. I have cable so you can watch anything you want. Movies...news....anything."

"You hungry? I don't have much here. You watch some TV and I'll run out and grab some grub. Do you like pizza?"

Seeing the quizzical look on Evan's face, "Never mind, I'll just grab a couple of burgers. Be back in a jiff."

Jude went out the front door. Evan sat back on the couch, going from channel to channel.

EIGHTEEN

At nine o'clock at night, Los Angeles International Airport was still a hub of bustling humanity. There was a heavy percentage of incoming travelers, but still plenty of people trying to escape the sprawl of ever spreading buildings and life pressures.

Flight 224 from Nevada was unloading from gate 69B at the end terminal 6, and there was less traffic. So as the passengers disembarked, there was only a smattering of welcoming parties to greet them. U.S. Marshal Jim Dobbs was the third person to emerge from the causeway, and after pausing to get his bearings, he headed to the nearest restroom.

Dobbs was a private person as well as a gun carrying member of law enforcement, and even though there is no one else around, Dobbs chooses to use a stall to relieve himself. He was standing at the toilet with the door propped open by his ample backside, when he became aware of a presence behind him.

"Hey, I'm using...."

He started to turn and was smashed on the back of the head. As he collapsed, his attacker caught him, turned him and got him sitting on the toilet bowl. A yellow handkerchief appeared and was pressured against his nose and mouth until he was dead. The mugger quickly closed the stall door and made a hurried exit. The whole episode took less than a minute.

Jude let himself into his apartment. He had a couple bags of food. He turned from the door to see Evan sleeping on the couch with the television left on, playing an old western movie.

NINETEEN

At eight o'clock the next morning, Evan was once again sitting in Captain Harrison's office. Harrison walked in and though it was still early, he had beads of moisture on his forehead. He patted his shirt pocket, and then his pants pockets. Not finding what he wanted, he began opening drawers on his desk.

"When is that damned air conditioner getting fixed?" he bellowed at no one in particular.

Finally, finding a yellow Marshals handkerchief, he wiped his face, sat back and looked over at Evan.

"Well, we did some research. Guess you might be who you say you are. We talked to the lab and we looked you up in the historical rolls. Seems there was a U.S. Marshal named Evan Longview in the late 1880's. It also gave a little biography, in which it states you were a pretty hard man. Take no prisoners kind of guy, very bloody trail."

Evan looked amused, "That was a long time ago."

Captain Harrison looked closely at Evan to see if he was joking.

"Funny," he smiled, "well, that's all history. According to this report, your last assignment was being sent to Los Angeles to pick up a witness…mmmm, says here…"

The phone rang on his desk. He picked it up.

"Yes?...yes sir, we've been waiting for him to check in."

He listened for a minute, a frown creasing his brow. He grabbed a pad and started to jot down some notes.

"Ahh, Christ… got it." Harrison hung up the phone and sat back. He looked out into the outer office, spotting Cavelot at his desk.

"Cavelot, get in here."

Jude ambled in and stood in the doorway, looking from Evan back to Harrison.

"Yes sir."

"Cavelot, you came out of Nevada originally, correct?"

"Yes sir, I transferred here a few years ago," he was grinning, "wanted change of scenery, be near the ocean air, palm trees, bikinis…followed in your footsteps."

Harrison waves impatiently, "Yea, yea, I get the picture. Well I have a new assignment for you. Do you know a character named Frank Lucias Johnston, apparently some bigwig in Nevada City?"

Jude glanced quickly at Evan who had stiffened and was sitting at full attention.

"Yes sir, I know of him. His family has been in that area forever. Own half the county and a bunch of businesses around town, not all of them legit."

"Well, it seems Mr. Johnston has gotten himself arrested for murdering his wife. The only witness is his step daughter, who just happens to be here in Los Angeles. Now, I just got off the phone with the Western District office and apparently the Marshal they sent to escort the witness back to Nevada just turned up dead at LAX. LAPD is handling that scene, but you get your ass out to the airport and find out what happened. One of our own just got dusted in our own backyard and I don't like it. Also…we have been instructed to pick up the girl and do the escorting to Nevada. I am assigning you to this because you have a history with these people. Can you handle that?"

"Yes sir, thank you sir."

"Cavelot, I don't need to remind you, you've had some problems lately."

"Yes sir."

"Get this job done right and maybe we can see about getting you back on regular assignments….oh, and Cavelot, we're keeping this low profile. It would seem pretty obvious Mr. Johnston doesn't want his daughter getting to trial. Now get going and I will have Ms. Stanton set up your travel."

Evan stood up, facing Captain Harrison.

"Sir, I would like to accompany Marshal Cavelot on this assignment. I know the terrain between here and Nevada City and believe I can be of some help."

"I appreciate the offer, Marshal," but the *terrain* won't be much of an issue these days, and besides, this is official Marshals business."

"Well sir, last I looked, I was still a U.S. Marshal. In fact, I probably have seniority over everyone here."

Harrison, with a pained expression, looked over both men in front of him.

"Umph, okay, Jude could probably use the extra body and what are we going to do with you anyway."

Harrison turned to Jude, "but see if you can't find him a different gun and holster. Going through the airport with a gun strapped to his leg…"

TWENTY

Jude and Evan hurried through the morning commuter crowd, at LAX, toward terminal 6. Evan was awed by the mass of people in one place, carrying or pulling bags of all shapes and sizes, hustling quickly to unknown destinations. Jude, with a strained look on his face was moving quickly, with little patience for Evan's inquisitive talk. As Evan glanced out a window, he saw the monstrous planes waiting to be loaded or unloaded. He stopped when he came to a series of pictures on the wall showing the evolution of airplanes from idea to jumbo jet.

"Do these go up in the air? What keeps them up? They carry people?"

Jude stopped and retreated back to where Evan was standing. "I can't explain exactly, but they are kept up by size, shape and angle of those long wings on the sides. And they are powered by huge engines which keep them going, and yes, they carry people, lots of them. To any place in the world, now come on." He tugged Evan's shirtsleeve to get him moving again.

They came to a small crowd of people, but can tell it's the crime scene by the yellow tape keeping everyone away. They approached a police officer doing crowd control and showed their badges. He lifted the tape and they slid under. He pointed to a man in street clothes with a badge on his belt, "That's the detective in charge."

The man turned as they approached, "John Lardas," he held out a hand to shake, "and *yes* that's how it's pronounced."

Jude shook his hand, "Marshal Cavelot, and this is Marshal Longview." Evan also shook hands.

"Right, well, what we got is one of yours. A Marshal Dobbs, who looks to have been whacked from behind while taking a whiz and then smothered till he was dead. We'll know more when the ME finishes. What do you guys know?"

"Well," Evan began, "all we really know is he was coming in from the Nevada to pick up a witness for a murder trial."

"Yeah, well, looks like somebody didn't want that to happen. Your murder suspect has a long arm."

Jude moved toward the bathroom opening and looked in. "Any clues? Don't suppose the hitter left any evidence behind?"

Lardas looked out over the crowd, "Not that we've found so far. And unfortunately, we have no idea who went in and out as the security cameras don't cover this door. We're canvasing passengers up and down, but with flights leaving in and out, going to have to get real lucky to find anyone who saw something."

Evan also moved to the door. He can see three guys with CSI on their jackets working around the bathroom. "How do you know how he died?"

"There's a baseball sized bump on the back of his head, but we can tell by the discoloration of his skin that he was smothered. The ME will confirm all this, but it would work. Nice and quiet, in and out."

They stood for another minute, looking around. Jude finally moved to get a business card from his shirt pocket. "Alright…you let me know directly if you find anything. Just call this number. We'll work on the suspect list from our end of things. See if our murder suspect has any contacts our here on the coast. We'll let you know if we find anything."

Everyone shook hands again and Jude and Evan moved under the tape and headed back toward an exit.

TWENTY ONE

Sitting at his oversized desk, Frank Johnston was looking over some paperwork. He is attired today in a dark green, crushed velvet smoking jacket and black lapels, his hair slicked back as usual and the obligatory gold medallion resting on his shirtless, black hairy chest. A cigar is smoking in the ashtray. As he looks up out the window, the phone on the desk rings. He absently picked it up,

"Yeah?" He listened for a minute. "You don't say...okay, we'll take care of it."

He hung up the phone, picked up his cigar, and leaned back, puffing it to get it started again. Looking out through the glass doors at his boat house and the lake beyond, his features went through a series of twisted changes, distorting as if each side of his brain is wrestling with the other side. Slowly, calm descended over him. His eyes came back into focus and he looked back toward the double doors that lead into main hall.

"Johnny... get in here!"

Johnny Lang immediately stepped into the room, having been lurking just outside the door, waiting for just such a summons. Lang is a hood, a street punk from the neighborhood. He is a big man,

6'4" tall and broad shouldered, but his size is equal in proportion to his lack of intelligence. He isn't stupid, more clever, but most of all, he is loyal. He grew up with Frank Johnston and has been his sidekick/bodyguard since the day in 7th grade when Frank had faced down a group of 8th graders trying to dump a confused Lang upside down into a trash can. They backed off when Johnston brandished a switchblade and told them he would sneak into their homes and cut off their balls while they slept. They'd been inseparable since, and it only helped that Johnny had grown into his size 15 shoes. He didn't talk too much, which was fine with Johnston, and over the next 30 plus years, they had developed an intertwining relationship in which each one of them got something. Johnny got an authority figure who treated him fairly, and Johnston, a sounding board that didn't talk back and carried out his instructions to the "T".

Johnny moved to his familiar spot in front of Frank's desk. "Yeah Boss?"

"It seems our old friend in California did his job and got rid of the Marshal sent to escort my little girl back to Nevada. But now, they assigned a couple of their own to bring her back to us." He looked directly into Johnny's eyes, "I want you to take a few of the boys and go out there. Make sure they don't make it back here…understand?"

"Yes Boss"

"I'll have Jack fly you over tonight." Johnston added, "You should be able to pick them up tomorrow. Get the boys and get out to the airfield. Jack will have all the details when you get there.

TWENTY TWO

The late morning sun was pouring down through the bedroom window of the Venice apartment. Tanetia was sitting in the overstuffed chair in the corner, watching Susan pack a few final things in her travel bag.

"You sure you want to do this?" Tanetia asked.

Nodding, as if to convince herself. "I have to."

"Why"

"Because I cannot hide the rest of my life. Other than my testimony, there isn't much evidence to counter Frank's version. He'll get acquitted and get away with murdering my mother. *That's* not going to happen." Susan sat down on the edge of the bed.

Tanetia looked at her friend. "Are you nervous…I mean about traveling back to Nevada and the trial?"

Susan thought about it for a second. "A little, I suppose, but I just want it over with so I can get on with my life, as boring as it was."

The doorbell rang down the hall. Susan zipped up her bag and lifted it off the bed.

"After all this excitement," she laughed nervously, "maybe Toby Gentry wouldn't be so bad after all."

TWENTY THREE

While Jude drove, Evan looked through some paperwork from a file on his lap.

"Well, what does it say about our witness?" Jude asks.

"Her name is Susan Aiello…uh, I thought her father was Frank Johnston?"

"Stepfather probably," Jude ventured a guess, "her real father's name was probably Aiello. Maybe he died and the mom remarried this Frank jerk, but Susan kept her maiden name."

Still reading, "Okay…she's 25 years old. She's a nurse. Apparently, she came downstairs in their home to see her stepfather beating her mom to death with a fireplace poker…geez, poor kid."

The SUV came to a stop sign and Evan glanced out the window at a very dirty man in many layers of ragged clothes with a sign standing on the corner.

"Wha…I mean, who is that?"

Jude chuckled, "Him? He's just a homeless dude. We have them all over the place. Mostly people who did too many drugs or drank themselves out of home and family. They become derelict and end up living anywhere they can find shelter. They live on money they can bum off other people. I'm sure you had the same kind in your day."

"Drugs?" Evan had quizzical look on his face.

"Mmm...you know how the Indians smoke a pipe? Maybe have some peyote buttons...from the cactus. Supposed to change their perspective on things? Well, now the world is rampant with all types of drugs like that. Some are natural grown, like marijuana. That's tobacco that makes you hungry and paranoid. You probably had that back in your day. Others are manmade, from natural plants grown around the world,...cocaine, heroin. The worst though are the ones that are made in a laboratory. Those really whack you out. All of them are illegal...considered worse than drinking booze, all pretty addicting. Problem is, they're big business. They may be illegal, but millions of people use one type or another, and where there is a demand, there is a supplier. The drug business is huge."

Evan was about to ask more about drugs when he spotted a couple of girls in bathing suits walking on the sidewalk.

Turning his head quickly toward Jude, he blurts, "Those women...they're walking in public practically naked!"

Laughing, Jude says, "they're wearing bathing suits...you know, something to swim in." Chuckling, "we've come a long way baby!"

Evan swiveled his head back and forth as he spotted one intriguing sight after another. A young boy was skateboarding down the sidewalk, passing a black man sweeping in front of his store. At the next light, a car pulled up on Evan's side and began to bounce up and down on hydraulic lifts. Evan looked to the other side to see two men walking down the sidewalk holding hands.

"Is that two...?"

"Yep, welcome to today's America."

Jude made a few turns off the main street and slowed to look for the numbers on the houses. After a minute he pulled to the curb.

"Here we are. Why don't you keep an eye out for any unsavory characters and I'll go and get her."

Jude got out, went around the front of the SUV, to the front door, and rang the bell. After a minute, the door opened and Tanetia and Susan step out.

Addressing Susan, Jude asked, "Ms. Aiello?"

"Yes, I'm Susan Aiello."

"How do you do ma'am. I'm Marshal Cavelot, and we're here to escort you to Nevada. Are you ready to go?"

"Yes," she turned to Tanetia, "Okay, I guess this is it. I'll call you when I get settled, should be sometime tonight."

Don't worry about it, baby, I'll be here for you."

The two women hugged and Tanetia, looked over Susan's shoulder at Jude, "You better take care of this girl."

Jude tipped his hat to Tanetia, "Yes ma'am we will."

Jude picked up the luggage and they turned for the SUV. Evan scrambled out and opened the back door for Susan. He nodded, "Hello ma'am, I'm Marshal Evan Longview"

"How do you do?" Susan answered as she climbed into the back seat.

Jude put the luggage in the back and moved into the driver seat. Susan looked out her window to wave goodbye to Tanetia, who nodded toward Evan and gave Susan the thumbs up. She waved as the SUV pulled away from the curb.

TWENTY FOUR

The worn out looking, single storied, wooden shed, sat sadly behind the stately science hall on campus, looking a lot like a left over WWII Quonset hut. The only hint of internal existence was the sign on the outside of the door saying, "Outward Imagination", but on the other side, it had very few, if any, signs of imagination. The room was sparsely furnished with nothing but a reception desk, minus the receptionist, one chair in front and one behind. There were no pictures or paintings on the walls and no windows. Even the coloring was boring, a cross between institutional grey and baby poop green. There was a single door behind the reception desk with a paper sign taped to the frosted window, reading, R & D. Through this door, at least there was activity, if still no outward sign of caring for work environment. The room took up the other three quarters of the building and it had two windows one on each side. It had the same lack of any discernable color on the walls, but there was the sound of soft rock drifting through the stale air. The room was littered with tables and chairs in no organized pattern. A picnic table was sitting near the door with a small dorm room sized refrigerator next to it. There was a self-standing wash basin next to that and then a hand built wood box with a toilet and shower behind the badly hung door. There was a computer on almost all the tables and a few odd machines, in various states of repair.

It was here that Tom Davidson and his vagabond troupe of scientists and interns, toiled away to make their ideas come to life. It was obvious by their surroundings, that the funding they received was not one of full commitment.

"We're never going to get this fixed," a frustrated Yoshi complained. "There's just too much sand everywhere. It would be easier to just replace the components."

"Yeah…well, unfortunately, that's not in the budget," an equally frustrated Davidson responded.

Another intern, Peter who was working at another table said, "but after you told the board about the Marshal, wouldn't they be all over this, throwing money at us to get it working again, asap?"

"Maybe," Tom replied, "if we could produce the Marshal. They said they would check with their sources, but he seems to have disappeared again and nobody is talking. The Marshals office is playing mum."

Emily, the only female on the team, chimed in, "Well, I'd like to find him…do some testing on him myself."

Peter shook his head, "Niiiiice."

"What? I'm just saying."

TWENTY FIVE

"Ok, let's go," an out of breath Jude said, "gate 7E, down that way."

Even late morning on a weekday doesn't lessen the mass of humanity flowing through Los Angeles International Airport. With three million people moving in and around the city, there was always a very hefty number traveling to and from. After finally finding a parking spot in long term parking, they hustled into the terminal. Evan and Susan sat seated in a waiting area, as Jude was returning from acquiring tickets to Nevada City. It had taken about twenty minutes and Evan was, of course, amazed by all of the people, the different nationalities, clothing and languages. He was too stunned to even ask questions. He just sat and soaked it all in.

They had checked Susan's case at the counter, but Jude and Evan each had a small carry on. They gathered their things and moved down the hall toward their gate, with Susan between Jude and Evan.

Stepping from behind a large column, Johnny and a couple other men moved in and formed up around them. Johnny was walking next to Jude, while one man took up a position in front and the other stepped in behind.

"Hello Susan," Johnny nodded, "just keep walking gentlemen, let's don't do anything stupid." He patted his pocket, "We have you covered. We're just going to walk out that door like one big, happy family."

Evan looked to Susan, "Do you know these men?"

"They work for Frank"

"That's right," Johnny interjected, "so we're just doing our jobs here."

The sliding double door opened and they exited to the side walk outside.

Susan looked toward Johnny, "Where are you taking us, Johnny? Frank murdered my mother. I have to testify. How can you work for a scum like him?"

"I'm sorry Susan. I always liked you. I wasn't too fond of your mother's cooking, but I am sorry for what happened to her."

The other two men chuckled and nodded as they entered the parking structure.

Johnny pointed to a black SUV up the ramp a little. "Let's go, over there."

They started to move toward the SUV. Evan caught Susan's eye. He threw an elbow backward into the throat of the man behind. Susan kicked the man in front behind his knee and he collapsed to the ground.

"Run!"

Jude turned and pushed Johnny into the staggering man behind and followed Evan and Susan up the ramp. They ran up and around to the next level. Johnny was the first to recover.

"You," he pointed to the man on the ground, "get the car." Johnny and the other man ran up the ramp, following Jude, Evan and Susan.

As the evading trio climbed the ramp, a man was just getting into his car.

"Sorry," Jude pushed the man aside, "Marshals business."

Pushing the unlock button, everyone climbed into the car. Jude threw the car into reverse, backed out and tore down the ramp, passing Johnny and his sidekick. They either didn't want to attract too much attention or they were caught by surprise and couldn't get their guns out in time. They turned and sprinted back down to their own waiting SUV.

Jude maneuvered the car through the heavy, airport crowd and out into the city traffic. Just making a yellow light, he turned quickly onto the first side street he came to.

"Get out."

They quickly exited the car and Jude led them back to the main street. In a few seconds he saw what he was looking for and flagged down a cab. The cabbie had a surprised and confused look on his face.

"Closest Amtrak station and hurry."

The taxi pulled away from the curb and entered the flow of traffic in the right lane.

Jude, who was sitting in the front seat, looked out though the back window and yelled, "Get down."

Evan and Susan ducked down in the back seat as low as they could go. In a minute, Johnny's SUV raced past.

TWENTY SIX

"You two go sit over there out of sight," Jude pointed to a bench behind a large pillar. "I'll go get some tickets and be right back."

Jude went off to the ticket counter. Evan and Susan moved to sit on the bench.

"You alright?" Evan asked when they were seated.

"Yes…I think so. Do you think they'll find us here?"

"Not sure…where are we?"

Susan gave him a quizzical look, "We're at the Amtrak station."

"Amtrak?"

"Yes, it's the train that runs all over the country."

Evan tried to look understanding "Oh, yeah…the train."

Across the way, Jude stepped away from the ticket window. As he looked around and then over to Evan and Susan, he pulled a cellphone from his pocket and stepped behind another pillar to make a call.

Susan took a closer look at Evan. "Where are you from Marshal Longview?"

"Evan"

"Ok, Evan….where are you from?"

"Nevada City, Nevada originally"

A look of surprise jumped on Susan's face, "Really, so am I. What part?"

Looking around for Jude, a distracted Evan said, "Where is Jude…uh, what part?"

"Yeah, what area, what street?"

A faraway look came over Evan's face. "Oh, I have a ranch about two miles out of town, over on the river."

Susan furrowed her brow in thought, "Mmm…what school did you go to?"

"Well, there's only one…"

Just then, Jude walked up waving some tickets. "Ok, we got lucky. We're booked on the 11:00 for Chicago, with stops in Bakersfield and Nevada City…which means if we hurry, we can make the train."

Susan had been looking at Evan with her head tilted in confused thought. They all looked furtively around as they made their way to the gate.

TWENTY SEVEN

A warm breeze was blowing across the pool, but it was barely enough to affect the scorching desert heat. Frank Johnston was sitting beneath a large umbrella. The mist from the ceiling pipes feeding some coolness was all but useless as the breeze was blowing most of it over his head. Frank's tasteless attire is, as usual, straight out of a bad fifties movie. Oversized swim trunks with an ugly flower pattern, a cotton towel coat with short sleeves and the obvious gold necklace resting on his matted black chest hair, slick with sweat. The whole ensemble is capped off by slip on rubber flip flops and a pair of oversized Hollywood sunglasses. The cell phone sitting next to his fruity cocktail with an umbrella began to vibrate on the mottled glass table top. Frank glanced down at the number and picked up the phone.

"Well, nice of you to call, you piece of shit. What are you thinking? This girl can put me in the chair…" He listened, "Ok, but this time, stay out of the way…."

Frank pushed the off button and then dialed another number, "They're on an Amtrak train heading to Chicago. #327. They'll be in Bakersfield by 3:00 and here by 8:00 tomorrow morning. Make sure they don't get off that train, got it?"

He pushed the hang up button and threw the phone down. "Fuckin' morons!"

TWENTY EIGHT

The landscape outside the window was flying by and Evan was again overcome by the speed of the world. How do you enjoy the land, the rivers, the mountains? All you get is a glimpse. He turned back to the interior and looked around the lush compartment.

"This isn't like any train I ever been on."

Susan, sat across from him, again watching him with a questioning look on her face.

"Where did Marshal Cavelot go?"

Evan brought his focus back to Susan's eyes. "He went to check the other cars."

"Who are you, Marshal Longview…err, Evan. I mean, you seem out of sorts. Where are you really from? I've lived in Nevada City my whole life and it certainly has more than one school, and you act like you've never seen a train before. So….who *are* you, really?"

Evan looked intently at Susan. After a long moment, he broke his gaze away and took a deep breath.

"Ok…my name *is* Evan Longview and I *am* from Nevada City." He paused to gather his thoughts.

"I was born in 1865. I was coming across the desert to pick up a witness to my wife's murder when I came through some sort of time machine and ended up in this time period. Marshal Cavelot was at the scene, and I ended up at the Marshals office with him. I believe your murderer, Frank, is the great grandson of my wife's murderer. When I heard his name, I got myself assigned to your service in hopes of getting more evidence against Lucias, so that I could go back and put him in the ground..." Evan exhaled.

"Oh…ok, that explains it," Susan retorted with a sarcastic tone. She turned away to look out the window.

"Really, Susan, believe me. I'm as out of water here as you probably feel."

A thought occurred to Evan and he dug into his shirt pocket.

"Here, this is the card of the scientist who had the machine. They were experimenting in the desert when the machine went on by accident just as I came along."

Glancing down at the card, Susan asked, "Your wife was murdered, by Frank's great grandfather?"

"Yes, him and his gang...had their way with her first, on our wedding night...that was three years ago. I joined the Marshals service and have been taking out my anger on any thief, killer, or cattle rustler that came across my path. All I really want, though, is to look Lucias Johnston in the eye as I put a bullet through his black heart."

"Oh Marsh...Evan, I am so sorry. That's a terrible story."

It was Susan's turn to look Evan in the eye, "I guess we both have something in common then. I watched Frank Johnston beat my mother to death with a fire place poker, after she confronted him about him having an affair with the maid. He didn't show any remorse....just anger that she was actually questioning his actions."

Susan wiped the back of her hand across her eyes as they were beginning to moisten from tears. "That's why I have to go back and testify in court, because I want to see that bastard fry in the electric chair!"

Susan began to sob from pent up stress, sadness and anger, Evan moved to sit beside her. As he put his arm around her, she snuggled into his shoulder. She began to settle down and they sat quietly for a few minutes, with Evan staring off into the night streaming by.

As Susan began to nod off, she whispered a last question. "Evan, how did Johnny know we were at the airport?"

TWENTY NINE

Outside the window, the terrain had changed from flat desert to low hills with bigger mountains looming ahead. Susan was still sleeping on Evan's shoulder. Jude was sitting across from them. Evan, lost in thought, was still looking out at the dark shapes of trees and mountains as they trundled past.

"She's really crashed…she slept through the last two stops." Jude cocked his head to the right, "Take my advice buddy, don't get too attached to her. Women always find a way to break your heart."

"I wouldn't know. The only woman I ever loved never had the chance." Evan pulled back from the window and looked at Jude. "Why don't you call your captain, ask for help? Tell him somebody tried to bushwhack us."

Jude shook his head, "How do you think those guys knew we were at the airport? No, I can't call in. There must be a leak in the office. I wouldn't know who to trust."

Evan looked at Jude. "What did your captain mean when he said you'd had some trouble?"

"I made some bad investments with my money and when the bad guys came to collect, I shot one of them in self-defense."

"You mean you had some gambling debts."

"Something like that…anyway, the Marshals service kind of frowns on that kind of behavior and I ended up on suspension for a month. When I got back to duty, I was given the shit jobs, like babysitting a bunch of snot nosed science punks. So there I was when you came out of nowhere."

Evan continued to tug on the thread, "He also mentioned you had a connection to Nevada. What did he mean by that?"

"You don't miss much, do you?" Jude chuckled and then looked at Evan, "Well, I'm originally from around Nevada City, grew up there. Like I told the captain, I needed a change of scenery, so I moved to sunny Southern California."

Jude averted his eyes and looked down the car. His eyes grew wide with surprise.

"Aw shit, those mugs are on the train. They must have boarded at the last stop… com'n, get her up, we have to go!"

Evan looked down the car to see Johnny and friends coming through the door at the end. He shook Susan hard, dragged her up to her feet and began to push her toward the opposite end, pulling his gun at the same time.

"Wha..?"

"Com'n, we've got to go. Your friend Johnny is on the train."

Susan, now fully awake, looked back over her shoulder, "Oh no!...how did they know where we were?"

Johnny came through the end door and let off a wild shot. One female passenger screamed and everyone ducked down behind a seat. The other two thugs filed in behind Johnny and they moved up the aisle. Evan shoved Susan through the door and turned to fire his gun. He was already turning to follow Susan when he saw a red spot blossom on one of the men. Evan didn't wait to see if he went down. They escaped into the vestibule and moved into the next car.

"Everybody down!" Jude yelled.

When the passengers saw three people rushing up the aisle, two of them with guns brandished, they quickly followed orders and dove to the floor behind seats.

Evan, Jude and Susan continued to move forward till they got to the conductor car. As they arrived at the last vestibule door, Jude reached up and pulled the emergency stop cord. The train shuddered and shook as the brakes kicked in. They squeezed through the last door, and as the train began to slow, they burst out a side door and jumped to the ground, stumbling and falling as the momentum carried them away from the tracks. Johnny and his crew had been thrown to the floor as the train lurched to a stop. Rising, he spotted Evan helping Susan up from the ground and the three fugitives running for the roadway, two hundred yards away.

Jude reached the roadway first and flashing his badge and gun, flagged down an oncoming car.

"U.S.Marshals business, we need your car, sir, right now!"

"Hey, I'm on my way home…you can't do this!"

Evan and Susan ran around to the passenger side as Jude grabbed the man by the shirt front and pulled him away from the car, "Sorry sir, we gotta go!"

The driver began to move around the back of the car toward the passenger side, "Well then, I'm coming with you, to make sure noth…"

A gun shot rang out as a bullet smashed into the back fender next to the driver. He turned to see Johnny and crew sprinting toward them, guns waving. The driver started running down the road in the opposite direction.

"You guys go ahead, my card is in the glove box…let me know where you leave it…"

This last statement fell on an empty space as Jude threw the car into gear and bolted away. Johnny reached the road and stood with his gun out pointed at the next vehicle coming along, a SUV. As it came to a stop, one of his crew dragged the driver out the door and flung him aside, down the embankment. They loaded up and tore out after other car.

In the front car, a frightened Susan looked out the back window. "How did they know we were on that train?"

"I told you," Jude said, "there must be a leak at the station…look, we're never going to out run that truck in this piece of shit car. We're going to have to lose them or stop them somehow. Help Evan get his seatbelt on, this is going to get crazy."

As they raced up the mountain road, the trees flashing by are dark and dense. The guard rails along the edge are the only barrier between the cars and the dark abyss beyond. For the next few miles, the cat and mouse chase continues. The bigger engine in the SUV helping it pull close on the straight a ways, but the smaller car building a gap on the tight mountain curves.

As they begin to crest the top of the mountain and start down the backside, Evan turns to Jude.

"Jude, do you know these guys? Do you know who they work for, this Frank Johnstone?"

Jude hesitated and then with a hangdog look said, "Yes..I..I used to work for him, a long time ago."

Susan leaned forward from the back seat. "Have you been feeding him information all this time? Are you the leak?"

Suddenly the smaller car is smashed from behind as the SUV had closed the gap and run right up into its quarry.

"Shit… hold on," a panicked Jude called out. He was fighting the wheel, but the blunt force from behind had pushed the smaller car into a sideways slide and he couldn't gain control. With another sharp curve coming right at them, the car slid right into the barrier.

"Look out!" Evan shouted.

Susan screamed.

The momentum of three thousand pounds of steel hit the barrier, which proved no match for the speed and force it was designed to stop. The car flipped up and rolled over the edge, down into the dark forest below.

The car rolled over again before landing on its roof and crashing down the hillside, caroming off trees and brush like a violent pinball. Sliding sideways, it hit a tree stump leftover from the last great wind storm and flipped once again onto its side before coming to a crushing stop up against a huge, ancient redwood tree. For a long minute there was no sound except the hissing of the motor gasping out its last dying breath.

Hanging sideways from the passenger seat, Evan was the first to regain some semblance of consciousness. For a few seconds he let his mind work its way down his body to make sure all parts were attached and functioning. He had been uncomfortable when Susan had helped him into his "seatbelt" harness, but was now thankful that it seemed to have done its job. He felt warmth on his arm and looked to see blood soaking through his shirt. He ignored it and looked around the interior of the car. A moan came from the back seat and Evan turned his head to see Susan stirring awake. She also was still buckled into her seat. Shards of glass covered the whole back seat area, but miraculously, she seemed to be okay.

"Susan…Susan, are you alright?"

Susan looked up at Evan for a second before answering, "Yes, I think so."

Looking back to Jude, who was collapsed on the door, unconscious, Evan could see a large, bloody area forming on the ground below his head.

"Jude! Jude! Can you hear me?....I think he's knocked out."

Beginning to unbuckle herself, Susan said, "We've got to get out of here before it blows!"

"Blows?"

Susan crawled up and out the hole where the back window used to be. Jumping down, she moved around to the front of the car. Speaking through the smashed windshield, she said, "The fuel that runs these cars is very combustible. Any little spark and the whole thing could go up like a bomb….at least it does in the movies."

"Movies?"

"Never mind, let's get Jude out of there."

Evan, who was now unbuckled and bracing himself from falling on top of Jude, reached down and worked the seatbelt loose. He grabbed Jude's arm and tried to lift him but stopped when a shooting pain ran up his arm. "I don't think I can lift him up, he's too heavy."

Susan stepped back and looked up the mountain and then back to the car. "Hurry, climb out and help me. We'll have to push the car back over on it wheels and then we can drag him out his door or through the window."

Evan scrambled up and out his door window. He dropped to the ground and moved around the car and down the hill, next to the tree. As luck would have it, whatever luck they had, the car was tilted at an angle which allowed them to push together, relatively easily, and the car fell back on its wheels with a loud crunch. Evan grabbed the door handle and yanked hard. The door opened, but only a few inches. He braced his feet and pulled as hard as he could. Slowly, with a metal scraping screech, he was able to make the opening wide enough to pull Jude out and clear of the car. They each grabbed an arm and dragged Jude down the mountain another fifty feet. They propped him up next to a tree. As they are setting him down, Evan noticed another bloody spot on Jude's stomach. Jude began to awaken with moans of pain.

"Jude, Jude, can you hear me?"

Jude opened his eyes, his chest was heaving and his breathing was coming in short spurts.

"Ahhhh, I think I crushed my chest...my head hurts something fierce." He looked up the hill as events began to come back to him. "You guys need to get out of here."

Evan was shaking his head, "You're going to be okay, we'll get you to a doctor."

Jude grabbed Evan's arm, "No, no, leave me...not going to make it. Look, I'm sorry... I *was* leaking our location. You were right. I had gambling debts...Frank bought them up. He figured it would be good to have some law enforcement under his thumb. Guess he was right."

Jude closed his eyes and began to breathe faster, "I'm sorry"

Evan looked at Jude, "Did you kill the Marshal at the airport?"

Jude's eyes snapped open with a look of bewilderment. He tried to summon the effort to speak, but nothing came out except his last dying breath.

Susan took the gun from Jude's holster, and grabbed Evan's shoulder, "We've got to go, now. There's nothing we can do for him."

Evan stood and they staggered off down the hill.

THIRTY

Up on the dark mountain road, the SUV had to drive another one hundred yards past the crushed railing to find a place to pull off the road. Johnny found a flashlight in the glove compartment and with his two associates ran back up the hill to the exit point. They stood and looked down into the darkness. A few noises carried up to them and then a sound like nails on a chalk board reached their ears.

Johnny shoved the man next to him, handed him the flashlight and ordered, "Sid, go down and make sure they're dead."

Sid looked down the steep mountain side into the darkness, "Me, why me, why not Joe?"

Johnny cuffed him in the back of the head, "Because Joe got shot, dumbass, that's why."

Turning to face Joe, Sid whined, "Shit, it was only a shoulder graze, he's fine, ain't ya Joe?"

An angry Johnny stepped forward, "Fine, both of you go. Make sure!"

Sid and Joe stepped over the bent railing and began to slip and slide down the mountain side, getting very little grip in their smooth, soled Italian loafers. Even with the dim flashlight, there was little to no visibility, the going was slow as they ran into trees, banged their shins on rocks and twisted their ankles in soft dirt. After a few tortuous minutes they saw the car next to a tree. Sid shined the light around, and spotted a body a little further down the hill. He and Joe exchanged a worried glance. They started to move down toward the car when it exploded into a fiery ball of flame, throwing both of them back to the ground.

Further down the mountain, Evan and Susan were working their way slowly through the trees. Suddenly they heard an explosion and the sky was lit up by the ball of fire up the hill above them.

Susan stopped and looked back, "Um, guess the movies got it right."

Evan took her hand, "Com'n, got to keep moving...movies?"

"Uh...it's a story told in a series of moving pictures. You watch it on a big screen or a TV. Sometimes they're mysteries, sometimes they're love stories. They're even historical. There are hundreds of movies made that take place in your time...If we get out of this, we'll have to go see one together sometime, like a date."

They started to move down and around a large bunch of bushes and rocks. Evan stopped and looked at the wall of bushes close by.

"Hang on a second." He climbed back up a little, poking into the bushes. "I know this mountain. I used to come up here all the time when I wanted to clear my head or just ride. See that rock formation over there? There's a cave there. We can hide out there. It's not likely anyone will try to follow us down the mountain in the dark. It's getting cold and we need to find shelter. We can rest up in there."

Johnny was stamping his feet impatiently at the top of the mountain. He could hear his men coming back up, cursing and thrashing the brush. Sid and Joe reached the top edge and clambered awkwardly back over the rail.

"Well, nice to see you didn't blow yourselves up. What'd ya see?"

Sid, breathing very hard explained, "The car blew before we could check it out...we saw one of the Marshals dead near the car. Maybe he crawled out but the other two were stuck inside and must have got blown up."

Johnny stared at him, "Or maybe they escaped and are heading down the mountain." He paused to think a minute. "Ok, let's go before the cops show up. I need to check in."

Frank Johnston leaned back in his office chair, puffing on his usual pungent cigar. "Who was it dead?...not sure...Christ, what a clusterfuck...if they survived, we might get lucky and they'll die on the mountain, they might be injured or something...ok, drive down and hole up somewhere, I need to do some thinking."

Johnston put the phone back into its cradle and blew out a plume of smoke...

"Shit."

THIRTY ONE

The musty smell in the darkness was brought on by the moisture seeping from the walls of the cave.

"If I remember right, this goes back far enough for us to be out of sight, but we won't be able to have any fire."

With hands extended, they found the back wall and a spot with no wetness. They sat down with their backs against the rock and tried to get comfortable. Susan leaned into Evan and he put his arm around her shoulders to keep her warm. A small smile curled up on her lips.

Susan snuggled in closer, "Evan, if we survive this, what are you going to do?"

"What do you mean?"

"Well, after you deliver me to the District Attorney, where will you go?"

"I don't know…I suppose I'll try to get a hold of that scientist guy and see about getting home."

He looked down at her, "What about you?"

"Well, I really haven't thought about it. The trial will probably take a while. I suppose the D.A. will have to keep me locked up some place away from

Frank. If all goes well, and he goes to jail, I'll be free to do what I want."

Evan put his head back and closed his eyes. "Will you go back to your friend's house? She seemed....uh, colorful..."

Susan sat up abruptly, "Things have changed Evan. Blacks aren't slaves anymore. You should know that. I mean, things still aren't perfect, but things have changed quite a bit since "your" day."

"I'm sorry, I didn't mean anything by it, it's just that where I come... uh in my time, you don't see a lot of white people being friends with black people."

Susan settled back down under his arm. "Well, there is still a lot of hostility, not quite as obvious and not nearly as tolerated. Tanetia and I went to school together. We're best buds. Don't know what I'd do without her."

Evan closed his eyes again. "So, will you go back to her house?"

"I don't know. If Frank goes to jail, I might get control of his empire. Maybe I'll set myself up to be the next Don Corleone...oops, sorry, movie reference. With my mom gone, there's nothing really holding me there. Maybe I'll just sell everything and retire to a tropical island. You could come along and be my cabana boy."

"Is that like a slave…I thought that was outlawed?"

Giggling, Susan purred, "More like a sex slave…it would be strictly consensual, of course."

Now Evan was embarrassed, "Uh…we should probably get some rest, going to need our strength to stay alive tomorrow."

They snuggled closer and Evan tried to corral his thoughts. In a few minutes, the only sound in the cave was the quiet breathing of two exhausted people.

THIRTY TWO

Tom Davidson ran toward the burning building, but was stopped by the intense heat when he was still fifty feet away. The bungalow squatting next to the science lab was engulfed in towering flames.

"What the hell happened?" He turned to a spectator standing nearby.

"I don't know, man, sometimes students come outside the lab building to take a smoke break. Maybe one of them didn't put his out enough."

Tomas Linkley arrived on a run, breathing heavily, "Oh my God! What happened?

"We're screwed, that's what happened. Everything was in that lab."

"Crap, crap, crap…I've got some mechanical drawings at home, but all of the software and designs were on those computers. Some of the molds for the bigger pieces are at the plant, but it's going to take…shit, I don't know, at least a year to get all the components made and assembled again…crap, crap, crap!"

Tom collapsed to the ground, his head in his hands. "Don't even know if our investors are going to be willing to foot this bill all over again…like I said, we're screwed."

THIRTY THREE

The sun leaked through the bushes at the entrance to the cave. Small particles of light splashed on the floor and walls like tiny shards of glass. A blue jay cawed loudly in a tree at some perceived nuisance. Evan's eyes opened and his head blurted out to him loudly that his body was very sore all over. He slowly took in his surroundings, vaguely remembering the chase, but reliving the crash in full detail. Glancing down, his eyes locked onto Susan's, as she was staring up at him.

"Good morning sunshine," she smiled

"Good morning…it is morning, isn't it?"

"Yes, I watched the sun rise a little from what I can see."

"Man, I feel like I got thrown off the wildest buck and then got stepped on for good measure."

"Wow, was this what that feels like? I can see why rodeo is so popular. Who wouldn't want to feel like *this*."

Evan began to get to his feet, wincing as pain shot through his arm.

"Hey, you're hurt; let me take a look at that."

"It's nothing, just a scratch."

Susan pulled him back down and began to unbutton Evan's shirt. "I'm a nurse, remember?" She gently worked the shirt off his shoulder and down to his waist. "I won't hurt you...much."

"I'm telling you, I'm fine," but he let her touch his arm and look over his would.

"Hush, just shut up and let me look."

She reached down and tore a strip from the bottom of his shirt. She turned and wet the rag from the moisture leaking from the walls. She began to dab and wipe the blood from the wound.

"It's not too deep, just a little gash. We don't have any bandages, so just hold this against it for a little bit, should stop any bleeding."

"Told you it was nothing...but...thank you." He looked at Susan, his eyes roaming up and down, "You seem okay, no visible cuts or ...gashes."

They sat for a minute, staring out toward the sunlight ahead and the day to come.

"Evan?"

"Yes?"

"Let's don't go back"

"What do you mean?"

"I mean," and now Susan sat up on her knees, facing Evan, "I've been thinking, this is crazy. We're going to get killed...and I don't want to die. Let's just hide out here."

"And what do you propose we live on "out here?""

Susan began to get a little heated, "I don't know, you're the westerner. I'm sure you can hunt and fish. We can make clothes from animal skins...like Jeremiah Johnson."

"Who"

"It's a movie with Robert Redford, where he becomes a mountain man and lives off the land. Just disappears from civilization."

"What about Frank," Evan asked, "what about what he did to your mother?"

Susan's shoulders slump, "I don't care about that anymore." She turned her eyes away, Testifying against him is not going to bring her back. And besides, guys like Frank don't go to jail. They have slick, expensive lawyers. They buy off jurors and judges. They make backroom deals. He'll be free and keep coming after me," Susan began to shake. "I don't want to live looking over my shoulder forever." She leaned forward into Evan and he took her in his arms.

With Susan collapsed in his arms, Evan stared out of the cave into the rising sunshine. His mind began to create a familiar, nightmare scene. He saw Mary getting hit, Lucias getting up off her, buttoning up his pants, looking down at her, a slight smile on his face as he raised his foot and stomped down...

Evan jolted back to reality. He pushed Susan away and holding both hands on her shoulders, he looked into her eyes. She was startled, as she could see the depths of his anger. Anger that was familiar to all the thieves and rustlers he had cornered and arrested in a previous time.

"I can't do that, Susan. First of all, I'm a terrible fisherman, and not a very good rancher. And I can't run away. I can't run away, for Mary, for your mother. You said it, guys like this Frank, like Lucias, never go to jail. They think they're above the law. There are never any consequences for what they do." He reached down and touched his badge, "Well, I'm the law and what I *am* good at is catching the bad guys and making sure they pay for their sins...I'm the consequences."

Evan stood up and looked down at Susan, putting out his hand. She looked up into his eyes for a second and then reached up to take his hand. He helped her to her feet and they headed out, Evan leading Susan down the mountain side.

Evan was moving carefully. "Geez, this sure seemed easier when I was a kid or had a horse." He stopped to look down the mountain, "There's a ranch down there. We can probably get some help there."

Right then, Susan stumbled and lost her balance.

"Shit!"

She fell and dropped Jude's gun as she rolled down the hillside. Turning at the sound, Evan braced himself and caught her, stopping her slide.

"Whoa there, you alright?"

A breathless Susan looked up gratefully, "Yes, thank you"

They looked at each other. Evan leaned down and gave Susan a kiss, but pulled away quickly, embarrassed. Susan pulled him down for a longer kiss when all of a sudden a gunshot rang out and dirt kicked up a few feet away.

Evan grabbed Susan and they scrambled toward some trees for cover, another gun shot and another puff of dirt chasing them.

Peering out from the edge of the tree, Evan pointed, "The shot came from that direction, so maybe we can still get to the ranch for help."

Susan took a quick look around the tree, "How do you know that?"

"Because I can see the shooter…c'mon, keep low."

THIRTY FOUR

A black SUV moved steadily down the old, country road. Sid was driving, and Joe was sitting in the backseat behind Johnny, who was in the passenger seat looking intently out the window. A long range rifle was standing between his legs. The base of the mountain began to rise up on their right across a field of mowed hay. The landscape to their left was flat. It alternated between more fields of mowed hay and pastures with a smattering of horses.

Suddenly Johnny yelled out, "There they are, stop the truck!"

As the truck slid to a stop, Johnny was already out the door. He ran around to the driver's side and threw the rifle up on the hood. Bending down and looking through the attached scope, he saw Evan and Susan slowly making their way down the mountain side. He was about ready to fire when Susan stumbled and fell down. As she slid down to Evan, Johnny realigned his shot.

"That's niiice, look at the hillside lovers."

Just as he was pulling the trigger, Sid jumped out of the truck to watch. The loss of weight rocked the truck and Johnny's shot missed its mark.

"You fucking dumbshit!"

He yanked back on the bolt and loaded another bullet. This time, he didn't use the truck, just threw the rifle up to his shoulder and took quick aim. Evan and Susan were running as fast as they could across the hill toward a group of trees. He fired again, but this time, he missed slightly behind them. Before he can reload again, they had disappeared into the trees.

Johnny ordered, "Get back in the truck, now!"

He looked out the window and saw Evan and Susan moving down the mountain again.

The three men loaded back into the SUV and Johnny pointed up the road ahead of the truck, "That's the only ranch in the nearby area. Get this piece of shit moving, we gotta make that house before they can get to a phone.

THIRTY FIVE

At the base of the mountain, Evan and Susan reached a fence meant to keep the livestock from wandering off up the mountain. Evan put a booted foot on the top layer of bobbed wire and pushed, bending the fence down and snapping the nearest fence post in two. With the fence lying low, Susan jumped over and continued running full speed through the pasture. Evan jumped clear of the wire and took off after Susan. Off to his right, a couple of Paint horses were watching them with bored indifference. To his left he could see the black truck racing toward the farm. Straight ahead was the main farm house. A nice, typical, two story wood planked home with a wraparound porch. Standing a little closer to the pasture and more to the right, Evan looked at the farm barn, a hulking building with large, open double doors and hay bale pulley swinging above.

Evan's longer strides caught him up to Susan. He yelled breathlessly, "Head for the barn, got an idea."

They raced across the pasture. Susan was almost out of breath and strength, but the panicky feeling inside and the memory of the bullet next to her created a second wind. They made the other side, and climbed over the wooden gate. The black SUV pulled into the yard and skidded to a stop in the gravel as they disappeared into the barn. Everyone piled out of the SUV, with guns drawn. Warily, they approached the open door of the barn. Johnny nudged Joe and signaled for him to circle around behind. Joe turned and slipped around the corner. Johnny and Sid eased through the open door into the darkness. It took their eyes a second to adjust, but when they did, it was just in time to see a large horse with Evan and Susan riding double, racing out a back door into the field beyond.

"Shit! Back to the truck."

They sprinted back to the SUV. They climbed in, Sid floored it, spraying gravel every direction until the wheels grabbed traction and they shot off around the barn, slowing down only to pick up Joe.

THIRTY SIX

With no time to put on a saddle, Evan just grabbed a bridal hanging from a nail and went quickly into a stall. Inside was another healthy looking Paint horse.

"Don't know why you aren't outside with your friends, but glad of it."

Waiting out in the runway, Susan looked furtively toward the main door. She saw the SUV slide to a stop and the doors open. She turned back to the stall.

"You might want to hurry up with your new friend there. We're about to have unwanted guests."

Leading a horse out of the stall, Evan stepped around and jumped up on its bare back.

"Sorry, it won't be comfortable, but best I could do on short notice."

He reached down and pulled Susan up behind. They headed toward the back and pushed through a back door. Evan gave a little kick in the side and the horse responded, leaping into a full gallop. Evan saw a man coming around the corner out of the corner of his eye, but they were already out and running across the pasture.

Susan had both arms around Evan and was hanging on as if her life depended on it, which it did. Evan, with both knees squeezing tight, to keep them both on the horse, turned his head and called over his shoulder.

"You ok? You said you could ride."

"Don't worry about me, cowboy. You just worry about those guys." She took her hand away to point back at the SUV.

Evan looked back to see the black SUV bouncing and sliding as it charged across the grassy pasture.

"We won't be able to outrun them for long. Let's head back to the mountain where the truck can't go. Maybe we can lose them in the trees."

Evan angled the horse toward the mountain looming to the right. As they got closer to the tree line, Evan looked back to see the SUV had gained ground and was almost upon them. A gun shot sounded and the bullet zipped by, just missing on their right. Another shot went off, seemingly right behind them, and though it hit nothing, it had another desirable effect. The horse they were riding was used to easy gallops and quiet morning grazing in the pasture. The exploding sound of gun shots was new and shocking and he reacted accordingly. He jolted to a halt, shaking his head left and right, trying to get control of his own actions. Evan was fighting the reins as best he could, but the SUV swung around to their right and the horse panicked and reared up on its hind legs, spilling Susan hard to the ground behind them. Without the extra person, Evan was able to calm the horse down. As he slowly got the horse to stand still, the SUV came to a halt and the three men inside, piled out with guns waiving. Johnny looked down at Susan, who was sitting up slowly, and then back up to Evan

"Alright, why don't you get down off that horse buddy. I don't know who you are, but you've been a major pain in my ass long enough."

As Sid leaned over and pulled Susan to her feet, Johnny approached Evan.

"Don't do anything stupid or the girl gets hurt."

While Evan stood still, Johnny patted him down and removed his gun. After checking for any ankle weapons, he stood up, looked into Evan's face and with lightning speed, smashed Evan across the face with his gun, dropping him to one knee.

Susan cried out, "Don't!"

Sid, jerking her arm, snarled, "Shut up bitch, or you get one too."

Evan looked at Johnny and slowly stood back up.

"That's for making us run you down all the way from L.A."

With another quick movement, Johnny hit Evan again, sending him back to a knee.

"And that's for shooting Joe back on the train." Evan slowly rose back to his feet.

"Get them in the truck…and tape their hands, we don't need any funny business on the way back."

THIRTY SEVEN

District Attorney Justin Stocker was usually a tidy, dapper man. His tie never loosened, his shoes always polished and not a hair out of place. He had pale blue eyes, a ready smile and a friendly demeanor that made him easy to underestimate. And there were plenty of inmates in Nevada jails whose attorneys did just that. But today, he was leaning over his desk, a hand clawing at his tie, trying to get any extra air he could find.

"What do you mean you don't know where my witness is? You had her...damn it. Captain, first one of my marshals gets killed in your airport, and now you've lost the star witness to the biggest murder case in states history!" He paused to listen, breathing hard. "Shooting on an Amtrak?...what the hell does that have to do with my case?"

He listens for another minute. His eyes clenched closed in frustration.

"So, let me get this straight. My witness never got on a plane, eyewitnesses say there was a shootout on an Amtrak train, a women and two police types were seen running away from some other guys with guns and everybody hijacked cars and disappeared...what the fuck is this, some sort of Hollywood movie?"

He listened again for a few seconds, "Well, that's *great*, they were last seen heading in the general direction of Nevada…thanks for all your help, Captain. Hope I can return the favor some day!"

Stocker slammed down the phone and yelled through his closed door.

"Kruse, get in here!"

Asst. District Attorney Donald Kruse stepped into the office. Kruse was a career city attorney who had a deep seated dislike for any person or persons who wanted to break the law. His career was like his personality, methodical, persistent and direct. No case was too small or too big, he had prosecuted everything from drug possession to murder. Standing well over six feet tall, with a withering stare, no one underestimated him in court.

"Yea boss"

Stocker ran his hands through his quickly greying hair, "Seems our witness is in the wind. Probably heading our direction, but with Frank Johnston's goons in hot pursuit. Get on the phone with the police and let's get someone out to the Johnston's place."

"Yes sir." Kruse turned and went out. Stocker leaned forward

And put his head back in his hands.

"Shit"

THIRTY EIGHT

Frank Johnston was sitting at his desk. The midday sun was falling through the glass doors on his left, the heat shimmered off the lake down at the end of the grass. He was holding a pistol loosely in his hands as he waved it in the general direction of Susan and Evan, who were sitting side by side on the couch, their hands still taped together in front of them. Johnny lounged casually by the door to the hall.

"Oh Susan, you've been a busy little girl, what with your little chase across Southern California and your plan to testify against me."

Susan held his eyes, "You're a murdering son of a bitch, and I'm going to see you dead!"

"Tsk, tsk…what language for such a sweet thing, but we both know your lying."

Susan just glared back defiantly. Johnston turned his attention to Evan.

"And you Marshal, you've caused quite a stir. Johnny here says you shot one of my men and led this merry chase across the country…that is, after my good buddy Jude died. Pity…it's always good to have a couple law enforcement types on the payroll, helps to smooth the way sometimes."

Evan had been looking around the room, his eyes resting on the painting over the fireplace. The old anger is rising up, and he let it come.

"You're just like your great grandfather, he was a jackass also."

Frank dropped his fake smile, "What *are* you talking about? My great grandfather built this empire."

A slight smile curled on Evan's face, "Well, I'm a little bit of a history buff, and I say he was a chicken shit, murdering, rapist who gained this *"empire"* by brute force, thieving and murder."

Leaning back in his oversized chair, Frank looked intently at Evan. After a few seconds, he chuckled and said, "Well Marshal you may be right, but I have to admire a man who goes after what he wants and doesn't let anything get in his way…in fact, I have a letter he wrote."

Johnston sat up and opened a desk drawer on his right. He dug around in a file drawer for a second and then sat back, waiving a piece of old yellowed paper. "Here we go."

"Found this is in a box of his belongings after my Daddy died…let's see.."

" ...she had the greenest eyes you ever saw and with her flaming red hair, she was easily the prettiest girl in the county. But she had a weak spot for that fool, Longview. I never could understand what she saw in him. Just a poor, dirt farmer with a small pooch of land, I could have given her the world. Well, no matter, I got the last laugh. Took her, before he did. Knocked him upside the head and had my way, on their wedding night, no less. She was a sweet thing and wild...had to let my boys take her also...take some of the fight out of her. When they were through, though, I kinda lost my taste, and I couldn't let her talk, so while she looked in my eyes, I put my foot on her neck and stepped on her till I heard the snap..."

Johnston looked up, a wild look in his eyes, his breathing a little more rapid. "...so yeah, you're right, he was a low down murdering rapist." He let out a low chuckle.

Evan was boiling over with anger, and he had tears running down his cheeks. He leaned forward to jump up but Frank fired a bullet over his head into the wall behind Susan's head. Glaring at Frank, Evan sank back into the couch. Susan reached over and put a hand on his arm.

"Mmm, hit a tender spot, did we?" Pointing the gun at Evan now, "Well, no matter, ancient history now. Johnny, take the Marshal here down to the boat house, and see if he can swim with a cement block tied to his legs. Susan and I have a little history of our own to make."

Johnny jerked Evan up to his feet and pulled him out the glass doors towards the boat house. Evan turned to look back at Susan.

Asst. D.A. Kruse rushed into his boss's office, "Sir, the police just found a Marshals hat in a local field and the rancher is saying a big black SUV was chasing a man and women on horseback. The police think the man and woman were taken away in the SUV!"

District Attorney Stocker stood up so fast his chair went flying over backwards. He grabbed his jacket off the coat rack, "Christ, that's them! Get those patrol cars out to the Johnston place, now!!"

****

Johnny pushed Evan roughly through the boathouse door. It was a small room with just enough space for a new looking 13' Boston Whaler sitting in the only slip. There was a thin walkway beside the boat leading to the side wall covered in boating equipment, extra paddles, life preserves and some nets for scooping up fish. With his gun in Evan's back, Johnny goaded him down to the walk way and quickly stepped around him. Watching Evan, he squatted down and untied the rope from the dock cleats. As he stood back up, his gun hand drooped slightly and Evan stepped forward with a hard head butt to Johnny's nose. His hands flew to his face and Evan kicked him as hard as he could in the groin. Johnny immediately folded forward in pain. As he was moaning in agony, Evan stepped back to get a good angle and brought his taped hands up in a brutal uppercut, standing Johnny up and backwards. As he staggered back, his eyes went from dark pain to open surprise as he impaled himself on a protruding oar peg. As Johnny took his last living breath, Evan looked around for his gun. Spotting it on the walkway, he picked it up. Searching again, he found an old rusted fish knife on a shelf next to Johnny and cut himself free of the tape. He moved quickly toward the door. As he reached it, he heard a voice. "Johnny, you okay in there?" Sid called out.

Evan quickly stepped behind the door. Sid pushed the door open and stepped inside, with gun hand extended in front of him. As he cleared the door, Evan quickly smashed his gun down on Sid's head and he collapsed to the ground. Evan stepped around him and ran up the walk towards the house.

****

A police cruiser pulled into the driveway. Officer Kaminsky stepped out of the car and heard a gunshot. Pulling his pistol, he moved toward the front door.

****

Frank watched Johnny pushing Evan down the walk to the boathouse. He turned slowly back to Susan.

"So...do tell, why did you wack your own loving mother?"

Susan's face was flush with anger as she spat out her reply. "Because she was a pathetic lush. After my father died, she gave up on life and stopped caring about anything...me. She became selfish and dependent, marrying you and your disgusting gang of thugs. Every time I looked at her, I wanted to slap her. After listening to her cry about and the maid, scared of losing you instead of standing up to you, over and over, I finally couldn't take it...."

Chuckling, Frank stood and moved to her. "Well, you probably saved me the job of doing it myself. And now, alone at last, I've wanted this since the day I met your mother and you. It was almost worth the torture, being with that sow, just to have you around. I can't tell you how much I'm going to enjoy this."

Susan shrank back into the couch, "Stay away from me, you bastard, I'll kill you too!"

Frank grabbed her by the wrists and jerked her to her feet, dragging her toward his desk. He tried to throw Susan onto the desk, but she kicked back at his knee and broke away. Grabbing the fireplace poker from the rack, she turned to face Frank.

"My, this must seem like déjà vu."

As he took a step toward her, Evan smashed through the glass patio doors. Rolling over, he came up to his knees just as Frank turned toward the crashing sound, and shot him in the heart. The gun blast spun Frank around to face Susan who was bringing the poker down on his head. Just before she made contact, another shot rang out and blood appeared on her blouse. She was knocked backward against the fireplace. She dropped the poker, looked sadly at Evan and collapsed to the floor, dead.

Evan was staring at Susan as she slid to the floor.

"Police, Put your gun down!"

Evan slowly lowered his gun and turned to the door. Officer Kaminsky was standing in his firing stance, pointing at Evan with smoke coming from the end of his shaking gun.

The front driveway looked like the circus came to town. There were police cars and ambulances, all with flashers set on high. A CID van was pulled up in by the front door with technicians loading up their kits. D.A. Stocker was on the phone next to his car. Evan was sitting in the backseat of a patrol car, though the door was open and he was not wearing handcuffs. Detective Ivarone was off to the side, speaking with Officer Kaminsky, taking notes.

"...as I was getting out of my car," Kaminsky was explaining, "I heard a gunshot. I pulled my gun and approached the front door. It was unlocked and as I entered, I heard voices coming from the study across the hall. As I neared the door, I heard Ms. Aiello talking about how she had killed her mother and then tried to pin it on Mr. Johnston..."

D.A. Stocker hung up his phone and walked over to Evan, who quickly folded a piece of yellowed paper and stuffed it into his front shirt pocket.

"I just spoke to the States attorney. There won't be any problems with Frank's death. It will be classified as self-defense. Same goes for the asshole in the boathouse. We'll round up the rest of his goons. You probably won't have to testify in court. If you identify them as the guys who kidnapped you, I'm sure they'll spill for lesser charges."

He paused for a second, looking intently at Evan. "Pretty surprised about Susan Aiello, though, didn't see that one coming." Stocker reached out to shake hands with Evan, "We'll be in touch, Marshal. Good luck."

Evan looked around at all the activity and lights. He reached up and put his hand on his shirt pocket. For a second, the old anger rose up to his eyes, but quickly subsided. Hearing a sound above, he looked up to see an airplane flying overhead....

FUTURE JUSTICE

ONE

His eyes fluttered open but he lay motionless, staring up at the ceiling fan spinning endlessly to its own clacking beat. The surrounding room was barely visible as the morning sun was just beginning to wake, stretching its rays over the eastern sky. He knew it was a little after six thirty, because he had been waking up at the same time for as long as he could remember. The difference now was this was the most comfortable bed he had every slept in and he really had nowhere to go or anything to do.

When you grew up in the harsh west during the 1800's, you rose early to take care of the animals and work the fields. Most likely, your bed was a layer of straw, stuffed into a cotton bag, draped over a wooden cot. Guilt was not an unfamiliar feeling each day, but U.S. Marshal Evan Longview wasn't living in the 1800's, he was waking in a very comfortable bed, in a nice, but small, house in Los Angeles in the late 1900's. Having been thrown, literally, into the next century six months ago, Longview had already lived through a harrowing high speed chase across the mountains, a terrifying crash down a mountain side, and a couple of shoot outs, all ending with the deaths of the only two people he really knew in this century.

So every morning, Evan lay in bed and thought about where he was, how he got here, where he had come from and his losses. His beloved girl, Mary, had been raped and murdered on their wedding night. He'd spent a few years of frustrating and angry pursuit of all types of thieves, murderers and rustlers. And just when he had finally been on the trail of his long hated nemesis, and his wife's killer, he had stumbled through some time machine contraption built in this century. It had been accidently tuned to the wrong direction and he wound up one hundred years out of his element. Though he had a part in the downfall of a notorious felon related to his own wife's killer, the ever present embers of hatred still burned in the pit of his stomach. The lines between justice and revenge remained but they were becoming more blurry by the day.

Longview threw back the covers and sat up, putting his feet on the floor. Looking down at his striped boxer shorts, he sat for a minute, thinking about how Deputy Marshal Linder had convinced him that "boxers" were better than "briefs" as they allowed a little more breathing. To Longview, they just seemed a closer match to the long johns he usually wore. He had to admit, though, the pictures of mostly naked men in different types of underclothing gave him an uncomfortable feeling. Much different than the feeling he got when Linder showed him the pictures on the female packages.

Deputy Marshal Linder had been assigned to help out and watch over Longview by his boss, Captain Harrison. After the shootout in Nevada ended, Linder had been dispatched to retrieve Longview. He arrived by automobile after Evan's hesitant attitude regarding flying in the sky.

Linder was fairly new to the Marshals service, but his twenty five years in this century still gave him a leg up on Longview's three weeks. Captain Harrison welcomed Longview back from the deadly mission, thanked him and then took his gun away. He made it clear that Evan could no longer be an active US Marshal in this time period as he had no formal training or even knowledge of the new world in which he was now living. Evan did, however, keep his badge, as it was his from 1887.

Captain Harrison did not turn his back completely. He made arrangements for Evan to use Jude Camelot's house and truck. Marshal Cavelot had been with Evan on his death race across California. Now being recently deceased and without family that could be found, the house and truck would just sit idle until the legal stuff was sorted out. Harrison assigned Deputy Marshal Linder to be his minder and guide indefinitely or until something else could be worked out. Linder was given a packet of money from the Marshal's slush fund and told to turn in receipts when he needed more.

Since Longview hadn't really had any time to get used to his surroundings previously, Linder agreed to temporarily move in with him and show him the new world. Three months later, Evan was pretty familiar with most of the local stores, bars and restaurants in his neighborhood. He really enjoyed walking about, going in and out of all types of stores and businesses. He didn't speak often, but when spoken to, was humble and polite. The money part was fairly simple, though he was always flabbergasted at the price of everything. The sheer amount of people always around still made him a little nervous. He just wasn't used to so much activity in such a small area. Linder explained that in Southern California, this was the normal scenery.

Cavelot was obviously single, and must have eaten out a lot, as his kitchen was a little short of everything. He did have, to Evan's amusement, an odd contraption called a Keurig. When Linder said this was a new invention and told him it was used to make coffee, Evan was a little more enthused. He was

173

downright ecstatic after making and tasting the first cup of normal, steaming hot black coffee he had had in a while.

On the fourth day as roommates, Linder could sense that Evan was getting a little weary of all the constant commotion and information overload. After the usual two cups of coffee and some scrambled eggs and bacon, they went out and climbed into Cavelot's Chevy Tahoe. They drove a few blocks and turned into the large parking lot of a closed down warehouse.

Linder opened his door and climbing out said, "Come on, your turn."

Not understanding, Evan got out of his side and met Linder at the front of the SUV.

"Time for you to learn to drive," and he held up the keys.

Evan stared at Linder for a second, then shrugged, "Um... ok."

After all, he had been watching the whole world drive something, how hard could it be?

He hit the first light standard he came near and just missed the second one before he was able to get the feel of the wheel and the brake pedal. The gas pedal took a little more time, and he learned how to reverse when he drove up into the bushes at the end of the lot. After an hour or so, though, he was fairly competent and was able to drive around the lot without further damage.

"Now, there is a ton more to driving than just stop and go," Linder warned. "There are rules of the road, signs to read and lots of moving objects. We can practice some more tomorrow, and in the meantime I will explain things as we drive about."

That was a few months ago, and though Evan could now drive alone to the local market, he still preferred to have Linder in the truck with him most of the time. Linder had moved back to his own place a month ago, but he still came around most days. Each day was filled with driving lessons, sightseeing, lessons of the land and occasionally a drive out of the city where Evan was reassured that there was still some country side. He had seen the desert, but now had been to the mountains and some lakes in the area. They had also frequented a couple local bars where Evan showed Deputy Marshal Linder how to drink.

During this time, Evan had found the card given him by Tom Davidson. Evan had heard rumors in his day of a device which allowed talking over great distances, but had never seen one. Linder had to show him how to "dial" the numbers on the phone that matched the ones on the card. It took all of his calm to not drop the phone the first time he heard a voice spoken in his ear.

Davidson was the leader of a group of scientists who invented the time machine that brought Longview to this era. He and Evan had spoken an awkward couple times, but there had been little progress to remake the machine. This was why Davidson was on his way. He was taking Evan with him to meet with the investors. He felt sure that if they could see and talk to Evan, they would be rejuvenated in their belief and interest to fund the new machine.

Longview stood, stretched, and padded barefoot into the kitchen. He wasn't sure about the upcoming day, but he was sure of his new friend, Keurig.

TWO

When your favorite book growing up is H.G. Wells "The Time Machine", you're a geek, especially when the other books on your shelf are some old copies of Tom Swift, Boy Inventor, and a stack of well-read Scientific America magazines. While the other kids are outside kicking a soccer ball or throwing baseballs through neighboring windows, you are busy putting together your first telescope. The friends you do have are also geeks.

Tom Davidson was a geek. Born from middle class parents, his father an insurance salesman and his mother a travel agent, he grew up in Saugus, a stable, if uneventful suburb of Boston, MA. Arriving into the world in 1970, he spent many snow frozen winters buried beneath blankets, reading of faraway places. It became evident early on that he was exceedingly intelligent. It wasn't that he didn't like sports, (he knew who the Red Sox were), he just had a stronger desire to learn more about this world and beyond. So while his contemporaries were listening to Blondie and smoking pot, he was finishing high school early and getting accepted to MIT.

When his dad received an offer to join his cousin's insurance firm on the other side of the country, his parents decided they could spend their later years in a more moderate climate. Geek or not, and having an adventurous spirit, Tom found a sister program at CIT, and went along to sunny Southern California.

When his favorite professor suggested he needed to get out more and enjoy life, Tom discovered that he was fairly adept at surfing. At six foot tall, a slim build and now much less pale, you could find him most mornings, paddling out through the pacific swell. As the rising sun peaked over the coastal hills, it warmed up his brain synapsis as well as his back.

Surfing was one of those individual sports that allowed him to get exercise for his body and thinking time for himself.

It was at a small cocktail party thrown by Dr.Sussel, for his best doctoral students, that Tom first publicly voiced his enthusiasm for time travel. Standing with his mentor and another fellow student, and on his third mojito, he began an excited discourse about the possibilities.

"I'm telling you, I was breaking down through this beautiful tube yesterday, and it hit me. If we could just find a way to roll *with* the tube from one end to the other, we could essentially end up in a different place."

"You do realize," fellow Jr. physicist Phillip Doone countered, "you're not the first to believe that."

Dr.Sussel also chimed in. "Some of the greatest minds of all time have attempted such ideas, only to be left ridiculed by society."

"But they have been trying to make the *leap* from one time to another. I am talking about sliding along the tube or portal." Tom is beginning to get worked up.

"Well, it has always been an intriguing dream," Dr. Sussel soothed, "and perhaps one day you will find the answer, but not tonight. Tonight we celebrate your graduation and your next step in this adventure called life."

Not willing to concede any points, Tom looks down at his empty glass, "Perhaps," he mumbled. "Well, the surf is supposed to be good tomorrow, so thank you for your hospitality and I will see you tomorrow in your office.

After graduation, having been courted by private enterprise as well as government entities, Tom accepted a compromise, taking a job with a private think tank that had strong government contracts. Now three years in, and though the work was challenging, Tom remained restless and unfulfilled, his lifelong dreams of time travel and exploration lingering at the front of his thoughts. It wasn't that his current bosses were unsympathetic; it's just that it wasn't what they were getting paid to think about. They assured him that funding for such a pipedream would be next to impossible to acquire.

When you're sitting on your surfboard two hundred yards from shore, waiting for the next good wave, it is easy to strike up a conversation. It was just such a conversation that changed Tom's life. The long, blond haired surfer was easy to notice as he was by far one of the better board men in the water. That he had been hitting the waves for most of his life was evident. And even though they had shared the same beach and many waves together for a while now, this was the first time they had been side by side in a calm sea.

His name was Tomas Linkley, a southern California native. He graduated from a nearby university with a Master's degree in mechanical engineering and like Davidson, had an itch to explore wider boundaries. Davidson's grasp of space and time and Linkley's conceptual vision, together, made them a modern day DaVinci.

As their bond became tighter, their time in the water became less. They would still hit the waves each morning, but their sessions soon became shorter, as they spent more and more time scribbling theories and figures on napkins over coffee and breakfast burritos at the Surf and Sandwich. They would go off to their respective jobs and then run back to one of their apartments to drink Corona and plot into the night.

One night, with the rain falling in sheets and lightning flashing, Tom climbed out of his late model Ford Explorer, pulled the hood of his sweatshirt up over his head and sprinted up the stairs to Linkley's apartment. In his excitement, he didn't even knock. He burst through the door, already talking fast and loud.

"We got it! We got it!"

Tomas came in from the kitchen, "Easy man, slow down. Got what?"

"Money, we got money." Davidson shed his damp sweatshirt and threw it on the floor. "Old man Sussel spoke with some contact, who might be interested in funding our machine!"

Linkley laughed, "Ok, that's great news, but a name is hardly a check."

"No, no, I already spoke to the guy. I have a meeting with him tomorrow. He is definitely interested."

"Alright, just relax and have a beer. Let's order in some pizza and talk about what you're going to say."

And that's how it began. Davidson met with a gentleman who represented other men. They met for lunch at a nice restaurant in the hills overlooking Los Angeles. Tom explained his background, his idea and how with the help of his mechanically minded friend, they could build a time continuum capable of allowing travel to other times in history. The gentleman seemed duly impressed and agreed to speak with his partners. After a long, nerve wracking week, Tom was contacted and once again found himself in the restaurant in the Los Angeles hills. After an opening cocktail and some uncomfortable small talk, they got down to details. The consortium had agreed to fully fund the time continuum project. This would include a working laboratory, manufacturing costs, whatever other assistants might be needed and livable salaries for both Davidson and Linkley, so they could focus their attention full time. In return, the investors would have the right to thirty five percent of any and all revenues resulting from the completion and use of the machine. Davidson agreed and they were in business.

It had been the most exciting eighteen months of their lives. They finagled the use of an old Quonset hut on campus and convinced three brilliant students to work for peanuts. They spent their days working on manufacturing and assembly and their nights working out the next bug and obstacle.

Whether it was tempting the laws of nature, bad luck or just a series of unfortunate incidents, Davidson and his merry band of dreamers suffered a cataclysmic set back. After a dust storm shut down their successful, though backward, maiden attempt at time travel, their entire lab and all contents therein, were destroyed in a freak fire.

The only evidence of their work and success was a couple of notebooks and US Marshal Evan Longview, late of 1888. Longview had contacted Tom out of the blue one day and they had stayed in contact. They met once for lunch, where Evan filled him in on his deadly chase across the west, and Tom retold his own tale of woe. Unfortunately, there had been even less contact with the investors. The bad taste left in their mouths regarding the loss of their substantial investment had made them lose their adventurous appetites as well.

Knocking on the front door of the house where Evan stayed, Davidson hoped their meeting with William Pensor would rekindle their interest. Producing a US Marshal from the 1800's would certainly go a long way to substantiating his request. It had worked once, and he was sure he could convince them it could be done it again.

THREE

The door opened and Longview stepped out, pulling the door closed behind him. Knowing this was an important meeting, Evan had brushed his worn boots as best he could. He was wearing something called Dockers pants, a button down white shirt and a sport coat he found in the closet. Deputy Linder had taken him shopping for some extra updated clothing, but he occasionally wore outfits he found leftover in Cavelot's closet. They were a little big in the shoulders, and a little short in the sleeves, but still comfortable enough. Deputy Linder had been over the night before and helped him pick out his outfit, before taking today off as Evan's minder.

"Good morning, Tom," he greeted as they shook hands.

Davidson was dressed similarly, though he wore loafers instead of boots and he had added a colorful knit tie.

"Good morning. Thanks for coming along for the big day."

It was a typical southern California day. The sun was pushing up on midday, without a cloud in site. Didn't matter what time of year it was, this was the weather most days. Tom had been out early in the surf,

184

clearing his head and preparing for today's meeting. They turned and headed to Tom's SUV.

As they headed through the customary city traffic, Tom rambled on about what he was expecting.

"We are meeting at Mr. Pensor's home today, something about being more private and intimate. I have to warn you, he can be a little abrasive. He doesn't do small talk. We'll just introduce you, and hope the fact that you're living proof of concept will be enough to loosen his purse strings again. I have the video we got at the site of your arrival. Pensor will want to verify our story. Maybe show him your badge, you brought it, right? It looks pretty authentic."

Evan was listening and nodding, but as always, seemed more focused on watching the city scape and people moving past outside the truck. As they moved away from the western fringe of Los Angeles and got closer to the hills rising over the northern skyline, he noticed the neighborhoods and stores become a little nicer and kept up. The people walking also seemed to look and be dressed appropriately to match.

As they passed through an intersection, Evan was looking at an approaching building, next to an empty lot. It was a little worn and in need of a paint job, standing apart from its neighbors, which is probably what caught his eye. It had four apartments, two bottom and two above, with a set of stairs going up the middle, separating them like two towers. Each apartment had a window facing out over the street. It was a flurry of movement in one of the upstairs windows that caused Evan to shout out.

"Stop the truck!"

Tom hit the brakes, thinking something was going to jump out in front of him. "What?"

"Just stop. Something is happening in there." Evan opened the door and jumped out before the SUV came to a complete stop.

"Hey, where are you going?" a confused Davidson called after him. "We're going to be late to Pensors."

Evan ran back down the sidewalk and turned to sprint up the apartment stairs. When he got to the upper landing, he turned right. With no hesitation, he took three running steps, put his shoulder down and smashed into the apartment door. It was an older building, not well maintained, and the door burst open upon impact. Longview stumbled into the room.

What he saw brought immediate flashes of recognition and rage. There were two men who seconds before had been salivating their good fortune, but now looked startled and shocked. A woman was sprawled on the couch, screaming in fright. One man was trying to keep the woman's arms pinned, while the other man was standing over her in the process of pulling his pants down. Evan took one stride and launched himself at the man at the end of the couch. With his pants half way down to his knees, the two boots in his backside sent him flying over the coffee table where he rolled up against a lounge chair in the corner. Longview's momentum carried him right up to the second man. Who, letting go of the woman, tried to get up off the couch, only to be met by a right fist raining down from above. He collapsed back onto the floor where Evan continued his forward movement, stomping down on the man's face, breaking his nose and knocking him unconscious. Still moving in fluid motion, Evan stepped to the first assailant and grabbing him by the front of his shirt, dragged him to his feet. He then proceeded to pummel him with punch after punch, visions of his wife's rape and murdered, lifeless body feeding fuel to his blood.

The pounding in his head was so loud, he at first didn't hear. "Evan! Evan!"

Davidson, reaching the top of the stairs, ran through the smashed door to find one man down on the ground and Evan punching another man over and over. Running past the shocked woman sitting up on the couch, Tom grabbed Evan from behind.

"That's enough, man. You're going to kill him!"

He got two arms around Evan in a light bear hug, the long unconscious predator dropping to the floor like a bag of flour meal.

"I got you Evan, I got you. You okay?" Davidson let go of Evan, who slowly looked down at the targets of his rage and then over to the woman on the couch.

Breathing heavily, he asked her, "Are you all right ma'am?"

She was a pretty lady. At thirty eight, she kept herself in good shape working out at the gym four days a week and playing tennis the other three. Today, though, her hair was a mess from struggling with her assailants and her makeup was running and smeared on her face. Looking down, she smoothed her skirt and glanced nervously at the two men beaten bloody on the floor.

"Yes, thanks to you." She put out a shaking hand, "My name is Lisa. Lisa Levin."

Evan took her hand, "how do you do, I'm Evan Longview, and this is my friend Tom Davidson." He pointed a thumb at Tom who was on his cell phone across the room.

"I saw you in the window, ma'am. You didn't look like you were trying to get fresh air."

"No, no. These men attacked me outside Nordstrom's as I was unlocking my car. They threw me into a van and brought me here. When we got up to this apartment, they shoved me into the room and I ran straight over to the window, hoping to get someone's attention."

"I am very grateful you saw me," she glanced again to bodies on the floor, "and that you were brave enough to take action."

Across the room, Tom closed his phone and said, "The police are on their way,"

Looking around the room, he looked disappointed. "I'll have to call Mr. Pensor and tell him we will be late or reschedule. We're going to have to hang around for a while and give statements." He took out his phone again and stepped into the kitchen to make his call.

Looking around, Lisa asked, "Could you hand me my purse over there? I don't think I'm ready to stand up yet."

Evan looked where she was pointing and went to retrieve the purse from the corner. Handing it to her, she opened it and scrambled around till she came out with a tissue and a compact. Looking in the small mirror and wiping her face she said, "I must look a fright."

FOUR

The police came and both Evan and Tom gave statements. The two assailants were still not awake when taken into custody and the paramedics moved them to the security ward of City Hospital. They would be questioned later. The officer doing the interviews was a little wary of Evan's story, but when Mrs. Levin gave her statement, backing him, there was not much choice but to let him go with the usual warning about being available for further investigation. There was a general agreement among the officers present, that the two attackers had been working this area for a few months with no leads and all in all, this was a positive result, regardless of the violent hero.

During the interviews, Lisa Levin had called her husband and he had arrived shortly thereafter in his black town car. While the driver remained at the car, Richard Levin ran to his wife, who was now sitting on the front steps of the apartment building. They hugged and she explained what had happened, assuring him she hadn't been violated or harmed in any way. When the police were finished speaking with Evan and Tom, they began to walk toward Tom's SUV. Richard broke away from his wife and hurried to catch up with them.

"Excuse me, Mr. Longview?"

Evan and Tom turned to face him.

"My name is Richard Levin, I am Lisa's husband." He was perfectly groomed. Someone accustomed to manicures and probably pedicures. His skin the perfect tan from living in sunny Southern California and the best tanning salons money could buy. His teeth were so white, you winced when he smiled.

Tom seemed a little surprised. "*THE* Richard Levin, producer of Street Justice? I love that movie."

Swelling a little with pride, Levin responded, "Yes, among others. I'm glad you liked it. But today I'm just Lisa's husband. And I want to thank you for what you did." He reached into his front shirt pocket. "This is my card. Your name will be on a list and if you call, you will be put through straight to me. If there is anything, anything I can do for you, please don't hesitate to call."

He reached out to shake both their hands and then turned abruptly back to Lisa.

"Man, Richard fricken Levin." Tom stared after him. "That guy's got more money than GOD. I read somewhere that he had inherited a fortune from his father, who got it from *his* father, something about railroads and hotels. He turned it into even more with investments in some big electronics company and now he produces movies and hangs with all the stars. I hear he throws the best shindigs in town. And believe me; this town knows how to throw a shindig."

They turned and headed back to the SUV.

"I spoke to Mr. Pensor and he said if we could get there by two o'clock, he would still meet us." Tom reached over and brushed some dust from Evan's shoulder. "Since we're all dressed up, let's make it a day."

FIVE

"I'm not sure if you were being brave or foolish back there."

The SUV was moving up into the hills above Los Angeles. The streets packed with stores and people gave way to tree lined lanes with eclectic cottages and bungalows. At midday, most of the joggers and dog walkers had completed their workouts, leaving only occasional stay at home moms pushing baby strollers through the quiet vicinage.

"I didn't think about it." Evan had his head turned away, looking out his side window. The driveways were getting a little further apart as the cottages became mansions with iron gates and ten foot fences.

"My wife was raped and murdered on our wedding night." His voice so quiet, Davidson could barely hear.

"Ah man, I'm sorry. I didn't know."

In a rare moment, Evan told a little more of his story. "I was on my way to pick up one of her rapists when I got caught in your little experiment. When I was in Nevada, a while back, I found evidence confirming the guilty party." The old rage began to rise again, "So that's why I really want to get back to my time. So I can get the bastard responsible!"

Squinting to see street numbers, Tom turned right into a driveway blocked by a medieval looking gate.

"Here we are. Well, let's go get you started."

Davidson pulled up next to a little box on a pole, pushing the button on its face. The gate split in the middle slowly opening inward.

They entered the gate and drove up a short circular driveway till they were parked in front of a large two story monstrosity which could only be described as gothic. Built stone upon stone, it had two gabled upstairs windows. Each window had a steeple rising above it, being guarded by its own gargoyle. The stone had aged to a mottle of dark brown and grey with splotches of moss up and down its face like an adolescent male trying to grow a beard.

Climbing out of the SUV, Tom gave a low whistle. "Jesus, no wonder the guy is cold as ice, he lives like Dracula."

There was a large upside down horse shoe on the door and when Davidson lifted it to knock, a deep tone echoed from inside like an ancient Chinese gong.

"Hey, that's pretty clever," Tom said, "a door bell disguised as a door knocker."

After only a few seconds, the door was opened by a solid looking man about thirty years old. He was dressed nice but casual in black slacks, loafers and a black sport coat over an open necked white dress shirt.

"Hello." He had a deep baritone voice and sounded like it was beneath him to be answering the door.

"Hi, I'm Tom Davidson and this is Evan Longview. I believe we have an appointment with Mr.Pensor."

"Of course, come in." He stepped back and waved them into the entry way. "Mr. Pensor is expecting you."

Tom and Evan stepped across the threshold into a small entry and were immediately surprised by the setting. Straight ahead, there was a hallway leading further into the house, with a wide staircase going upstairs on its right. There was a bright colored rug running the length of the hall and where you might expect the standing suit of armor, there was a small elegant secretary style writing table supporting a large assemblage of bright flowers. There were closed double doors to their left and an open entry way on their right. Through this, they could see a large living room. It was well lit with modern furnishings. From their limited view, Tom could see tasteful art on the walls and more vases of flowers spread throughout. The only alliance to the outside being the rather garish stone fire place with a large old fashioned portrait hanging above. The subject being a heavy, grey haired gentleman in a jacket and waistcoat, the obligatory watch draped in the breast pocket.

"Wait one moment please." The man stepped through the double doors on the left for just a second.

Holding the right side door open, he again waved them to the next room, "This way gentleman."

Evan and Tom stepped into a large study. Keeping with contradiction, this room was dimly lit. The heavy curtains were partially closed over the large front window on the left, and what light did enter was absorbed by deep cherry oak paneling. There were rows of books covering the wall to their right and a large antique desk at the far end with a single desk lamp on the front corner. There was a brocade covered chair to the left of the window, a standing lamp behind it. The baby grand piano and bench to its left was resting on an expensive Turkish rug. To their right was a couch with matching brocade fabric.

"That will be all, Sam, thank you."

The man speaking was sitting in a large overstuffed chair behind the desk. Wearing a white dress shirt and dark waistcoat, he was a slimmer version of the portrait over the fireplace. He had dark hair with grey highlights left in strategic places to help cultivate a younger, more distinguished look. A long thin nose and a small mouth, which was in a constant state of creased vehemence. A serious intensity radiated from the depths of his small dark eyes.

SIX

When Adolf Hitler attained a position of prominence in 1933, Walter Penzig was away from his home, working in North Africa. Penzig was a geologist. He was also a Jew, and despite disturbing stories and a few sporadic incidents, he was a German, hard headed and determined. So he kept his head down, kept his family close and went about his life, trying to ignore the world around him.

In 1943, his neighbors were dragged from their home in the middle of the night, their dog yapping at the heels of the Gestapo. With two infant sons and the eruption of a new reality, Walter Penzig made immediate plans to leave Germany. Acquiring papers from a friend of a friend, Walter and his family left Germany, boarded a ship and sailed for America. When they landed at Ellis Island, the Pensors were welcomed to America. A Finnish family seeking a new beginning was what America was all about.

For the next two years, Walter kept his family fed and clothed taking odd jobs, working their way south where his skills as a geologist began to turn their lives around. Working as a roustabout on a pipeline through southwest Texas, he would often borrow a horse and ride for miles around the surrounding plains.

He studied the rock formations, the plant life and often times, getting down from the horse to feel the dirt.

One day after such a ride, he approached the job foreman.

"I would like to speak to the owner of the pipeline."

The burly union boss looked at him like he was crazy. "Look bub, I have no idea who the owner is, just a company name. And even if I did, you just can't go walking into the Texas South Oil Company demanding to talk to the owner."

But that is what Walter did. Risking the loss of his job, he took an extra day off and traveled to Houston. After sitting in the waiting room for over an hour, he was finally ushered into the managing partner's office. Explaining his background and current position, he told of his belief that there was more oil in a certain area he had found in his wanderings. Oil companies have one ultimate goal, to make money, so the word was passed and they made an exploratory dig where Walter suggested. When the gusher was finally capped, Walter's future was set. He moved up from pipe layer to working with the company geologists. After a couple more strikes, he renegotiated his way to partner and became rich.

Walter moved his wife and two sons to Houston where he continued to reap money from oil, and began to grow his fortune with investments in manufacturing and real estate holdings. Eventually, William, the heir apparent to Walter's empire, went off to college to study business. The other son remained behind, something not quite right about him. If he wasn't following his brother Walter around, he was out in the garden cultivating a variety of flowers, which when picked, adorned rooms throughout the house. He was a mystery though, as he could be lovingly working his flowers one moment, and then be viciously torturing a captured bird the next moment.

When his father died of a massive heart attack a year after he graduated college, William Pensor became one of the countries youngest and richest CEO's. When his mother died within the year, William liquidated much of the company's local holdings and moved his operation to the west coast. Tired of the Texas dust and heat, he would begin to build *his* legacy in the new western frontier of Los Angeles.

Twenty five years later, by shrewd maneuvering, brute will and vicious action, he had amassed one of the largest private fortunes in modern history. Money by itself can be liberating, and the challenge of acquiring it can be exhilarating. Along with that challenge, though, comes the addiction to power each new conquest brings. William Pensor was a very rich man, but it wasn't enough anymore. The two men sitting in front of him now represented the opportunity to vault him to the pinnacle of that power.

SEVEN

The bottomless dark eyes turned their focus to Evan. Sitting just outside what little light there was, Evan could barely make out the man behind the desk, but he could feel the intensity of his scrutiny.

"Have a seat, gentlemen."

Evan and Tom moved forward and sat in the chairs facing the desk.

Tom spoke first. "Thank you for seeing us this afternoon. It's been an eventful day." He laughed nervously, nodding towards Evan, "he had to make a quick stop to break up a rape in progress."

Pensors eyes never left Evan. "How admirable."

"Yes, uh well, this is Evan Longview. The Marshal I told you about. He's from 1888."

Evan stood up to shake hands across the desk, "nice to meet you sir."

Pensor didn't move, just nodded. "I'm sure."

Evan remained standing for an awkward second before pulling back his hand. He slowly sat back down to an uncomfortable silence.

"We have someone you can call," Tom started up again, trying to break the tension. "Captain Harrison, Evan's boss."

Pensor put up a hand to quiet Davidson. "I have already spoken with Captain Harrison. He has convinced me of Mr. Longview's, how should we put it....authenticity."

"Great, then you can see why we need to get back on track. We've proven we can make the machine work. We just had some bad luck."

Once again, Pensor cut off Tom. "I don't believe in luck, Mr. Davidson. I'm sure you noticed my door chime, the upside down horseshoe. It usually symbolizes bad luck. I don't share those beliefs. What I do believe in is research and determination. A man must have a clear view of what he wants and the will to take it."

Evan has been sitting quietly. He's heard this kind of talk before. Looking around the room, he had a strange feeling. He couldn't put his finger on it, just a tingle on his spine. He turned his focus back to the conversation.

Tom was pushing back, "Luck, fate, bad timing, whatever you call it, we had it. I do believe in my machine, it works. We proved that," again nodding toward Evan. "We just need to retrace our steps. Recreate it."

Pensor leaned back in his chair, his fingers steepled together on his chest. There was a palpable drop in the room temperature. A minute passed as he gazed across his desk, his eyes shifting from Evan to Tom and back. His lips pursed like he was contemplating his next chess move. Tom was shifting uncomfortably in the silence, his hands in a constant slow washing motion. Evan was like a statue, returning the stare with one of his own.

"I believe in your machine as well, Mr. Davidson."

Tom's body deflated as he let out a visible sigh of relief.

"However, the proof as you put it," Pensor pointed a finger at Evan, "puts events in quite a different light."

Tom is suddenly on edge again, "What is that supposed to mean?"

"Come now, you must understand." Pensor leaned forward, his forearms resting on the edge of his desk. "Everyone dreams of time travel. There are hundreds of movies and books describing the possibility. Each one showing what can be accomplished with the opportunity to go back in time to right a wrong, or learn of something before it happens. Or to go forward to see what the future holds. Surely you have thought about this, or you wouldn't have gone done the path you chose in the first place."

"What do you want?" Evan asked quietly.

Pensor swiveled his head, his eyes boring into Evan. "What do I want? The same as everyone else, that opportunity to right a wrong, buy stock in Microsoft early. Screw that girl in college I found out later wanted it. Whatever, the possibilities would be endless."

"What do you *want*?" Evan's eyes locked with Pensor's.

Pensor slowly leaned back into his chair. He pulled his stare away from Evan and turned back to Tom.

"I will fully fund the project again. You'll get a new facility, this one with a little more security. I have an unused building over in east LA, you can use it. Fair salaries for all the help you need. You can get your old team back or start a new one, I don't care. I don't expect to understand every purchase order you submit, and I don't expect you to work a hundred hours a week. I do expect, though, that you work steady. Days, nights, doesn't matter. You built the last one in about a year. I am sure you can do much better this time."

It was Tom's turn to ask, "And what do you want in return for all this generosity?"

"I will have a contract drawn up. We will form a company. I want seventy five percent ownership of the working machine. That's seventy five percent of all monies earned from its use. And," he pauses to move his gaze back to Evan, "I want exclusive use or approval of use rights."

A stunned Davidson jumped to his feet. "That's absurd. It's bullshit! Build your own machine."

"Sit down Mr. Davidson. I will not have a discussion with a ranting madman."

"Madman?" Tom walked a circle behind his chair. "Madman? You're the one demanding the whole pie."

"Sit down, Mr. Davidson. Please."

Tom stopped pacing and looked out the window. He took a deep breath, turned and sat down in his chair.

"Thank you. Now just listen to reason. I am putting up a lot of money, I've already put out a lot of money. You will be paid well while you do the work. Once completed, you just sit back and collect your twenty five percent, which believe me, will be substantial."

"And what about me?" Evan asks. "How will I get home?"

Pensor kept his eyes on Tom, "Of course, we can make arrangements to send you back if possible," he waved a hand dismissively.

Tom moved forward to the edge of his chair getting as close to the desk as he could.

"Mr. Pensor, what about my dreams, my ideas? I have spent most of my life envisioning the day I could step into another time and place. You think I don't want to bonk that girl in college also? I'm sorry, sir. I know you have already spent a small fortune and it didn't end very well, but I cannot in good faith, to myself or my team, just sign away all control of something we have given our lives to. Our time, our sweat, our dreams, those are a worth something more than just money."

Pensor glanced out the window, his interest ostensibly waning. He reached under the desk and pushed a button.

"Well gentlemen, I'm sorry to hear that. I wish you luck with your machine. Sam will show you out."

The door to the entry opened behind them. Sam stepped into the room.

"What, that's it?" A flabbergasted Tom was on his feet again. "No discussion, no negotiation?"

"I don't believe you are in a position to negotiate."

Evan stood up as Tom leaned over the desk. "They're my plans, my machine. I can find another investor."

"I will give you two days to accept my offer."

"Or what, is that a threat?"

"Two days."

Evan took Tom by the elbow and guided him out. Sam closed the hall door behind them and opened the front door. He didn't say a word as Evan and Tom moved down the walk to their SUV.

As soon as the hall door closed, a section of the book shelf on the wall pushed open and a man stepped into the room. He was slim with a thin nose, dancing green eyes and a mouth in a seemingly perpetual grin. He was wearing black slacks and a bright red button down shirt, open at the collar.

"That didn't go very well." He said as he crossed the room and looked out from the edge of the curtain.

"Maybe, maybe not, we need to have our other option ready to go, just in case."

Outside, Davidson moved around to the driver's side. As Evan opened his door and began to climb in, he glanced back at the picture window. He saw movement at the edge of the curtain. There was a flash of red and a familiar face.

EIGHT

As they leave out the driveway, Evan started to mention the face at the window, but Tom angrily jumped in.

"The nerve of that guy, who does he think he is? Seventy five percent. Exclusive rights. That's bullshit. I mean, I get that he is putting up a lot of money, but exclusive rights? That *ain't* going to happen."

Still bothered by the strange face, Evan turned to Davidson. "How did you meet that guy?"

Driving down the canyon, the neighborhood was reversing itself. The homes got smaller as they approached the bottom. The view of the city sprawled out before them coming sporadically into view as they wove down the hill. The afternoon sun was sitting lower in the sky as it began its slow shuffle to the other side of the globe.

"My old college professor introduced us. Apparently he and Pensor's old man had done some work together in Texas when they were younger. Dr. Sussel loves to throw cocktail parties. When I thought I was getting close to making it all work, the good doctor threw us together at one of his little soirees.

Come to think of it, he may have had the party just to get us introduced."

They continue heading back the way they had come. Passing by the apartments where Evan mounted his violent rescue, there was a loan police car and a crime scene van still parked at the curb. No one was in sight.

Tom was still ranting, "But friend or no friend, I'm not giving up everything so that little weasel can get richer. I need to talk to Tomas and maybe the team, but looks like we'll be back to square one financially as well as production wise."

Listening to Davidson and watching the crime scene slide past, Evan involuntarily reaches up and feels the card in his shirt pocket. His mind is already tugging at the thread of an idea.

The SUV came to a stop in front of Evan's house. He climbed out and closed the door. The window slid down and Davidson leaned over to talk to Evan.

"Hey man, it's been a pretty long, eventful day. You did good back there, saving that lady and all. And I'm sorry we may not get our money soon. I know you want to get back home, but we'll get there. I'm going to go over to Tomas apartment right now. We'll brainstorm and come up with something, don't you worry."

The window slid up and Davidson pulled away from the curb. Evan gave a little wave as he drove off. The sun was almost down. Standing on the sidewalk, he looked toward the dark house up the walk and then down the street. A dark green sedan moved past going in the same direction as Davidson. The driver had his hand up to his face, rubbing his forehead. Watching the car with detached interest, Evan made a decision and rambled off around the corner. It *had* been a long day and the emotions roaring inside him made a roast beef sandwich and a couple cold beers sound pretty good.

Two hours later with a little more stagger than swagger in his walk, Longview turned up his walkway and entered the front door. He stood for minute to adjust his sight and thoughts. He stepped into the kitchen, turned on the light and picked up the phone. Taking the business card out of his shirt pocket, he squinted at the numbers to dial.

"Hello, Mr. Levin?...

NINE

Darkness has descended on the city. Not pitch black dark, like out in the desert, but with its usual sky glow. Light rising into the atmosphere from incompletely shielded sources, such as hundreds of thousands of neon signs, street lamps and automobile headlights.

After a quick stop at 7/11, a twelve pack of Corona beside him, Davidson turned out of the parking lot and continued on to Tomas Linkley's apartment. It was going to be a long night. One block back, a dark green sedan pulled away from the curb and took up a position behind two other cars.

Davidson turned into the entry of the underground parking below Linkley's third floor apartment. The apartment was only accessible by an elevator at one end of the garage. The green sedan slowed down as it passed the driveway. When it reached the end of the building, the engine revved up and it sped off down the street. With a bag of beer and a financial problem to solve, Davidson and Linkley would most likely be holed up for most of the evening.

Twenty minutes later, a few miles away, a vague figure moved silently down a cement driveway, beside a darkened house, toward the small door on the side of the garage at the rear of the property. It had been converted into a comfortable studio apartment. When the husband died, the nice old lady living in the front house rented it out to supplement her social security.

The shadow had little trouble picking the lock and quietly entered the small apartment. There was a glow from the next door neighbors back porch light coming over the closed curtains. The intruder stood still for a minute, letting his eyes get a feel for the layout.

It was a simple room with a brown leather couch facing away from the door. A coffee table and wooden Ikea chair are beyond it, facing a TV sitting on an antique looking cabinet. To the left of the TV, around a half wall, are a square table and two chairs. There is a short waist high counter separating the table from the small efficient kitchen. On the far right wall, there are two doors. The left door open to the bathroom and the right presumably the bedroom.

The kitchen table is strewn with papers and a couple notebooks. The stranger took four strides and picked up one of the notebooks. With seemingly no fear of discovery, he pulled a small penlight from the pack he was carrying and quickly flipped through a few pages. Grunting with satisfaction, he put his pack on the floor and pulled out a large camera.

Awkwardly, with gloved hands, he opened the notebook to the first page and with one hand to hold and turn the pages, began to snap pictures with the camera in his other hand.

After eight minutes, he had finished with both notebooks. He quickly went through the loose papers on the table, taking pictures of a few random sheets. Standing up straight, he listened for a second. Grabbing his pack, he moved quietly across the room and opened the bedroom door. Using his penlight, he took a quick look around the room. It was empty except for the double bed in the middle of the back wall and a single night stand on the right side. The Ikea dresser against the left wall had nothing but clothes in the drawers and a single framed picture of an older couple on top. After a quick search of the night stand and small closet, the intruder moved out of the bedroom and headed for the side door where he hesitated. Turning back, he once again stepped over to the kitchen table. He picked up the second of the two notebooks. He turned to the last three pages and bending over, carefully tore them out. Exiting the garage apartment, he locked the door behind him and staying to the bushes on the edge, snuck back down the driveway to the street. Peering around the corner of the house and seeing no one in sight, he moved out to the sidewalk and leisurely walked down the street.

When he got a half a block away, he opened the driver door and slid into a dark green sedan.

TEN

The two cars climbed the winding tree lined street and turned into the only driveway near the top. The first car stopped at the humongous ornate wood gate with a carved RL emblem at the top. The gate split the letters as it opened inwardly and the two cars moved forward up the hill to the peak. The second car, an aged Volkswagen bus struggled to climb the steep incline, its engine whining in low gear as it tried to keep up. As they crest the top, the passengers of both vehicles are overpowered by the sight of a castle resting in the middle of an enormous green meadow. It was resplendent with actual towers at each corner and merlons cut along the top of each wall between them. There was even a large banner flapping in the breeze in the front left corner tower. It was red and gold with the same designed RL embroidered upon it. The whole of Los Angeles city was visible in the distance beyond and down the back side. The driveway wound like a river through the front lawn and widened like a delta at the front door. Tom Davidson's SUV and the Volkswagen bus pulled to a stop twenty feet short of the door, perhaps subconsciously feeling unworthy of parking directly in front.

Davidson, Evan and Tomas Linkley climbed out of the SUV. When the VW bus came to a stop, the front doors popped open and a young man stepped from each side. The side door slid open and a young woman crawled out to stand beside her friends.

Yoshi Turang, Peter Smithson and Emily Jepsen are all dressed in their Sunday best, at least the best for mid-twenties, southern California grad students. Yoshi and Peter are wearing similar khaki pants, patterned button down, long sleeved shirts and comfortable loafers. Emily is in tight fitting blue jeans with a silver pattern sewn on the back pockets, a loose fitting flowery blouse and sandals. Yoshi and Emily both have earrings.

For a minute, the whole party just stood and stared up at the monolith before them. It looked authentic enough, from moss covered stones to the open holed windows high up in the towers.

"Okay, guys, let's get our act together." Davidson gathered his team around. "We don't want to seem too overawed. Mr. Levin isn't going to want to give his money to a bunch of drooling idiots."

"Yea, but dude, is this a real castle, in Los Angeles?" Peter reached out a hand to touch the stone wall. "I'm mean, who heats this place."

Evan moved away from the group and stepped into the deep recess of the doorway. Pressing the only possible button, a shield with two swords crossed over it, he heard the sound of trumpets heralding their arrival. The rest of the group gathered behind him. The solid oak door creaked open and they were greeted by a handsome middle aged woman. She was wearing a dark business skirt, no nylons, a loose white blouse, black loafers and her jet black hair tied in a tight bun behind her head.

"Hello and welcome," she offered, not necessarily warmly, "if you will come with me, Mr. Levin is waiting for you on the terrace." She waited till everyone was inside and closed the door behind them.

She moved to the head of the pack and led the mini troupe through what looked like a huge living room, but was in reality just the foyer. It was lined with a few tasteful landscape prints and a spacious thick rug covering almost all of a very expensive looking travertine floor. There is a door to their left and two more to their right, but they moved across the room to another opening leading to another cavernous room.

If the outside looked like a real castle, the inside was a bit more contemporary. The new room they passed through was designed and decorated like you might imagine a rich person would do. Keeping with the castle theme, there are huge beautiful tapestries hanging from the walls, starting high up near the vaulted ceiling. The walls themselves are finished in modern textures, no stone blocks, and painted in light grey tones. There was a large fireplace in the wall to the left, and the room itself was well lit by two prodigious skylights in the ceiling and eight stylish, wall mounted lamps. A full size bear rug lay sprawled in front of the fireplace hearth, covering a floor of real dark oak wood. It is surrounded by two overstuffed leather chairs.

As the group passed through, most of the right side was an opening to the dining room. A beautiful cherry wood table set for twelve people, surrounded by hand carved, plush cushioned chairs. Topping it off was a monstrous chandelier straight out of Phantom of the Opera hanging overhead.

Their focus shifted back forward as they approach a crystal clear glass door. As they got close, the glass parted in the middle allowing passage to the outside without lifting a hand.

Like most expensive properties in Los Angeles, the view is what creates the value. The castle of Richard Levin is not the exception. As Evan and his group walked through the parted doors, the effort to cloak their awe was forgotten. Once through the doors, they found themselves beneath a beautiful, white painted, lattice covered patio. Lush green vines winding their way from ground to cover on every support post. At the far edge, three wide red stone steps led to an Olympic sized infinity pool, the crystal clear water sparkling under the refulgent southern California sun. The opulent green lawn continued beyond the pool, but from the terrace view, the whole Los Angeles basin seemed to be a fingertip away. At the far end of the pool, a lady in a very small bathing suit reclined in a chaise lounge, her body shimmering with oil in the midday sun. As she peered beneath her large floppy hat and over her Hollywood sunglasses, she gave a small wave to the ogling crowd.

Leaping up from his chair, Richard Levin bounded over.

"Welcome, welcome to my humble abode." He extended his hand and enthusiastically shook hands with everyone. "Thanks for making it up here on a Saturday. I hope you found it with no trouble."

He turned slightly back to the glass table, gesturing to a man rising from his seat. "This is my attorney and friend, Myron Brewster," and swinging his arm back toward the pool, "and I know that a couple of you know my beautiful wife, Lisa."

Brewster was dressed in casual clothes. White linen pants, dark blue polo shirt and canvas boat shoes with no socks. He was very thin with an equally thin mustache. His full head of black hair was shoulder length, and swept back into a little pony tail. Looking like a young Errol Flynn, he stepped forward and shook hands all around.

Davidson spoke first. "Yes," nodding toward Lisa, "and no, we didn't have any problems. I must say, sir, you have an extraordinary home here, the view is fantastic.

Moving from left to right, he gestured, "This is Tomas Linkley, our mechanical engineer, Yoshi Turang, Peter Smithson and Emily Jepsen. They are the builders and sounding boards to our little baby. We all lean on each other to question, suggest and support the work." Turning to Evan, he put a hand on his shoulder, "and this as you know, is Evan Longview, a US Marshal from 1888."

This last sentence dropped like a brick and a blanket of silence enveloped everyone. Levin stared at Tom, slowly looked to Evan and then turned to glance at Brewster. After a couple seconds, a smile spreads over his face and he began to laugh out loud. Looking a little unsure, Brewster chuckled a little under his breath. The rest of the group was smiling, but no one was saying anything.

Levin looked around at the faces and not seeing much support, stopped laughing abruptly and facing Evan said,"You're serious?"

Evan just looked back at him.

"Okay, let's sit down and talk about this."

They all pulled up chairs and gathered around the glass table. Levin pressed the button on a box on a side table. In a second, a young man appeared through the sliding door.

"Yes Sir?"

Levin looked around the table. "Joseph, bring a pitcher of margaritas please." He looked around the table again, "who wants salt?"

After everyone had given their preference, Levin spoke first.

"Ok, maybe we should start over. The other day, I said you could call anytime for anything." He chuckled, "The same day may be a record for calling in a favor, but I agreed to meet with you and your friends as you requested. So why don't you tell us what this is really about."

Davidson cleared his throat a little and put a hand on Evan's arm. "Maybe I can tell the story. I will try to keep it succinct and you can ask questions when I finish"

Leaning back, Levin waved a hand to begin.

"While I was a physics student at CIT, and with a lifelong belief, I came up with an idea to make time travel a possibility. I met Tomas, here, and together we figured a way to make it work. My mentor in school hooked us up with an investor and we went to work creating our dream."

Joseph came through the doors with a cart full of glasses and drinks. After everyone had a drink in front of them, Levin leaned forward, nodding, "go ahead."

"Tomas and I recruited Yoshi and Peter from our time at CIT. They had the qualifications to do the work, the ability to dream *and* the willingness to work for very little money. Emily here, heard about our little adventure through the school grapevine and showed up on our door all full of energy, and degrees of accomplishments, also willing to share the dream for little pay." Tom paused to sip his margarita.

"After a year of long hours, questioned belief and a few hundred Corona's, we had finished our girl and went out into the desert for her maiden voyage.

225

"I don't know why it has to always be seen as a female?" Emily spoke for the first time.

Davidson waved her away with a smile. "While we were setting up, the Marshal chaperoning the project, accidently flipped some switches and before we knew what happened, Evan here, was lying at our feet."

Reaching into a bag he had been carrying, Tom pulled out a video tape.

"This is a video, taken on the spot, of what I just described." He slid the tape across the table.

"We had barely recovered from the shock when a huge sand storm blew over us and we had to dismantle the machine. Evan was swooped up by the other Marshal and they took off back to LA. If that wasn't bad enough, after a month of cleaning and repairing as best we could, our work shop was burned down in a fire, losing all components and computers. All we have now are my notebooks and some paperwork at Tomas's.

Tom took another sip of his drink. "When I finally hooked back up with Evan, we went to visit our original investor, hoping that Evan being proof of function would convince him to fund us again. Unfortunately it had an adverse effect. Without going into too much detail, we have chosen not to do business with him again and are looking for alternative funding."

Davidson sat back and for a whole minute, not a word was spoken. Yoshi was looking down into his drink. Peter was watching Lisa Levin in the sun. Emily was staring across the table at Evan who is looking out over the LA horizon. Levin is looking at everyone, trying to digest what he just heard.

He turned his gaze on Evan. "What is *your* story? Is this the truth?"

Evan pulled his gaze back from the view. "I don't know about the early stuff, or any of the technical words. I was just riding my horse across the desert on the way to Los Angeles when he tripped in a hole and threw me over his head. When I landed and looked up," he waved around the table, "all these people were standing around me."

Evan paused to gather his thoughts. "All I really know is I was born around 1865. I became a US Marshal when my wife was raped and murdered. I somehow ended up in this time period and I have spent the last few months trying to get my mind around what happened to my world, and how I can get back to avenge her death."

He looked around the table and quickly reached for his margarita, drinking it down in two gulps.

Levin stirred his drink with his finger, swiping some salt from the lip of the glass. He looked over at Brewster, who just stared back.

"Why don't you guys go take a little walk in the gardens around the side of the house while Myron and I watch your video, discuss your little tale, and try to decide whether it should be a documentary, a science fiction or a comedy."

Everyone stood and Peter and Yoshi refilled their drink glasses. They all shuffled off the terrace and worked their way down a path to the side of the house, which opened into a vast multitude of roses and flowers.

As they wandered around the paths, taking in the view and the smells, there was a smattering of conversation.

"Do you think they'll go for it?"

"That Myron guy is kind of creepy."

"Levin is a little odd himself, but I guess when you have his money you can be any way you want."

"His wife by the pool is so Hollywood cliché."

"Pretty good margarita."

Davidson was walking beside Evan. "What do you think?"

Evan stopped to look at a patch of vibrant red roses. "I don't know. I don't understand anything, this lifestyle, this place, all the people. It's all so.... fast"

Tom put his hand on Evan's shoulder as Emily called out.

"They're signaling us back."

The group made their way back to the terrace and took their seats again. Levin looked around the table, pausing for effect on each face, his hands folded together on the table.

"Ok, I believe you."

There was a noticeable sigh around the table.

"Hell, I take risks every day to make movies with not much guarantee what the public will buy. We just try to put out as many as possible and hope a few stick and make money. So, pending some verification of who you say you are, I will back you 100%. Put together a list of expenses and we will have a contract drawn up."

"Excuse me Mr. Levin," Davidson looked apprehensive, "what exactly will you be expecting in return for your generosity?"

"Well, that should be obvious. For my 100% backing, I get 100% of the movie rights and all profits derived from it therein."

ELEVEN

Once again, the overhead fan was quietly clacking above the bed. The sun was probably on its way up, but it was hidden by a cloud cover that seemed ready to burst into tears at any time. The warm wind was pushing the trees out of its way as it hurried to reach a faraway destination. Evan had been lying awake for some time now, his usual thoughts of past and present. There was a slight prejudice to the present now, as the possibility of returning home had been upgraded with the agreed backing of Levin.

After a night of beer, tequila shots and "screw Pensor! shouts," Evan spent most of yesterday recovering. He also tried to think about what he would do to keep himself occupied while the rebuilding of the time machine was being accomplished. Deputy Marshal Linder had spoken of a shooting range where they could practice. He would definitely make it there a few times. Captain Harrison may have taken his issued gun, but he still had his Colt and holster and he still had plans for its use, sometime in the future.

Sitting up and spinning to sit, Evan put his feet on the floor and headed to the kitchen for the day's first cup of coffee. While he waited for the Keurig to warm up he watched the clouds break outside and let their pent up retention rain down on the world below.

He thought about the consequences of the rain now and back in his time. A heavy rain in the 1880s made travel by wagon almost impossible as all but the most packed roads turned into long running mud ponds. Even a man on horseback was slowed by the muck and had to be careful of getting a hoof stuck. Today, with the hard covering the roads had, it didn't seem like much of an issue. Then again, seeing the vehicles they used, Evan wasn't sure if anything slowed down. He had seen a couple accidents, though, and the results were much more catastrophic compared to a broken arm being thrown from a horse.

His coffee beeped finished and with mug in hand he moved back to the bedroom. It still amazed him how the morning rituals of going to the bathroom, shaving and showering had become so easy and convenient. The razors to shave with were odd, but effective. He had yet to cut himself once since starting to use them. The shower was his favorite part of the morning. The constant pressure and controllable temperature allowed him to relax and put his thoughts in order for the day to come. Had he been younger with no plans, it would have been hard to get him out at all.

Stepping through the steam, he grabbed a large towel from the rack to dry off. Before he could finish, the doorbell rang, interrupting his rumination. He wrapped the towel around his waist and made his way toward the front door, using his hands to comb his hair as he went.

Looking through the peephole, Evan was surprised to see his visitor. Throwing the deadbolt, he pulled the door open.

"Emily, hello."

Emily Jepsen took a step back as the door opened and she was confronted by Evan wearing nothing but a sheen of water and a towel.

"Oh, I'm sorry, I didn't…

"No, come in, out of the rain"

Evan moved aside as Emily stepped into the foyer. "What brings you here?"

"I wanted to talk to you."

"Ok, but come in to the kitchen. I was just about to have another cup of coffee. Would you like one"?

"Sure, do you have any Hawaiian Nut?" Emily giggles.

Evan gave a small smile, "No, just plain ole' black coffee."

He led the way to the kitchen and Emily couldn't help observe the bunched muscles in Evan's back and legs.

Emily was wearing red sneakers, a tight fitting white t-shirt with a printed image of Stevie Nicks and light blue jacket with the sleeves rolled up. The usual shorts have surrendered to a pair of snug, high waisted, blue jeans in deference to the inclement weather outside. Her reddish, brown hair normally pulled up and back is loose and flowing down below her shoulders, the wetness from the rain adding a hint of vulnerability.

Evan took this all in as they stepped into the kitchen and he waved her to a stool at the counter. He grabbed a coffee mug from the cabinet and inserted a coffee pod into the machine.

"Is black okay? I have sugar, but no milk." He turned to find her appraising him from head to toe.

"Black is fine," A small smile on her lips.

Realizing what he was or wasn't wearing, he started for the door. "I'll just go put some clothes on real quick."

Another giggle, "Oh don't go on my account."

Evan hurried from the room. Emily got up to get her coffee. As she slowly sipped, she looked around at the sparse room out beyond the kitchen counter. There were only a few pictures on the walls, two prints in a set of the beach at sunset and across the room a large framed, mediocre painting of a farm with horses running in the field behind the barn. An EZ boy recliner was kept company by a worn out cloth couch and a large television resting on a cheap wooden table.

Hearing movement behind her, to her disappointment, Emily turned to find Evan fully clothed.

"I like what you've done to the place. So…guy simple."

"Well, I haven't done anything. This is how Jude had it. It's not my house nor is it going to be permanent, so I don't feel the need to make any changes."

Evan was back to his normal blue jeans, boots and button down shirt. His hair was combed back.

"How's your coffee?" Evan stepped to the kitchen and started another cup for himself.

"It's fine." Emily moved around and back onto the stool. "Evan, have you talked to Tom recently. I'm mean yesterday or today?"

"No, I spent most of yesterday with my head in ice water and trying not to throw up, why?"

"Well, I tried calling but no one answered and when I went by his apartment, he didn't answer there either."

"Did you try Tomas? Maybe he's been staying there."

"Not yet, you live close, so I just came here after going by Tom's."

"Do you have his phone number, let's call him now."

Emily reached for her purse and after rummaging around, pulled out a small book.

"My lifeline to the world, I would be lost without this."

She dove back into her purse and brought out her cell phone. After dialing the number, she listened for a minute. "No answer."

Evan looked at Emily. "Let's drive by again. Maybe he was just at the store or in the shower."

They agreed to take Emily's car and as Evan locked the door and turned to follow her down the sidewalk, it was his turn to observe that she seemed to have curves in all the right places.

There was still no answer at Tom's and after looking through windows as best they could for signs of foul play, they decided to head to Tomas' place. There was no answer there either, but as they were heading back to the car, Tomas appeared from around the corner with his surfboard under his arm and his wetsuit down around his waist.

He saw Emily and Evan standing on the sidewalk in front of his apartment complex. "Hey, what's up?"

Emily was looking over his shoulder, thinking maybe Tom has been surfing with him.

"Is Tom with you, or have you spoken to him recently?"

The smile slipped from his face. "No, not since the other night, why?"

TWELVE

36 Hours Earlier

The taxi pulled up to the curb, the driver unsure if he had the right address. His passenger was a little unclear as well as a lot drunk. His friends had helped pour the man into the back seat and handed him twenty dollars. He spent most of the drive hoping his rider wouldn't puke over the seat onto him.

"We're here, man."

Looking over his shoulder, his fare stirred from his stupor and fumbled for the door latch. Practically falling out of the door, Tom Davidson managed to right himself on the curb. He looked back at the cabbie with a lopsided grin on his face and gave him a "thumbs up". He turned toward the house, gathered himself and staggered off down the driveway.

The cloud cover had blown in early and added to the shadow of the trees lining the drive. Any light from the stars or city lights in the sky was masked out completely. In the pitch black and his foggy state, Davidson didn't see the large mass in front of him till he had walked right into it. Banging his knees, he fell forward, slamming his hands loudly onto the warm hood of a dark sedan.

"Oouch!" He shouted out, staggering back a step. "What the fu…., who parked…?"

The pain in his knees giving him a little clarity, he moved around the car and fumbled his keys from his pocket. After a few attempts, he got the key in the door and pushed his way into his apartment. It was just as dark inside as he reached back for the light switch by the door. The overhead light came on, momentarily blinding him. When he turned back from the door, he registered a face standing before him. He was able to just get out a gasp of recognition and surprise before his head exploded in pain and then all went black.

Long unused rooms can absorb and retain their last redolence. When the unused room is a warehouse bathroom and you add the normal mustiness of moisture and heat, the permeating bouquet can melt your nose hairs. Having this rankness seep into his consciousness, added to the pounding in his head from too much tequila, the throbbing pain in his nose and face was just piling on. The pain was temporarily pushed aside when Davidson tried to rub his face and his arm was jerked back by the handcuffs running from his wrist to the handicapped bar attached to the tile wall. Coming fully awake now, Tom took in his forced surroundings.

He was in a single room bathroom. The kind you see in most gas stations, just a sink and toilet. The latter which he was seated upon, chained to the wall.

Yanking on the chain again, he yelled, "Hey… hey, what the hell is going on. Anybody out there…hello?"

He jerked a couple more times on the cuffs and chain, but soon realized he was only going to hurt himself worse. Looking around, there was very little to see. The sink had rust all around the faucet and knobs, as well as a rusted drain at the bottom. The soap dispenser attached to the wall above the sink was missing its reservoir and was now just a piece of metal with no purpose. The towel box on the wall looked empty and lonely. There were a couple squares of toilet paper plastered to the floor near his feet and he subconsciously moved them away from any contact.

"Hey, anyone out there?" he tried again. "What the fuck is going on? You can't do this."

When there was no answer or any other sound, he slumped with his head on his chest. He figured he had only been here a few hours, as the pounding in his head again spoke up. "Remember me?"

"You're a what!?" Tomas collapsed back into the cushioned recliner in his living room. Evan was lounging on one end of a futon couch while Emily was sitting on the edge at the other end. There was a beanbag chair in the corner and a small TV on a coffee cart against the wall with a Play Station console on the second shelf. The table in front of them was made from snarled drift wood supporting a clear glass oval. The walls are adorned with posters ranging from Andy Warhol to Star Wars. There was a "Corona" neon sign hanging over the opening to the kitchen.

"I am an FBI agent." Emily stated again, sitting up a little straighter.

Opening her seemingly bottomless bag, she dug around for a second before coming out with a small, rectangular wallet. She flipped it open to reveal a badge and ID card. She passed it to Tomas, who looked it over carefully with a look of confusion on his face.

"But you were on campus. You were a student!"

"Pardon me, what is an "eff bee eye agent?" Both Tomas and Emily turned to look at Evan.

Tomas looked to Emily as he leaned over to hand the badge to Evan, "Perhaps you should take this one."

Emily gave Tomas a hard look before turning her attention to Evan. "The FBI is the Federal Bureau of Investigation. We are essentially the countries investigative police force. We are part of the Department of Justice and investigate crimes that are national in scope or have to do with crossing state lines, kidnapping, bank robberies and governmental spies. We assist local police with serial murder cases; we assist the US Marshals with manhunts across states. You haven't heard of us, because we didn't exist until the early 1900's."

Evan is looking at the badge while Emily is explaining. He is trying to understand his thoughts. He feels a mixture of confusion with a women working for a federal law group but also some sense of comradery.

Tomas is a little less exuberant about it. "What about our project? You're so…uh…young and cool. You seemed to actually know about….stuff?...and…and why?"

Emily looked at Evan and then back to Tomas. "Ok, let me explain, but I'm really thirsty; do you have anything to drink?"

"I have Corona or water."

Checking her watch, Emily shrugs, "What the hell, a beer sounds good, I'll take one."

Tomas got up and looked at Evan, "You want something?"

"Uh, sure, I'll have a beer also."

Tomas moved through the archway under the neon sign and the sound of the refrigerator opening is followed by a drawer opening and the pop, pop, pop of three bottles being opened.

Evan was looking at the different posters on the walls and Emily was gazing at the ceiling when Tomas came back to the room.

"I'm out of limes right now, sorry." He handed a beer to each Emily and Evan and sat back down in his chair.

Emily took a big swig of her beer. "Ok, my name really is Emily Jepsen. I am twenty seven years old. I graduated from UC Berkeley with a degree in computer technology and a minor degree in Political Science. Right before I graduated, I was approached at a party by a gentleman who eventually got around to asking if I would be interested in a job with the government. After we talked a little more, I agreed to meet him at his office the next day. It turned out to be the FBI office in San Francisco. I was intrigued, and a little excited, I suppose. It seemed kind of romantic to have a job working as Fed. I imagined myself helping to crack bank robbing rings, tracking down serial killers. I would be the next Clarice Starling."

Evan gave her a questioning look.

"She's a character in a movie."

"Does everyone tell stories regarding movie characters?"

It was Emily's turn to have a quizzical look. "Anyway, I agreed to come see him again after I graduated. Besides, it was a paying job with benefits, right out of school."

"I spent a year training and learning." She glanced at Tomas, "And yes, I can kick your butt."

"The Bureau heard from sources about your little project. They have "sources" everywhere. They planted me on the campus at Tech and told me to learn more and try to get involved. With my computer tech background," she paused to smile at Evan, batting her eyelashes, "and my natural feminine charms, it wasn't hard to get myself on the team."

She turned back to Tomas, "you know the government. If something big or new is going to happen, they want to know about it and get in on the action. I was the eyes and ears. I'm sorry."

The only sound for the next minute was three bottles of beer being tilted and gulped as everyone let Emily's story percolate.

Tomas was the first to speak. "Ok, now that that's out of the way, what are we going to do about Tom?"

Emily had thought about it. "Well, as you know, most law enforcement agencies will not get involved in a disappearance until the victim has been missing more than forty eight hours. Hell, we don't even know if Tom is a victim or missing. Maybe he just went somewhere. Clear his head. Plan our next steps."

"He *was* pretty drunk," Evan spoke up. "I knew a guy once that got so drunk; he wandered off into the hills, climbed a tree and slept for almost two days. It wasn't till he fell out of the tree that he woke up enough to wander back into town. He never did figure if the headache was from the whiskey or the fall"

Tomas shook his head. "No, he would have let me know. He wouldn't go off by himself. Something has happened to him."

"Ok, let's take this from both perspectives," Emily said. "I will check with my boss, but don't expect much. In the meantime, let's go back to Tom's place and see if we can find any more evidence pointing to where he might be."

FOURTEEN

As the sound of slow moving steps infiltrated Davidson's consciousness, his head jerked up, fully awake. It must have been a couple more hours as the pounding in his head had quelled to a slight agitation. He watched as the door lock was reversed from the outside and the door pushed open.

A man stepped into the small bathroom and Davidson's eyes widened in surprise. The previous night's recollection flooded back into his memory.

"You! What the fuck is going on?" Tom's face reddened with anger. "Did you knock me out? I told you on the phone yesterday, we didn't want your deal, didn't need it anymore."

The man standing before him was wearing tasseled loafers, khaki pants and a longs sleeved, dark green button down shirt. His hair was dark and a little too long at the collar. He had the slouched shoulders and round belly of someone not used to physical work. His thin nose and small mouth along with his wire rimmed glasses over small green eyes completed the picture of life long assistant manager in a small insurance office.

"I'm sorry sir," he spoke in a soft melodic tone, "we've never spoken before."

"Bullshit," Tom's voice echoed off the small, tiled confines. "I sat in front of your desk, just the other day and listened to your pompous demands for my work."

The man tilted his head to the right, giving Tom a look of bemused patience. "Again, sir, I am pretty sure we have never met or spoken."

Davidson leaned back and took a closer look at his captor. There was something different, the hair, the glasses, the casual clothes.

"Um, you may not be Pensor, but you look pretty damn similar. Who are you then and why am I chained to the wall in this crappy, pun intended, old bathroom?"

Ignoring the question, the man twitched a quick smile, "I am so sorry. I brought you something to brighten up your room."

He stepped from the room and Tom heard the man humming cheerfully to himself. A few seconds later he returned, pushing the door open with a rolling cart. Davidson couldn't see what was on the cart except a vase full of bright colored flowers.

"This place is such a grungy, blah room. I thought these might brighten up your stay a little."

Tom strained against his chain. "What do you mean my stay? You can't keep me here! Who are you?"

The stranger picked up the vase and set it on the back of the sink. "There, that's nice."

He turned and pushed the cart a little closer and Tom could now see a variety of instruments on the top shelf. Pliers, a scalpel, an ice pick and a couple other items he didn't recognize.

Tom's eyes widened in shock, "Hey, hey what the fuck?" Fear began to creep into his voice.

"Oh don't worry," the man purred, "I'm sure none of this will be necessary." He picked up an instrument that looked like a combination garlic press and a cigar tip cutter. He slowly stroked the edge of it with loving affection.

"It's very simple, actually. Since you won't accept the offer to fund your little project, we'll just proceed without you."

"What? That's not possible," Tom voice was beginning to sound even more strained. "You'll never figure it out. It will take you years to get to where we're at."

"Oh I don't think so," the stranger looked bored, "we have your notes and we have someone who can read them. And besides, if we get stalled, we'll just ask you." He gave his little smile as he caressed the tool in his hands.

"My notes, how did you get my notes…?

"Oh, you shouldn't be so naïve. You really should have put them in a safer place. Right on your kitchen table made things oh so easy."

Davidson tried to sound defiant, "There's way more to my machine than what is in those notes. Obstacles we came across on the way, things we solved on the spot. You'll never get it exactly right and I won't help you."

He looked nervously at the cart.

The stranger looked on Tom with a friendly smile. "You can call me Wendell, and I am sure we are going to get to know each other well in the near future."

He reached out and dropped the instrument in his hands onto the cart and then with mongoose like speed, he snatched Tom's unshackled wrist and held it with unexpected strength.

The smile remained on his face, but the light green eyes had turned a darker shade. His face distorted with a maniacal grin as he grabbed the middle finger and quickly bent it backwards till the crack echoed around the room.

The following sound was Tom's scream reverberating off the walls.

FIFTEEN

"Does Tom park his truck in the driveway?"
Evan was squatted down, studying the cement
driveway outside Davidson's apartment.

Emily was peering inside through the door
window on the side of the garage. Tomas had stayed at
his place in case Tom tried to reach him there.

"I don't really know, I've only been here once.
We always met at the lab to work or a bar to discuss
work. And by the way, where is his truck?"

Evan stands up, and strode down the drive
toward the street. When he got to the sidewalk, he
turned and looked up and down both ways. Returning
to the garage, he shook his head.

"It's not out there. Remember, though, he left it
at *The Wave* the other night. We put him into a cab. So
he is either out somewhere or it's still there."

Looking down at the driveway again, "But
look at these wheel tracks. Tom has a larger vehicle
and I'm pretty sure the wheels are wider than these."

Emily stepped over to see what he was
pointing at. She can barely make out a tire tread in the
light dust on the white cement. She looked up at Evan,
a mixed look of skepticism and admiration on her face.

"What?" Evan shrugs, "it's just normal to look at tracks. Every horse hoof print is unique and most cars have different wheel patterns as well. Different type of transportation, but same idea."

"Tires, they're called tire tracks," Emily explained. "The wheel is the metal part attached to the car. The tire is the rubber tube around it."

Evan took this in. "Ok, but there was a car parked here that was not Tom's"

They moved to the side door, and looked in the window again. Emily knocked on the door. After a few seconds, she knocked again, this time more firmly. She reached out and tried the knob, locked. She stepped back and began to rummage around in her bag.

"Here it is," a smile of triumph on her face. She pulled out a ring with a few odd shaped pieces of metal attached. Showing them to Evan, she saw the quizzical look on his face.

"Hey, I work for the FBI. I may not be a real "spy", but it doesn't mean I can't have some of their cool gadgets. One of my instructors at the academy taught me this."

She squatted down and picking out a couple of the odd shaped items she inserted them into the key hole on the door knob. A look of concentration masked her face as she *felt* for the right slot and chamber. After a minute of probing and twisting, she grunted with satisfaction. Turning the handle, the door pushed open into the apartment.

It was Evan's turn to look on admiringly. A light sheen of sweat had formed on Emily's forehead and with a *puff*, she blew a strand of hair out her eyes. For the second time that day, he realized how attractive she was.

She made a stately gesture to the door, "After you sir."

Evan stepped into the dark living room and Emily closed the door behind them as she followed. They stood side by side as their eyes adjusted. They took in the apartment. The couch in front of them, the TV against the wall, the two doors to the right and the small table and chairs and kitchen to the left. The table was strewn with paperwork and notebooks, but other than that, there didn't seem to be anything disturbed.

Emily was the first to speak. "Why don't you check those two rooms and I'll check out the mess on the table and the kitchen.

Evan moved off through the living room. There was nothing that caught his attention, so he moved to the first door on the left. It opened into a small bathroom and after a short cursory glance, closed the door and moved to the other door. Entering the bedroom, his first thought was that he wasn't going to be able to tell if anything was disturbed as the room seemed to be in a permanent stage of unkempt. The bed had been at least partially made by haphazardly pulling up the covers. There was a pile of clothes on the floor in a corner. Apparently Davidson didn't own a hamper. Evan diligently kicked through the pile anyway, just to make sure nothing was hidden. Keeping something hidden in a pair of dirty underwear might, in reality, work, though he wasn't sure what they were actually looking for. There was nothing of note in the closet or the dresser draw. He was just closing the last drawer when Emily gave a shout of excitement.

"Evan, come here, I think I've found something!"

Evan moved quickly out the door and found Emily standing over the small dining table holding one of the notebooks.

"These are Tom's notebooks, drawings and doodling's, for the time machine. God only knows why he just left them lying out on the kitchen table.

"Ok, so we know he didn't just pack up and leave us in the dark."

"No, but look at this," Emily put down the book she was holding and picked up the second one on the table. "Just glancing through this book, it seems to be the first one in sequence."

She leafed to the end of the book. "So the pages are numbered. This book has one hundred pages."

She put that book down and picked up the other book again. "This is an identical notebook. It is the continuation of the first. But look," She again shuffled to the back of the book. "This notebook ends at page ninety five. And look at this. You can see where the last few pages of been torn out."

She holds the book up to Evan's face to show him the binding close up. "Someone took the last few pages!"

Tempering Emily's enthusiasm, Evan offered, "What if Tom did it. Maybe he didn't want anyone to see the final steps. He did it to protect the project?"

Emily wasn't to be deterred. "I don't think so. I mean, look at this table. Does this look like the work of someone trying to hide something?"

Looking at the mess on the table, Evan could see the logic. Emily began to gather all the papers and notebooks. She stuffed them into her endless bag.

"Let's go find Tom's truck. We need more evidence." She froze for a second. "Oh crap, we're not wearing gloves. If something really did happen to Tom, this will be a crime scene." She thought for a few seconds, "screw it, if that turns out to be the case, they'll just have to do elimination prints."

Evan was totally confused. "What are you talking about?"

"I'll explain later." Emily pushed Evan outside, locked the door and pulled it closed behind her. She led him down the edge of the driveway, skirting the semi invisible tire tracks.

SIXTEEN

The door closed behind him and Carl Sussel turned to hear the click of finality and a feeling of entrapment. He turned back to face the room. The heavy curtains were only slightly open and the late morning sun coming through the large picture window sent a thin shaft of light across the room, illuminating the swirling dust. Sussel could barely make out the man sitting behind the large desk and the back of a vague figure sitting in a chair facing the desk.

"Dr. Sussel, welcome. Please come and sit down." William Pensor waved to the other chair facing his desk. "I believe you know Mr. Doone."

Sussel stepped through the ray of light, a look of confusion on his face. "Phillipe?"

"Hello Doc. Good to see you again." Phillipe Doone leaned over to shake hands with his old mentor, "been a while."

Sussel gave Doone a weak handshake. Looking over at Pensor, he warily sat in the chair next to Doone.

"Thank you for coming. I know you value your time, so I won't waste too much time on pleasantries."

"Yea," Doone interrupted, "Walter and I have been discussing a pretty interesting proposition."

Pensor's eyes turned to bottomless pits and he put up an impatient hand to stop the rambling.

"Perhaps our impetuous young friend here speaks out of turn." What might pass for a smile crosses his lips. "We *have* been discussing a project and I would like you to consider being involved."

"What type of project? I still have a few classes, and new doctoral candidates to shepherd."

"The type of project that will make you famous, a king among your peers, and one that will make you very rich."

Doone couldn't keep his mouth shut. "Oh yeah, we're talking adding a zero or two to your bottom line. No more kowtowing down to academics or giving your intellect for peanuts."

"*Mr. Doone*! If you can't suppress yourself," The color of Pensor's impatience was crawling up his neck, "I will be forced to have you removed from this conversation."

Phillipe shrank back into his chair. "Ok, ok, just wanted to help."

"Dr. Sussel," he turned back, "we have known each other for a long time. My father always considered you a close friend. And standing on that friendship, I agreed to help another protégé of yours." He paused to stare down Doone. "And now again, hoping to lean on that friendship, I would like your help with an historic undertaking of my own."

The ingratiating presence of Phillipe Doone and his oily pretense of friendship were making Sussel wary. And despite his father's friendship with Pensor's father, Sussel never felt the same connection.

"My life is very complete and satisfactory, so not sure what time I can offer you or what you can offer me to change it."

Pensor leaned back in his chair and steepled his fingers across his stomach. The little smile again fleetingly passed over his lips.

"Suppose I told you we have the opportunity to change history, mine, your's, the worlds. That you could right any wrongs, fix any regrets. What if your name could be up there, no, well above, Rockefeller, Carnegie, Gates?" Pensor's face contorted into an outright sneer, "would you be able to work that into your life?"

Stunned by the statements and the turn in Pensor's demeanor, Sussel questioned, "Those are some pretty big declarations, sir. How do you propose to accomplish feats of such magnitude?"

The crocodile smile slid back into place as Pensor leaned forward and opened a desk drawer. He pulled out a stack of papers and dropped them on the desk in front of him.

"I have recently come into possession of a set of instructions and drawings for building a... well, call it a time machine, if you will."

Dr. Sussel leaned forward, trying to get a glimpse of the pages. He turned to look at Doone and then back at Pensor. "Are those Tom Davidson's? That is what he was working on when I introduced you to him. Did he complete it? Does it work? Where is Tom?"

"Calm down Dr. Sussel," Pensor sat back, chuckling. "You'll give yourself a stroke, and we can't have that. How I came to possess this information is not important. What is important is that I require your services to build this machine and yes, it does work. I did a little research and found another protégé of yours here in Mr. Doone. He has agreed, for a substantial fee I might add, to assist you in this project."

Pensor paused to gauge his words so far. "You will be given free rein to use any other assistance you might require. You will have a well-equipped facility at your disposal."

Still unsure and having a little of his own anger begin to rise, Sussel sat up straight. "Is Tom alright? Has something happened to him? I don't believe I could be involved in this until I speak with him."

Pensor let out a sigh of resignation and glanced at the bookcase on his left. A panel in the middle of the wall began to open into the room. "I think that can be arranged."

The unimpressive man who steps into the room had a soft build, hair a little long to the collar and a pair of wire rimmed glasses. Other than that, he looked very much like Pensor. He also had a gun in his left hand.

"Gentlemen, let me introduce my brother, Wendell."

SEVENTEEN

"This sucks!" A disappointed Emily spit out.

She and Evan were sitting in her car in the parking lot of the *Wave Bar & Grill*. Directly in front of them was Tom Davidson's SUV.

"Well now, maybe he just came back to get it and is inside having a beer," Evan was trying to be the voice of reason.

"I don't know," Emily's fear persisted, "I got a bad feeling about this."

Evan reached over and touched her hand. "Let's not get ahead of ourselves. Let's just go in. I'm sure we'll find him. He'll be sitting at the bar with a large beer drawing on a napkin some new problem to solve."

She gripped his hand tight, "I hope your right."

They exited the car and walked side by side across the parking lot, their arms brushing together. Evan held the door and followed her into the dimly lit room.

As their eyes adjusted, they scanned the room for Tom. The early lunch crowd was scattered around the tables and there were three individual people sitting at the square bar in the center of the room. No Davidson.

"Nuts," Emily again lamented.

"I need to use the bathroom, so I'll check there," Evan said, "you go talk to the bartender." He sauntered to the back. He knew where to go, having been there two nights ago.

Emily approached the bar and caught the eye of the bartender. Seeing the comely young lady, he hustled over.

"What can I get for you?" His eyes were hoping for more than a drink order.

"Do you remember me? I was in here a couple nights ago with some friends." She pointed to a table in the corner. "We sat over there at that table. There were five of us."

"Yea, sure, I remember. Beer and lots of tequila shots."

"That's' right. One of my friends, Tom Davidson, left his truck outside. Have you seen him since?"

"Tom? I know Tom," disappointment edged into his voice. "He comes in fairly regular. That's why we haven't towed his SUV yet. We cut a little slack for the regulars."

"So you haven't seen him since that night?"

Evan moved in next to her, shaking his head at her questioning glance.

"Nope, haven't seen him." Mr. Business now. "So what can I get for you two?"

Emily looked at Evan, "We might as well get some food while we're here." She pointed to the same back table. "We'll just sit there."

The bartender pulled a couple menus from under the bar and handed them to Evan.

"I'll be right over to get your order."

Evan and Emily moved to the table. He pulled out her chair and held it for her and then went around and sat facing her.

As usual, as Evan studied the menu, Emily studied him. He looked up and caught her watching and their eyes stayed locked for a few seconds.

The moment was broken when the bartender appeared next to their table. "Ok folks, what can I get for you?"

They both ordered a chicken sandwich with fries. Emily had a diet coke and Evan ordered a cup of coffee. The bartender moved off and Emily looked back to Evan.

"Well, now what? I think I can get my supervisor involved now. I think we have enough to show something is wrong."

Evan shook his head, "I'm not so sure about that. He might just still be off somewhere. Maybe he left with someone else. Do you know all his friends?"

"No," disappointment in her voice, "I suppose that's possible, but I don't think so. He wouldn't just take off like this. Not with new funding and the work to get started again. I would think he would be all excited and pushing to go."

"Probably…" He was interrupted when a waitress arrived with their food.

They went about the business of prepping their food. When their hands met at the ketchup bottle, there was once again the awkward moment of intimacy. Evan withdrew his hand quickly, but not fast enough to avoid the jolt of sensuality.

Emily looked down to pick up her sandwich and took a big bite. With a glint of mischief in her eye and a mouth full of food, she asked, "So what's your story, Evan? What was your life like back then?"

The French fry froze halfway to his mouth. A look of pain fleetingly crossed his face to be quickly replaced by one of resignation. He had told this story too many times. The French fry moved again and disappeared into his mouth. With a deep sigh, he retold an abbreviated version of his loss and pain.

"I think you know most of my story. I was just a guy trying to work a sheep ranch and make a life for my girl. After she was taken from me, I went on a rampage against most of humanity. I found that it didn't really ease the pain, and it mostly made me hard to be around, but for a couple years, it served to keep me going."

Evan purposefully picked up his sandwich and took a bite, "What about you, where did you grow up?

Emily sipped from her drink before answering. "Well, I was born in a Northern California town called San Rafael. My dad owned a successful car dealership and my mom was a stay at home mom. She was active, though, in local school politics. I was an only child and because of that, spent a fair amount of time by myself. I had friends but I was more interested in my new computer. I was fascinated by the speed of which you could gather information.

She stopped to give her little giggle, "Of course it's much better and faster now." She took another large sip from her drink and continued with a distant look in her eye.

"It was such a growing field and I was so fascinated, it was an easy choice to pursue in college. The political science minor was just a by-product of my upbringing. I guess all those meetings and pamphlets my mother had must have had some influence on me."

Evan was looking at her with a bemused look. "Well, I certainly don't understand the computer. I see one on every desk, and wouldn't know what to do if I had one. I'll leave that to you."

Nodding for Emily to take the lead, he added, "What do we do now?"

EIGHTEEN

A scant couple miles from the hustle and bustle of the downtown Los Angeles business district is the seemingly abandoned area of the old industrial district. Before the skyscrapers and spider web of freeways, *this* was the heart of Southern California industry. A crisscross of railway lines that brought in raw materials and carried out finished goods. Progress waits for no man or city as it were and with the establishment of the Los Angeles and Long Beach harbors, importing finished products or shipping unfinished goods to other more industry friendly places began to erode the core of the Los Angeles work arena. Agriculture had migrated to outlying counties, tire companies and steel mills were gone to tax friendly states. Clothing was still a big business, but they had carved out their own little neighborhood a few blocks away. Los Angeles was still a booming destination, but Hollywood and Aerospace required much more glamorous surroundings.

In the center of all this decay, in a sad red brick building squeezed between two other decayed brick buildings, Tom Davidson was waiting for his lunch. His captors weren't starving him, but they weren't fattening him up for the kill either. He had spent his day and night standing and sitting to keep the blood flow going.

Now, sitting on his prison seat he heard movement coming down the hall outside the door. When the door opened he was expecting Wendell to step in, but was shocked when his old mentor Dr. Sussel and then Phillipe Doone stepped through the opening. The expected Wendell followed them in.

"My God," Sussel exclaimed, "Tom, what is going on?"

Even the normally smug Doone was looking pale.

Tom raised his free hand to give a slight wave, his middle index finger bent at an odd angle. "Hello Doc, welcome," he glanced around the small, dirty bathroom, "to my home away from home."

Sussel turned to Wendell. "What is the meaning of this? You cannot keep him or us here against our will. I demand you let this man go immediately!"

Wendell patiently waited for the older man to rant and then raised the gun and remarked pointedly, "Actually, I can, and I will." Wendell stepped aside and waiving the gun said, "Please, now that we're all together, let's go see your accommodations."

The Doctor stared defiantly at him for a few seconds, glanced back at Tom and reluctantly shuffled toward the door, the dumbfounded Doone in his wake.

They marched down the grungy, cement hallway for fifteen feet. "Turn in here to your right."

Sussel and Doone entered into another dingy, dusty bathroom. The only difference from Tom's cell was the cracked and chipped urinal hanging from the wall. The grime on the walls was so thick, even the original grey cement was invisible. There are no windows, only a nonworking vent in the ceiling. The pungent odor was almost too much to bear.

"Here we are gentlemen, your own cozy dorm room." Wendell let out a little giggle. "I hope you won't let the smell bother you. Actually, you won't be in here much except to sleep. We have much work to do."

Phillipe Doone finally found his voice and a little courage. "What do you want from us? I thought we were getting a laboratory, equipment. This is preposterous; I can't live here or work here!" He is almost on the verge of tears.

Wendell took a step forward, pointing the gun at Phillipe's face. Doone threw his hands up in a weak attempt to defend himself. Once again, with surprising speed, Wendell whipped the gun across Doone's face, knocking him into the toilet stall. There was no door and he stumbled into the far wall, banging his head on the wall as he collapsed to the floor.

Wendell quickly turned to Sussel, who threw up his hands in surrender. "Would you like to say anything else?" A friendly smile creasing his face.

Turning to leave, he sing songs, "Make yourselves comfortable. Dinner at six and then lights out, long days in front of you."

He pulled the door shut and the two new prisoners heard the snap as the lock was turned.

NINETEEN

"Tell me again why we're going to see this guy." Emily glanced over at Evan as she turned up the tree lined hill.

"Like I told you before, this guy was the original investor." Evan looked passively out the window as they passed the gated homes. "When Tom and I met with him, he wanted total control and use of the new rebuilt machine. Tom kind of blew his stack and we left. The guy was throwing around veiled threats as we left and I sensed there was more going on than meets the eye. I thought I saw someone else looking out the window at us as we left. Here it is, turn in here."

"Nice," Emily grunted under her breath as they pull up to the gate. "Who is this guy, Dracula?"

Evan glanced sideways at Emily with a slight smile, remembering Tom's exact reaction.

Once again, the gate opened on its own with no prompting. They continued down the driveway, but unlike Tom previously, Emily pulled up and parked right in front of the walk way to the door. Exiting the car, they approached the large wooden door, and like previously, Evan reached up and lifted the horseshoe knocker eliciting the gong within the house.

"Wow," her trademark giggle slipping out, "is some guy with a humpback going to answer?"

Her smile quickly faded as the door slowly opened and the stoic Sam was facing them. He was dressed the same as before in dark slacks, jacket and white button down shirt.

"Yes, welcome back," He nodded to Evan. There was no hint of emotion whatsoever in his face. Looking slowly in Emily's direction, he stepped back. "Come in. I will let Mr. Pensor know you are here."

They moved into the entry way and waited as Sam disappeared through the study door to announce their arrival.

Nothing had changed to Evan's eye except the fresh flower arrangements spread around in easy view.

Emily was taking in everything she could, "This seems fairly pleasant compared to the outside."

"Uh huh….maybe you should hold back on your judgement."

Emily gave Evan a quizzical look as the study door opened and Sam stepped out and waved them in. "Mr. Pensor will see you now." He moved aside as he ushered them into the dim lit room.

As before, the room was bathed in darkness with only partial light coming in from the curtained window.

William Pensor was sitting at his desk, deep in the shadows of the long room. There is another presence standing next to him and as Evan and Emily approach the desk, they can make out the trim man who looks a lot like the sitting Pensor.

"Come in, welcome back Mr. Longview. And welcome to you, Miss Jepsen."

A look of surprise came to Emily's eyes.

"Oh come now. I don't give a pile of money without doing my due diligence. I know you are part of the team that built the time machine, only to have it be destroyed, along with my small fortune investment."

Pensor waved to the two chairs in front of his desk. "But let's put that behind us."

Evan and Emily moved to sit in the overstuffed chairs. "Would you like something to drink, tea, water, or perhaps something stronger? I can have Sam round something up."

"No thank you, I think we are fine," Evan spoke for both of them as he stared at the man standing a little back from the desk in the shadows.

Noticing Evan's intense stare, Pensor cleared his throat, "Oh excuse me, where are my manners?" Turning his chair, he gently tugged the arm of the man, moving him closer to the desk.

"May I introduce my brother, Wendell." The likeness was remarkable. They are obviously twins, though Wendell wore his hair longer and his eyes are a lighter shade of green.

Forgetting his past slight, Evan stood and extended his hand. "Nice to meet you, Evan Longview"

Wendell looked down at the outstretched hand and hesitantly reached out to give a limp shake. As Evan pulled his hand back, he noticed brown dirt like smudges in his palm. He caught a quick glance at Wendell's hands before he could put them behind his back. They were stained dark.

"And Wendell, don't be shy, this is Emily Jepsen. She is one of the scientists I was telling you about."

"FBI agent Emily Jepsen," she corrected. She had seen the dirty hands of Wendell and so just nodded, refraining from any contact.

There was a slight tic in William Pensors eyes, but he quickly recovered. "FBI, well, that is interesting. I had thought maybe this meeting was going to be a little more congenial than our last encounter, but perhaps I was wrong."

Pensor leaned back in his chair and the steepled fingers appeared across his midsection. "So the FBI had a plant on the last team. Why would they do that?"

"Let's just say, the government likes to keep tabs on projects that could affect national security."

"I see. And speaking of your team, where is Mr. Davidson? I thought he was the ringleader of your little group. Have you come to negotiate for my help without him?"

It was Emily's turn to be the speaker. "No sir, we are here because Tom has disappeared." She paused, "and we were hoping you might be able to shed some light on that disappearance."

Through all of this conversation, Evan had kept his gaze on Wendell. There was something off about him. It's not a physical thing, but Evan's bad guy sense was picking up a feral heat radiating around him.

"Me? Why would I have any information? I barely knew the man." Pensor's eyes shrank to a squint as he leaned forward and his voice began to rise. "Are you accusing me of something...Agent Jepsen?"

Emily didn't blink or shrink back. "Well, you did make threats to him in your last meeting and he disappeared soon after that meeting."

"I did no such thing." Pensor sat back but was still a little red in the face. He swiveled his head to face Evan. "I simply stated my terms and gave a time limit to accept." Looking back to Emily, he added, "If you want to stretch that statement into a threat, then I guess I am guilty."

Emily held eye contact for a second before rummaging in her purse. "Ok, well this is a courtesy call. The FBI is looking into Tom's disappearance," she snapped a business card down on the edge of the desk, "so if you think of any information that might be helpful, please give me a call."

Pensor glanced at the card and then his eyes rose up to look at Evan. "and what about you Mr.

Longview? You're not really law enforcement. You have no power or jurisdiction. What is your roll in this charade?"

Evan stood up and looked first at William and then slid his gaze over to Wendell, he said softly, "I'm just the bloodhound."

Emily stood and moved with Evan toward the door. When they got a few feet from the desk, Evan turned and looked at Wendell and asked with a sneer, "Are you the gardener here. The flowers are lovely."

They go out the study door and walking past a slightly surprised Sam, they let themselves out the front door.

As they walk down the walk to their car, a fist clenched Wendell stood at the window watching them get into their car and drive away.

"Yes brother," William said in a calming voice, "that is going to be a problem."

TWENTY

"What are we doing, man?" Yoshi took a slug from his Corona, "Tom's disappeared, Emily is running around with that cowboy dude, and we're sitting here with our thumbs up our asses."

Tomas was leaning forward in his easy chair, rocking back and forth, his beer untouched in his hand. Peter was stretched out on the couch.

There were no lights on in Tomas' apartment and the setting sun through the blinds was leaving only small streaks across the worn brown carpet.

"I don't know *what* I can't get my head around more," Peter begins, "the fact that Emily is an FBI agent, or jealousy that she's getting it on with an old cowboy from the 1800's. It's just weird man."

"Uh…we don't know she's bonking him," Yoshi trying to take the high road, "and he's not that old."

"Come on man, she's been hot on him since he landed in the dirt at her feet."

"Maybe, but you've been just as hot on her since she hooked up with us. Finding out she's FBI just makes her more hot."

Peter takes a long pull from his beer. "Amen to that brother."

"All right you guys," Tomas came out of his revelry, "enough crap. Here's what we are going to do. We're going to keep going. We have to. There's plenty we can do." He looked over at Yoshi, "And when Tom gets back, we don't want him to find us sitting on our thumbs."

Peter sat up on the couch and Yoshi leaned forward in his chair.

"Tomorrow, you two start finding a us a new lab space. You know what we need. I will track down Mr. Levin and speak to him about Tom and the need to start work. We'll have to trust Emily and Evan to find him."

Peter and Yoshi are nodding agreement. "Now get out of here, I have a lot of notes to make."

TWENTY ONE

Two hours later and a few miles away, Emily's blue Toyota Corolla pulled up in front of Longview's house. Turning the engine off, she turned to Evan.

"Wow, two meals in one day," a little giggle, "is that like two dates?"

Blushing, Evan looked over and down on her. "It's been a long day. Not sure if we accomplished much. Tomorrow, I think we should look more into that brother. There's something not square with him." He turned to open the door.

Emily reached over and placed her hand on his arm. "Whoa there sir, aren't you going to invite a girl in for a nightcap?"

Evan froze for a second. He turned back as the flush again rose on his neck.

Looking into Emily's deep green eyes, he opened his mouth, but was momentarily paralyzed. He closed his lips and exhaled through his nose. He let a slight smile pull at the corners of his mouth.

"Sure, sure, why not, I think I can find something, come on in."

He climbed out of the car and went around to her door. They walked side by side up the sidewalk. At the front door, he dug the key out of his front pocket, unlocked the door and ushered her inside. They moved down the hall way and as they enter the kitchen, he reached out and flipped the light switch on the wall.

As Emily moved to the counter bar, Evan turned toward a cabinet above the refrigerator. "What would you like?" He looked into the cabinet. "We have whiskey, tequila, vodka…."

Sensing movement behind him, he turned to find Emily standing right in front of him. For a short second, a questioning look flashed across his face until she quickly stepped up into him and pulling his head down with a hand behind his neck, she kissed him full on the lips.

He tensed for another quick second, but just as quickly gave in and allowed the kiss to continue. After a few seconds, he pulled away and looked at Emily. Her flushed face and dancing eyes fire his own desire and he quickly bent for another kiss, this one lasting quite a bit longer.

Once again he pulled back. "Emily….I…haven't…"

She shushed him as she began to unbutton his shirt.

"No wait. I...I....haven't been with many women. I was saving myself for Mary, and after she died, I had a couple bouts with some local whores.....but..."

Emily pulled his shirt out of his pants and began dragging him toward the bedroom. "Well, as that was over a hundred years ago...I won't hold it against you."

Evan looked down on Emily and then upward for a second with his eyes closed. Seeming to come to a decision, his shoulders relaxed and he followed her into the bedroom, kicking the door closed behind him.

TWENTY TWO

"I'll take care of it."

"No, no you won't." A contemplative William Pensor sat back in his oversized chair, his customary fingers steepled across his chest. "You have enough to keep our friends on task. We need that machine to be finished. I have another idea."

Pensor leaned forward and pulled a soft, black notebook close. Opening it and finding what he was looking for, he reached for his phone and dialed a number.

"Hello Captain."

****

"We have to keep going. Play along." An exhausted Tom Davidson tells his fellow hostages.

His clothes looked like they haven't been washed in a week, which is in fact, the case. His face was streaked with dirt and sweat. There was no air conditioning in their warehouse laboratory. The only light was sunshine coming in from the high windows that line the upper walls. They only worked during the daylight hours as their captor didn't want any lights on at night. It would be the only building on the block to do so and that would stick out rather brightly.

"At least we're rebuilding the machine."

Dr. Sussel and Phillipe Doone looked just as grungy. Fresh clothes or even washing their existing outerwear didn't seem to hold any interest for Wendell. What did hold his interest was inflicting pain. And he was very good at it.

"What are you talking about?" an angry Doone snarled back. He was bent over a table full of small components, going back and forth between pages of instructions and parts in his hands. There was a faded blue bruise on his right cheek and a fresh red scab on his nose. "You think we're just going to walk out of here when this is complete?"

"I'm afraid Phillipe is correct, Tom." A very disheveled and cowed Dr. Sussel whispers. "I fear that as soon as we finish a working product, we will no longer be of any value." He also had a fading black eye to go with burnt skin around his right wrist.

"You know what?" finding some false courage, Doone spouts back, "If we're going to die, why do any of this then. Screw these guys… if their planning to kill us, let'em build their own fuckin' time machine!"

Suddenly the loud clang of the outer door slamming shut echoes around the warehouse walls. All three men turn and instantly become absorbed in the work in front of them. All their hands are shaking.

"Hello gentleman."

****

Six-thirty in the morning is a quiet time. Evan's eyes jumped open as he woke to another presence next to him. His heartbeat slowed as his mind quickly remembered the events of last night's activities. The all too familiar flush of embarrassment began to rise throughout his body until he realized it wasn't embarrassment but something else, lust?, contentment? He slowly turned to look at the body under the covers next to him. He reached out a hand and put it on the rise of Emily's hip as she lay turned away from him. A soft moan came from somewhere under the sheets.

Reluctantly turning away, Evan sat up and pulling the covers back, slid his feet into his slippers. He grabbed his robe, thrown widely on the floor, and moved quietly out of the room. He went to the kitchen and turned on the coffee machine. He stood for a second taking in the sounds of the house and early morning, letting the flush of last night's intimacy wash over his emotions. When his mind kicked into the present time, he headed down the hall to the front door. The newspapers from these times were so much more to absorb. He opened the front door and stepped out onto the porch. The early morning chill made him catch his breath.

Looking around, Evan spotted the paper by the flower bed to the right of the porch. The paperboy was always close, but could never seem to get it all the way up to the door. Evan stepped off the edge and leaned over to pick up the paper. When he stood up, looking down the street, he saw the flash and immediately felt the heat and pain in his head. His last thought was…."Emily"…. And he collapsed in darkness on the dew wet lawn.

TWENTY THREE

He couldn't remember the exact date when he recognized he was a bad man. Was it always in his heart? Are we preprogrammed from birth? Do we have a biological clock within us, just waiting for some physical episode or emotional trauma to set us off? Captain Jerome Harrison had thought about this question often in the years since he had turned to the dark side. He supposed he could track the beginning to when his mother had needed more help than he could provide.

It wasn't that he was completely bad, he *was* a US Marshal after all. He had done plenty of good in his life. He had actually spent most of his life fighting for the good of humanity. Two tours in Vietnam, four years as a city policeman, and now fifteen years in the Marshal's service. When the ravages of pancreatic cancer began to chip away at his mother's mental stability, Harrison, looking after her estate, found a mountain of problems. Unpaid doctor's bills, back mortgage statements, and enough credit card debt to buy a nice luxury car, which it seems is exactly what his mother had done. Pride and a lifetime of "doing the right thing," kept him from turning his back and putting her estate in bankruptcy. And a life spent in the employ of the government didn't exactly lend itself to one of excessive, leisurely pursuits. So having been able to send his mother on only one, long ago vacation to Hawaii, Harrison vowed to at least let her legacy rest with a clear balance sheet.

Unfortunately, like most people, he found that when you need them the most, the banks are less forthcoming than advertised. As a long time bachelor, content to rent an apartment and owning no sizeable assets, he had little to no collateral for the size loan he needed.

It started small, as it usually does, eight years ago. The early evening sky seemed even darker than usual as grey rain clouds hung low in the sky above Nellie's Pub, promising a wet weekend ahead. Sitting at the far end of the bar, facing the door as was his custom, Harrison nursed a Guinness beer, sullenly watching the week end crowd begin to fill the bar. 6:00 pm and already standing room only. He could have been at The Busted Shield down the street with other law enforcement types, but tonight he wasn't feeling very social, the most recent denial from the latest bank having left him feeling depressed and at a loss. Finishing his third dark beer and contemplating a fourth, he saw Vince McCally enter and move to a booth at the back wall. Being empty, Harrison could only surmise it had been reserved as his regular spot.

When he finally got the eye of the bartender, he raised his empty bottle, signaling for another. The beginnings of a bad idea were forming and he needed a little more liquid courage to either push it aside or take the next step. McCally was a low level loan shark with ties to a local businessman, who despite many legitimate fronts, was well known to have his hand in most of the illegal enterprises working around the county.

The beer arrived and Harrison tilted it back, drinking half of it in one pull. He sat motionless for a second before sliding off his stool. After taking a minute to steady himself, he took some money from his pants pocket and threw it on the bar. He grabbed his beer and made his way to the booth in the back. If McCally saw him coming, he didn't let on. When Harrison stopped next to the table, McCally was looking at a notebook open in front of him.

Looking up as the light dimmed over his reading, he asked, "What can I do for you Marshal?"

"How do you know who I am?" The words came out a little slurred together.

McCally looked at the Marshal a little more closely. "I've seen you in here occasionally, and I try to make it my business to know people." Gesturing across the table, "why don't you have a seat?"

Harrison dropped heavily into the padded seat facing McCally, his beer sloshing a little on the table. He wiped the wet spot away with his hand, looked around the room and finally settled his gaze on McCally.

"So you must know, in my position, being with you is not a great career stepping stone, but I find myself in a bit of a bind, and wondering what it would cost to have you help me out a little."

McCally's upper lip moved a fraction upward on one side as he asked, "I guess that depends on how much help you need."

Knowing how this worked, Harrison had decided to try for a small amount. He didn't want to get in too deep. "I need twenty thousand dollars." This would take care of most of the doctor bills. He was sure he could get the mortgage company and auto loan stalled.

McCally let out a low whistle, "Thought you said a little help. That's quite a first bite."

Harrison looks around the room, "Can you do it, and what will it cost?"

The upper lip moved a little extra this time. "I can get you the cash. It's usually a point a week, but as you're an upstanding member of the law enforcement community, I can let you use the money for half of that."

And that's how it started. Harrison was able to pay the interest only for a couple of months, but at one thousand per week, his savings dried up and he eventually began falling behind. When the mortgage company and the auto loan company began to put the squeeze on, Harrison was once again in the back booth at Nellie's.

"I need more time and I need more money." He was sober this time, and trying not to sound desperate.

"You're barely keeping up as it is, how much more do you need?"

Harrison, his head down, barely got out a whisper, "One hundred thousand."

"Excuse me?" This time, McCally was in full bore grin mode. "You're joking, right?"

Harrison just looked up at him, eyes moistening. "Please, you gotta help me."

McCally looked at the Marshal with nothing but contempt.

Thinking for a minute, he said, "Let me talk to some people. I'll get back to you. Give me a number I can reach you."

Two days later, he was sitting in front of the man himself, Frank Johnston. A caricature of the fifties mob man. Slicked back hair, big cigar, gold medallion resting on a mat of black chest hair protruding from an open collared shirt. Leaning back in his chair, blowing a plume of smoke, he looked across his big ugly desk at Captain Harrison.

"Well, Captain, I understand we have a problem."

Harrison, trying to be calm but confident, blurted out, "Look, I just need a little more money and more time to pay it back. I work for the US Marshal's office, for Christ Sake, I'm good for it!"

Johnston bolted forward in his chair, jumping up to stand over the desk. "Listen, you fuck, you're in twenty K deep, two weeks behind on your last loan and now you want more! What do I look like, a bank? I don't care if you're Jesus Fucking Christ himself, no one gets a ride!"

He looked down on Harrison, who was trying to make himself part of the chair. Taking a deep breath, Johnston scooted back to locate his chair and

294

sat down. He took a minute to locate and relight his cigar. Looking up, his shark smile spreading on his face, he said, "Ok, how much do you need?"

Harrison, trying to compose himself again, sat up and said. "I need one hundred thousand dollars on top of the twenty I already owe you."

"And what would you do with that money?"

"I need to pay the balance of my mother's, now my, mortgage. I can't afford to pay them and you. I am behind on all accounts. Not really sure how I can pay any of it."

Frank leaned back in his chair, took another puff on the cigar and looked thoughtfully at Captain Harrison. After a couple minutes of uncomfortable silence, Johnston leaned forward again, putting his hand on his desk in front of him.

"Ok, here is the deal. I will forgive the twenty K you already owe, pay off your mortgage, and I won't expect any cash repayment."

Momentarily stunned, Harrison sat back. The look of confusion was slowly replaced by one of horror and anger.

"How *do* you expect repayment then?"

"Oh, I don't know specifically. I'm sure we can find other services for you to provide."

"And what if I don't want to accept your offer?"

"Well, then you can pay me back my twenty thousand right now and we can go on our merry ways."

"But I don't have your money. That's why I'm here now."

"Ok, it's been nice knowing you Marshal." Johnston turns to a large man who has been standing by the door the whole time. "Johnny, get a couple of the boys and escort the Marshal here down to the lake for a swim. Make sure to give him the "heavy" swimsuit."

Captain Harrison jumped to his feet. "Hey wait a minute, you can't be serious. I'm an officer of the law!"

Johnny quickly produced a pistol and aiming it at Harrison, waved him back down into his seat.

The shark smile appeared again, "Ok, Marshal, what'll it be," Johnston pointed to the door leading into the front hall, "door number one," and sweeping his arm back to the glass doors leading to the lake, "or door number two?"

So that's when he had become a bad man. Oh, at first it was simple things. Get one of Johnston's thugs out of jail with no charges. Lose some paperwork here and there. Turn the other way when some illegal activity was going to happen. When he transferred to Southern California, it became less often, but then the ultimate had happened. By now he was so far intertwined with Johnston's activities, when the order came to kill the fellow US Marshal, he could do nothing but comply. He was pretty sure he had gotten away with it, and when Johnston was gunned down in his home, Harrison believed he had been released from the hold of his evil side.

Then his phone rang.

TWENTY FOUR

1 Month later

It is surprisingly quiet in a hospital late at night. There is the constant variety of beeps from a variety of machines, both near and far. The sound of rubber soled shoes moving up and down the halls. The occasional snippet of conversation or twitter of laughter from nurses and doctors gathered around their work station. And yet, despite all of that, there is an added aura of calm and quiet. Perhaps it is the absence of external sounds that leech in from the outside world during daytime hours. Or that most of the patients are sleeping, and so cutting the vocal acoustics to a mere murmur.

Emily had been sitting in the hospital room at various times of the day and night for a month now, between chasing dead end leads and fighting with her bosses to let her stay involved. After all, she was involved. She had been attracted to the tall, handsome cowboy the minute he had landed at her feet in the desert sand many months ago. When they had been working together for a few days to find Tom Davidson, the attraction had grown quickly, culminating in a wonderful night together and lingering thoughts of a future.

So here she was, dozing in an uncomfortable chair, in a quiet but dreary hospital room, looking at a comatose Evan Longview, wondering if anything was going to be the same again. The neurologist said the bullet that put a three inch groove in the side of his head had done no permanent damage, but coupled with the baseball sized bump on the other side of his head; his rattled brain had had enough and shut down. They talked confidently that he would come out of this state, but wouldn't go so far as to venture any time frame, or what his state of mind might be. By now, the bullet groove was almost healed and the bump from his front porch was down to the size of a walnut.

As the clock ticked away, crawling toward the midnight hour, Emily went over again how everything had come about. She thought about Tom's disappearance, her and Evan's meeting with the Pensor brothers, the over egotistical William and the super creepy Wendell. She was sure they were behind the attack on Evan, but with no proof of any kind, the investigation was going nowhere. The ballistics from the bullet came back with no matches and lacking any witnesses, she was not able to get any type of search warrant. Her superiors or any judge, for that matter, wouldn't give much credence to her gut feelings.

The time machine was at the center of all this, that much was obvious. But there wasn't one anymore.

So, was Tom taken to build another one? If that was the case, why not just pay him to build another one? He had a backer, Mr. Rich Hollywood. So it would have to be a different party. That left the Pensors. They wanted the machine, but strictly for their own purposes. They were the only logical choice. They had the money, the desire, and seemingly the balls to be treacherous enough. But why take a shot at Evan? What threat was he posing? Were they getting too close looking for Tom? Did Evan know something they were afraid of?

Emily's head was going to explode. Too many questions, not enough answers. She tried to clear her mind and relax. She began to think about her favorite movies. The quiet sounds of the hospital brought thoughts of scenes in hospitals. Her eyes were finally getting tired and just as she was contemplating going home for the night, she caught a movement from the bed. She jumped up and went to the bedside. She could see Evan's eyes twitching, fluttering beneath the lids. Suddenly his eyes flew open!

"Evan, Evan…can you hear me?" Emily clutched his hand at his side and squeezed. "Evan? Squeeze my hand, baby. Let me know you're there."

His eyes remained open for another three seconds and then slowly the lids closed again.

"No, no!" Emily brought her other hand to help squeeze his. "Come on Evan."

After a few minutes, she reached for the call button and summoned the nurse. She drew her chair next to the bed. Holding his hand, she rested her head in her arms.

Frustrated tears and scared sobs were barely audible over the hushed sounds of the hospital.

TWENTY FIVE

The long, tanned legs of the cute blonde surfer girl were keeping Peter's attention as she glided across the floor towards a booth in the back. The early evening crowd at the Wave was beginning to swell as the work day settled and the late afternoon sun was declining beyond the western horizon. Tomas, Yoshi and Peter were seated at the back side of the bar with the customary Corona within easy reach.

As Peter tried to catch the eye of any one of the female patrons who made up the constituency of their hangout, Yoshi was trying to absorb what Tomas was saying.

"Dude, this sucks. What do we do in the meantime, get a real job?"

"I don't know man," Tomas shrugged, "probably."

Dragging his eyes back to his friends, Peter joined in. "So let me get this straight. Mr. Movie doesn't trust us to do the work and is going to withhold funding until Tom makes an appearance?"

Tomas took a deep slug from his beer and wiped his mouth with the back of his hand. "Yea, well that and the fact that Evan is lying in a hospital in a coma from being shot, that pretty much sums it up. You can hardly blame the guy. Things have gone pretty sideways."

"Maybe he would hire me to be the pool boy. I could hang out at the castle, make a few drinks, and rub oil on the wife's back….."

Yoshi shook his head with a slight smile. "Man, this whole scene is one big clusterfuck."

"Look guys," says Tomas, trying to sound reassuring, "you're right, things are pretty messed up right now. But we have to keep the faith. I spoke with Emily and she said Evan came awake for a second last night. The doc said that's a good sign and shows he's fighting to come out of his coma."

He waved to the bartender hoping to catch his eye. "We gotta trust that Emily or the cops are going to find Tom, hopefully okay, and that everything will get back to normal."

The bartender nodded and moved toward them.

"Not sure if you are being optimistic or really naïve, man," Yoshi's said in a sorrowful voice, "but Tom has disappeared and Evan was shot…nothing is getting back to normal."

"What can I get for you boys:"

"Shots"

TWENTY SIX

As the last rays of daylight recede toward evening, splotches of rust, water stain and smatterings of bird droppings give the dirty grey walls of the warehouse a Jackson Pollack painting like look. Adding to the abstract oddity of the grim surroundings are vases full of bright, colorful flowers taking up space wherever it is afforded.

"This guy is a wacko, you know that, right?" Phillipe Doone looked nervously over his shoulder as he spoke, "We're going to finish this and then he's going to kill us all in some unspeakable manner."

"Phillipe, keep your voice down." Dr. Sussel also kept an uneasy watch on the back door. "Nothing will happen till we finish and hopefully by then we will be rescued." The tone of his voice made it clear that he didn't really expect this to happen.

Over by one of the walls, Tom Davidson was struggling to attach some parts to his time machine. It was taking shape and despite the pain and fear, he was also feeling the rise of excitement.

Darkness was approaching fast and Tom knew the day would end very soon. He cursed the Pensors for their lack of thought on the matter. If they had a real laboratory, they could work much longer hours and probably be finished by now. Spending their nights locked in dingy, filthy bathrooms and getting very little to eat wasn't helping their effort either.

Dr. Sussel was aging quickly before their eyes and seemed barely able to complete even the simplest task. Phillipe was becoming more and more manic, flip flopping between quiet sobbing depressions to loud boisterous bravado. He at least seemed still capable of doing the meticulous assembly required.

Tom himself was exhausted, but having completed this job once, was driven to finish and once again see his machine come to life. His was in constant fear, though, of how that life would be used. He knew the Pensor's ideas were for their own good, accumulation of more wealth and power, at any cost.

What were his aspirations? He reflected back to the beginning. Truthfully, he never really put much thought into what he would do if they succeeded. Sure, he and Tomas had spent many Corona buzzed nights talking about which teams to bet on for the Super Bowls of past, buying stock in Microsoft at the beginning or finally talking to some girl you lusted after, nothing too deep. The excitement was in the designing and building itself. Looking ahead to the completion and the satisfaction they had accomplished something phenomenal.

His thoughts of industry awards and a Nobel Prize were loudly interrupted by the frightening familiar slam of the outer warehouse door. A few seconds later Wendell appeared through the inner door, trailing his now spine chilling pushcart. The usual bouquet of bright flowers notwithstanding, everyone in the room had experienced fear and pain rendered by the other items on the top tray.

Pensor is wearing his usual black slacks and button down long sleeved shirt, green today. The ever present film of dark dirt is visible under his fingernails. And though he had his always present silly grin, his eyes have an extra glow of madness. You can almost sense the animal lust exuding from him.

"Good evening gentlemen. I trust your afternoon has been productive and rewarding." He glanced over to the area where Tom was working. "It seems you are getting very close. Tell me, how close are we?"

Despite the presence of the tray of pain, Phillipe stood and summed up some ignorant courage. "We'd be a hellava lot further if you took better care of us, a bed to sleep in, and decent food. How do you really expect us to function in these conditions?" The little outburst exhausting him, he collapsed back onto his stool.

"Phillipe, shush!" Sussel hissed, trying to keep the peace.

"Well, I am truly sorry to hear that," Wendell pouted, "but I don't think it's going to be an issue for much longer." He pushed his cart forward toward Doone's area.

Phillipe seemed to shrink smaller on his stool. He wanted to get up and run, but fear was gripping him and keeping him locked in place. His stomach was curdling and he battled to keep from soiling himself.

As the cart slid up next to him, he was shaking noticeably.

"Now, we feel we are getting very close to completion." Wendell reached down and picked up what looked like garden shears. "We also feel you might need some further inspiration…just to keep you focused as we near the finish line." As he finished the sentence, he bent over quickly, grabbed Phillipe's leg and snipped his Achilles tendon right above his left foot.

Phillipe let out a blood curdling scream. Wendell grabbed his arm to keep him on the stool.

"We also don't want you to have any ideas of running away."

Sussel was just sitting on his stool, unable to do anything but shake uncontrollably and began sobbing.

In a panic, Davidson searched around for anything he could use as a weapon. Spotting a piece of pipe, he grabbed it up and turned to attack Pensor.

"Stop!" Pensor was supporting the wailing Phillipe but was now holding an ice pick up to his temple. "Take another step and we'll see if a lobotomy improves his personality."

Tom freezes in his tracks. He held up one hand, "Ok, Ok, don't do anymore." He dropped the pipe and raised his other hand up in a stopping gesture. "Please, let him be."

"Please?...well that's nice." Pensor waved the ice pick, "Go stand over there next to Dr. Sussel, he looks like he needs the support."

Davidson shuffled past the waving ice pick, put his arm around Dr. Sussel and whispered in his ear. "It's gonna be alright. Hang in there."

But it wasn't going to be alright. When Davidson looked up, Wendell had a lopsided smile on his lips and looking directly at Tom, slowly pushed the ice pick into Doone's side, between his ribs and puncturing his lung.

"Now you boys be good." He slowly withdrew the ice pick from Phillip's side. "What was I saying before I was so rudely interrupted? Oh yea, we feel like you are close and needed some encouragement."

Doone was wheezing badly, trying to get air and at the same time crying from the excruciating pain in his side and leg.

Wendell looked down at the fear and pain on Doone's face. Still smiling his crazed smile, he grabbed his hair and pulled his head back. "Having trouble breathing? Let me help you."

With a quick motion, he shoved the bloody ice pick into Phillip's exposed throat with such force; the point broke through the back of his neck.

"Now maybe you'll learn not to interrupt." He giggled at his own joke as he let go of Doone, who collapsed and slid to the floor like a bag of wet mud, blood squirting from multiple apertures.

Grabbing a pistol from the tray, he turned to face Davidson and Sussel.

"Well, guess you'll you have to soldier on, just the two of you. Think you can do that?"

Dr. Sussel was frozen in shock and fear. He just sat and stared at the lifeless body bleeding out on the warehouse floor.

Davidson looked up from the body and glared at Wendell with open hatred. "You're insane. You're…."

The gunshot reverberated around the warehouse walls so loudly; Sussel covered his ears with his hands.

"I don't think you want to keep up the insults to the man holding the gun, Mr. Davidson." Wendell moved toward the two shocked men, waving the gun toward the door. "Let's go, time to go to your rooms."

Davidson helped Sussel from his stool and letting the older man lean on him, they started making their way toward the door to the hallway. Wendell wandered along behind humming an unintelligible song only he knew.

TWENTY SEVEN

The door slid slowly open and a black shadow appeared to slide into the room. The dull light from the hallway flashed only momentarily as the silent intruder quickly closed the door behind him. He stood for a quick couple seconds to let his eyes adjust to the darkness. He was a tall man, wearing a light windbreaker jacket and a ball cap pulled low over his eyes.

Glancing to his left, he could make out an empty chair. A rolling tray with a water glass and some empty dishes was sitting beside it. The bathroom door to his right was closed and there was no light coming from under the door.

The shadowy figure took a few steps toward the only bed in the room. The figure lying on it was quiet. There were many tubes and wires running from the wall of devices behind the patient leading to contact points all over the chest and arms of the inert body. The occasional steady beep from the monitor standing beside the bed was the only sound.

As the intruder took another step to move around the bed, his booted toe nicked the leg of a chair sitting near the end of the bed, making a loud scraping noise.

In frozen panic, the man listened hard for any commotion or change in the air. After what seemed like an hour but was just seconds, his breathing and heart beat came back under control. He reached behind his back and from under his jacket, pulled a pistol from his waistband. The gun had a large tubed silencer screwed onto the end but spotting a pillow on the chair he had kicked, he grabbed it up. Better to be safe.

Stepping up to the side of the bed, he placed the pillow over the face of the inert patient and put the gun into the pillow.

The first gun shot was loud, the second and third shots just as much. The body of the intruder flew backward away from the bed, hitting the window and breaking the glass. The gunman seemed stuck against the window for a second before slowly sliding down the wall, dead before he sat on the floor.

Simultaneously, as the second and third shots were being fired, Evan's eyes blew open and fighting panic to gain his senses; he clawed at the pillow on his face and sat upright in bed, tearing out some of the wires attached to his chest. Panting heavily and with wild eyes, his head swiveled first to the left to see the man sliding down the wall, blood covering his shirt and then to the right to see Emily standing in a shooters stance, arms extended and shaking, the bathroom door wide open behind her.

Seeing Evan awake and in her sights, she gasped, "Evan!"

She lowered her gun to her side and quickly moved around to the far side of the bed. She kicked the assassin's gun away from his hand and checked the pulse on his neck. Confirming he was dead, she stood and stepped to the bed and threw her arms around Evan, almost squeezing him back unconscious.

He hesitantly raised his arms and hugged her back, "Easy, now, easy."

The door to the hospital room burst open and a doctor and a nurse rushed into the room.

"What is going....oh my God." The nurse's hand flew to her mouth as she saw the blood smear on the wall and the head of a man lying on the floor behind the bed.

"Go call the police." The doctor grabbed her shoulder and turned her back to the hall. "Tell them to hurry."

Turning back to the room, he strode over to the bed. He looked over the bed at the dead man, glanced at the gun in Emily's hand and the sitting Evan. "Welcome back Mr. Longview."

An hour later, the body had been removed. Emily was sitting in the chair at the side of the bed. Evan still had a few tubes and wires, and was obviously uncomfortable. The police detective sitting in the other chair was large, barely fitting between the two armrests. His hat was pushed back on his head and he was scratching the side of his nose with the eraser of his pencil.

"Ok, Miss Jepsen, tell me again what happened."

A disheveled and tired Emily sighed..."I was in the bathroom. I stay here most nights, waiting for Evan to wake." She glanced at Evan and is bolstered by his silent thanks. "I had just hit the light switch off to come out when a flash of light came under the door. I put my ear to the door and thought I heard someone so I got my gun from my purse They were moving as if they were trying to be quiet, so I waited till I thought they were past the door. When I got the door opened just enough to see out, I could see the man picking up the pillow and put it over Evan's face. As he put the gun into the pillow, I pushed open the door and fired three shots into him."

She paused to gulp some air. "I've never shot anyone or even at anyone." She let out a nervous laugh, "I guess, from this range, even I couldn't miss." Evan reached over and took her hand, giving it a reassuring squeeze.

"And you, Mr....." the big detective looked down at his pad, "uh, Longview. You say you were awakened, it seems from a long coma, find Ms. Jepsen here, standing with her gun drawn and the assailant dead on the floor?"

"Yes sir."

"You've been in a coma for over a month now, according to the doctors. You had been shot previously along with a nasty bump from falling."

"Yes sir that is what I am told also."

"You mean you don't know? You don't know how you got here or why?"

"Well, sir, I just went out to get the paper and here we are."

"And you don't know why this man might have tried to kill you a couple times."

"No sir, but we don't know if he took the first shot."

"I think it is pretty safe to assume he came here to finish the job he wasn't able to get right the first time."

"If you say so sir"

"But you do know the man who has been trying to kill you."

"Yessir, its Captain Harrison. He's a U.S. Marshal."

TWENTY EIGHT

The man servant Sam set the tray down on the desk. He picked up the teapot and poured the steaming hot liquid into one of the cups. Looking up, he glanced over to the book shelf along the wall.

"It's okay, Sam, Wendell won't want any." William Pensor leaned forward, picked up the cup and gingerly sipped the hot tea. "Just leave it, thank you."

Sam set down the teapot. "Do you need anything else, sir?"

"No Sam that will be all."

Sam stepped back from the desk and quickly made his way to the hall door across the room. No sooner had the door closed behind him when the book shelf moved open and Wendell stepped out. He was carrying a large vase with bright, fresh flowers. Moving across the room he put them down on a small table near the big picture window. He reached up to pull the heavy curtains back so the sun was shining on the flowers.

"I don't know why you always have it so dark in here. You know the sun is so good for the flowers." Wendell backed away, admiring his work. "Of course, that new mulch I have been using recently hasn't hurt any either." He let out his little giggle.

William leaned forward and placed his teacup back on the tray. "Yes, well, that is what we need to discuss. "It seems our team has almost completed its task" Pensor frowned over at his brother who had taken a seat in front of the desk, "and it took a few extra days as the unfortunate Mr. Doone decided to leave us expectantly. And from your reports, Dr. Sussel is barely able to function and may not be able to proceed much longer. That is going to cause a problem and we might need extra hands to move the machine to the final destination."

Wendell, who had been looking dreamily at his new floral arrangement, turned to face his brother. "I have a plan to solve that little dilemma."

"I am sure you do. That is what concerns me. Our little project is getting complicated. We have multiple people missing, and from the light in your eyes, I suspect we will have more compost for your garden in short order."

"Well, big brother, you just keep thinking about all that money and power you're going to be able to acquire." He looked down at his dark stained fingers. "Let me take care of the dirty work."

The brothers sat for minute staring at each other when their staring contest was broken up by a buzzing on the desk. William looked down at his telephone with a contemptuous look as if to say, who would be disturbing me on this line?

He slowly picked up the phone, "Yes"

Listening, his face slowly grew darker and his eyes turned harder, as the person on the other end was obviously not bringing good news. After a minute, he leaned forward and put the phone back on its receiver. Settling back into his chair, he looked over at his brother.

"It seems our friend Captain Harrison has let us down. Not only did he fail to complete his task of making Mr. Longview go away, he was killed and that irritant, Marshal Longview, got up and walked out of the hospital.

"I told you I could take care of him."

"No!" The senior Pensor pointed his finger at his brother. "You get that machine finished and moved to the new location immediately." He hesitated for just a second, "and I don't care how."

The younger Pensor stood up and with a mock salute, said. "Yessir"

TWENTY NINE

"Good morning, Sunshine." A bubbly Emily stood in the doorway holding two cups of coffee. Evan, who was already awake and sitting up in bed looked grumpily over to his chipper companion. His dark demeanor quickly changed when he saw his waitperson standing sexily in the morning light wearing an oversized t-shirt and nothing else that he could see. He was still a little embarrassed and uncomfortable with the modern woman and her lack of clothes, but was quickly adjusting. The shapely, tanned legs from wearing shorts and skirts in the constant Southern California sun surely beat the alabaster ones, which, on rare occasions, he was able to see back in the day.

Emily handed him a cup of his favorite bold, black coffee and moved around to the other side of the bed. Sliding back under the covers, she sat shoulder to shoulder with him sipping her own sugar sweetened, cream filled mug. It was not an uncomfortable silence as they sat and listened to the now familiar clacking of the overhead fan.

"You know," she finally spoke, "you could turn on the air conditioner and turn off that fan."

Glancing up, Evan had a faraway look in his eyes. "I like it…it reminds me of the old windmill we had on our ranch. You could see it from anywhere on the ranch and hear it almost constantly throughout the day and night."

Emily reached over and put her coffee cup down on the nightstand beside the bed. She turned back and looked at Evan. She lay her head on his chest and put her hand on his flat stomach.

"You miss your time don't you?"

"Sometimes, it's just...it was so different. I didn't go through the change gradually. I was just then, and then I was now. So much happened in between, but I don't know any of that."

"I read a few books when I was younger. The setting was dated back in your time. It seemed like such a hard life, especially for the women."

Evan reached an arm up and put it across Emily's shoulder, rubbing her back. "I suppose it was. They did more forced physical work back then. Ranching, taking care of animals, gardening, cooking, cleaning... but they also were entertainers... you know, actresses, singers, whores.

Emily slapped his chest. "Ouch!"

"Ok, ok…but it just seems that women have many more choices now. Unlimited actually, lawyers, doctors, business owners…"

"That may seem so," Emily said, "but it didn't happen overnight. All that time you said you missed has been a slow uphill climb on the ladder of equality for women and minorities. And we have a very long way to go, especially in regards to minorities.

They lay in silence for another couple minutes.

Emily tilted her head up to look at his face. "Do you want to go back? Is that what we're doing, trying to find Tom so you can use his machine to go back?

After a second, Evan says, "I think so." He shifted his gaze from the circulating fan to look into the bright yearning eyes below, "Or at least I thought so. I have so much to finish. The past few years have been filled with nothing but rage to get vengeance for Mary. To make Lucias pay. But now I've been in this time for a while, and my head is filled with so many other thoughts, a different life, actual friends." He bent down and kissed Emily on the forehead, "maybe more."

"Have you thought about the changes you might be causing?"

"What do you mean?"

"Well, if you go back into the past and do something, it's going to cause different consequences than what has happened and things might turn out different. In fact they most certainly will be different."

Evan thought about this for a minute. "You're probably right, but what if the change is for the better? Who's to say every change has to be bad? Because, trust me, cleaning Lucias Johnston off this world can only be for the better."

And what about Mary and me? Emily wanted to ask, but was afraid of the answer.

"Well, first things first, we need to find Tom."

Evan started to sit up a little straighter. "I may have an idea on that. I remember William Pensor saying he had an old warehouse somewhere in Los Angeles he was going to let Tom use to build the machine. Maybe we could find it. If he really did kidnap Tom, that might be where they're keeping him to work."

"He could also have many properties throughout the city. It might take weeks to check them all out." Emily thought for a second. "My office is not being much help without any real evidence, but I can use the computers to find any properties Pensor might have in the area."

An energized Evan began to throw the covers back. "Great, let's get moving."

Emily grabbed his shoulder, "Wait, it's still early," she began to run her hand down his stomach under the covers. "A girl needs her exercise."

Evan leaned back on the bed, "Yeah? But the doctor was yelling to take it easy when we ran out of the hospital."

"Hmmm," Emily purrs as she kissed his stomach moving downward, "that didn't seem to be an issue last night."

THIRTY

By nine o'clock, the Wave was pretty quiet. Most of the regulars were of the younger persuasion and on a usual weeknight, they had slunk off home to conserve their monetary funds. The remaining patrons were a couple determined drinkers, a few stragglers from a local city sports team and last gasp loners finishing up after a long night of wishful thinking, Peter Smithson fell into the latter category.

The last few weeks had been unhappy ones for Peter. He was still attending an occasional class, but was finding himself sitting at the Wave more than a couple nights a week, slowly sinking into his own misery. The exciting project he had been involved with for the last year or so had collapsed into a pile of rubble. They had been so close to fame and fortune. His friends on the project had started to fade away into their own levels of melancholy. Yoshi, now doing some IT work at a small manufacturing company, was still taking classes, but no longer was the fun loving intellectual who liked to hang out and discuss politics and women. He too was looking for a kick start to the rest of his life. Tomas had all but fallen off the face of the earth. He had reverted back to his old surfing days. Hitting the waves every morning and then going off to a job that kept his rent paid, but hardly got his heart beat above a living rate. He spent his nights wandering around old haunts and contacting old acquaintances, trying to locate Tom Davidson.

Through his Corona fogged eyes, Peter took a last look around the subdued barroom, fantasizing about some lonely young lady who might see him through the same lenses. He caught the bartender's eye and signaled for his check. He threw a wadded up handful of cash on the bar, turned and made his way slowly out the door.

The cool ocean breeze swept over him and he hesitated as he looked up at the stars and then let his gaze drop to the ocean horizon a block away. The air was crisp and clear. The smell of salt water wafted into his senses. He really loved it here. *What was his problem? He was young. He could finish his Masters, get a good job. The girl of his dreams was just around the corner. Yea! Hey, when life handed you lemons, you made lemonade.* Peter sucked in a big breath of fresh sea air, pulled his shorts up a notch and stepped off smartly toward his car.

The cars were scattered sporadically around the lot, but there was a green sedan parked right next to his old Corolla. As he approached, a man got out of the driver side.

"Excuse me, I was wondering if you could direct me to a decent hotel." The man walked straight up to Peter. "I'm new in town and need a place to crash."

With a quick glance around at the empty lot, a gun suddenly appeared in the man's right hand. Standing very close to Peter, pushing the barrel of the gun into his stomach, he said. "Don't make a sound. Just move to the car and get in the back seat."

A stunned Peter was pushed over to the green sedan. The man reached around him and opened the rear door and nudged him to get in. As he bent his head, there was a sudden flash of pain and Peter collapsed onto the back seat. The man grabbed his legs and pushed him the rest of the way into the car. After another quick glance around, the man quickly jumped into the front seat, started the car and drove out of the parking lot.

THIRTY ONE

In one of the sunlit spaces of the dingy warehouse, Tom Davidson was bent over his workbench, soldering the final circuit board on the control panel. This close to completion, his excitement was making it hard to hold his hand steady, excitement and the frayed nerves from the last few weeks of abuse and fear.

Dr. Sussel was slumped on his stool, his head hanging down on his chest and his hands slowly kneading themselves on his lap. He was making sounds, but they were so mumbled as to make it impossible to understand. He had been this way for few days now, seeming only to be conscience when Wendell came around to bring in food and check on them, and then only to shrink into a scared childlike zombie.

Tom had tried to keep him cognizant by talking about places they would go when the machine was ready. Places with happier times. Remembering Sussel's fondness for cocktail parties, Tom talked of going back to Victorian days to host elegant parties with lots of students. Joking about the formal wear of the men and the frilly big dresses of the women and comparing them to the modern students of recent parties with their worn out jeans and wrinkled t-shirts.

"Com'n Doc, I'm just about done. Let's crank it up and give her a test drive."

Sussel just raised his head and looked at Tom with sad, defeated eyes. "We're done now Tom. The end is nearing."

"No seriously Doc, a couple more welds and I'll pop it in. It'll take a couple minutes to sync everything, but let's turn her on and go back to, say....that last party I attended. You remember the one where we were only beginning to discuss the possibilities of time travel."

Tom was cut off by the loud sound of a motor. To their surprise, the large roll up bay door on the side wall began to roll up. Tom had forgotten about the door. They had banged on it loudly the first couple days in captivity, but Wendell had heard them as he approached one day and gave everyone a severe beating with a rubber hose and a hammer. His left elbow and crooked nose still ached as a reminder.

When the door had completed its cycle to the top, the open space was filled with the rear of a U-Haul truck. It backed into the warehouse completely and the motor again screeched as the door began its descent back to the floor. Upon closure, the driver side door opened and a smiling Wendell jumped down.

"Hello, my pets. How's our project coming along, complete I hope." He walked around to the passenger side. "I brought you someone, a little helper. It's moving day and I can't help but know you're going to need another body." He opened the passenger side door, reached up and dragged an alive but cowering Peter from the truck. Pulling him along the truck, he tossed him onto the floor where Peter curled up to protect himself from further damage. He had a red splotch on his left cheek and there was blood caked on his left ear, which seemed to be only half there.

"Peter!" Tom exclaimed as he rushed to his friend's side. "Peter, it's me, Tom. Ah, Peter, I'm so sorry."

"Tom? Tom? What's going on? Don't let that guy near me." Peter was clutching Tom's arms.

"Yes…don't let me near him," Wendell chuckled. "Best to get him up and moving, you have work to do."

Wendell pulled the loading ramp up and out from the truck.

"It's time to move our project to another location for its christening."

****

When the bell tinkled from the opening door, Evan looked up from the newspaper he was reading. A flushed and excited Emily rushed into the little diner waiving some papers as she made her way to his table.

"I think I found something." She pulled out the other chair at the table and plopped down, slapping the papers and a little note book on the table.

"You know, it never ceases to amaze me, how much information is in each of these newspapers. I mean, you have whole sections for just what is happening in this city alone. And then another for all of the different activities, the uh…" He looked down, "sports section. Did you know that some guy named Michael Jordan makes thirty million dollars a year? Thirty million? A year? For what?"

Emily slammed her hand down on the newspaper. "Didn't you hear me? I may have found something."

Evan sat back and looked at Emily, a smile beginning to curl on his upper lip. "Thirty million, geez, we could spend the rest of our lives in bed making love and drinking delicious coffee at our leisure."

The subsiding flush is replaced by an embarrassed causing blush. "Well, I'm glad you've spent your morning sitting around imagining our future," she said with her own little smile, "but while you've been sitting here recovering from our very pleasant morning exercise, *I've* been down at the county clerk's office looking for properties tied to William Pensor."

"Ok, ok, what have you found?"

"Well, it's as I suspected. William Pensor is a very wealthy man and has many businesses spread throughout Southern California and beyond. Manufacturing plants, Distribution facilities, oil, hotels, etc...It would take us weeks to look into every one of them, unless we had more man power." Emily sat back with a satisfied look.

Evan gave her an appraising look and suspecting there is more said, "Uh... and that leaves us where?"

Emily leaned forward and with her patented giggle, "Well, glad you asked. Turns out, there is more than one Pensor who owns property in Los Angeles. Or at least Mr. William Pensor uses his brother's name, Mr. Wendell Pensor. And guess whose name is on an unused warehouse in the old business district over near Boyle Heights?"

Evan's mind immediately flashed back to a moving curtain and a flash of red while leaving the Pensor mansion. He remembered the cold, calculating eyes of William Pensor, sitting behind his big desk, demanding and arrogant. He remembered another time, another arrogant man. Forgetting the newspaper and his now cold cup of coffee, he pushed back his chair and stood up.

"Let's go, but I have to stop by my house for second."

****

The loading of the truck had been slow going. The loaders slowed by pain and fear.

Coming back down the ramp, Tom looked around the warehouse. "Ok, I think that's everything."

Peter was standing nervously near Dr. Sussel, who was still sitting on his stool, having not spoken or moved to help during the whole operation.

Wendell, who had been sitting comfortably in a chair, monitoring the work, stood up and looked around.

"Alright then, just one more item to load" He pulled his pistol from his jacket and in one smooth motion, shot Dr. Sussel in the chest.

335

"I would have liked to spend more time with you Doc, but we are short on that commodity and you probably wouldn't have been much fun anyway."

He pointed to a horrified Peter, who had jumped back away from the falling body. "Roll him up in that tarp over there and get him up into the truck, time to go."

THIRTY TWO

"Ah shit... I mean... uh excuse me." A peeved but slightly embarrassed Evan exclaimed as another gulp of coffee never made it to his mouth. "These damn rail tracks are making it impossible to drink this."

"Well never mind, according to my notes, that's the building up there." Emily, who was driving, pointed out the windshield to a disheveled, graffiti covered brick building up on the left.

She quickly turned down an alley a block away, slopping yet more coffee on Evans shirt. "Let's park here and walk the rest of the way."

Emily pulled to the right next to another rundown, aged brick building. It also had much graffiti and any window within reach was broken or missing altogether. They exited and met at the front of the car. Emily pulled her FBI issued Glock and checked to make sure it was locked and loaded. She did not put it back in her purse, choosing to carry it by her side.

Evan pulled his gun belt around his waist and secured it to his hips. He tied the two strands of rawhide at the base around his thigh to keep it down. Pulling his Colt 45 from the holster, he checked the load and the action, spinning the cylinder to make sure it was free and smooth. He spun the gun on his finger and deftly dropped it into the holster at his side.

Wide eyed, Emily watched intently. "Are you a good ole fashioned gunslinger?"

Evan looked up to see a bright light of excitement in her eyes. "Don't get all wide eyed on me now. We seem to be dealing with some pretty desperate and calculating men. Stay focused." He turned to head up the alley.

Embarrassed by her childlike emotions, an admonished Emily gathered herself, took a deep breath and started after Evan.

When they reached the end of the alley, he peered around the corner. The block in view was deserted. Most of the buildings look the same. Broken, worn out and unused.

"What do you think?" Though Evan was an experienced hunter of animals and men, this was not his time or his world.

Emily thought for a second. "Ok, if they *are* building the machine in there, it will most likely be in the back part of the warehouse. There's probably a roll up door they can use to access and move machinery.

So, I think we can go right to the front door. It will be the furthest away from where anyone might be."

The stepped around the corner and moved down the street in single file. When they reached the end of the building, they stopped again at the corner. Looking around the edge of the building and seeing no movement, they hurried across the street to the building that matched the address Emily had found. The front door was old and metal. There was also a metal gate, but it had long ago been bent back and torn from its purpose. Evan stepped back and started to raise his leg to try and kick down the door, but Emily put her hand on his shoulder.

"This requires a woman's touch. Remember?" She held up her group of odd keys. "Let's see if we can do this a little more quietly first." She knelt down and began to try different keys in the slot on the door handle. Evan stood next to her, turning left and right to watch the street behind them. Finding one that seemed to fit smoothly, she brought up the other little metal pick and inserted it into the lock. After a few seconds of jiggling and shaking, the sound of the lock popping brought a sigh of relief.

Emily stood and grabbed the handle slowly turning it, while pushing inward. The screech of metal on metal seemed to echo at a full ten decibels on the empty street. They both froze, listening. After what seemed like five minutes, but was actually twenty seconds, and with no discernable response, she pushed the door fully open and they stepped in. The "front" office was as decrepit as the outside of the building. There were two matching desks, one on each side of the room. Both covered in old paperwork, books, and an old fashioned dial phone. There were four file cabinets on the far wall, two on either side of a door leading towards the back of the building. The clock on the wall was stopped on five o'clock as if quitting with the end of the era. The opening of the front door had disturbed the thick layer of dust that engulfed every nook and cranny so much that Emily had to put her hand over her mouth and choke back the urge to cough drastically.

They moved through the room to the door opposite. Evan, taking the lead, quickly pushed open the door and stood aside. Beyond was just a short hall with another door twenty feet away. There was a door on each side of the short hall, each with a sign showing the appropriate sex for use. They moved down the hallway and stopped at the door. Evan put his ear to the door and listened for a few seconds. Not hearing anything, he took a deep breath and slowly turned the handle. Pushing the door open and with no resistance, but a little squeak, he stepped into the large open warehouse space. He had his gun out and was sweeping it back and forth. Emily squeezed in behind him and also looked around with her gun out in front of her.

Open before them was a single large space. If Evan had to guess, he would say it was one hundred feet across and eighty feet to the far wall. They could make out a wide metal door to their left. There was an old abandoned truck parked to their right, with a smashed in window and flat tires. In front of them was a myriad of tables, piles of scrap metal, and many machines in various states of decay.

They spread out and each moved forward down pathways winding throughout the debris. Emily, her gun held with two hands out in front of her, moved to the right, Evan with his gun hanging loosely by his side, moved down a path on the left.

Evan was almost to the large metal door, when he noticed spots on the floor. "I think I have something here." Kneeling down, he touched a finger to the semi dried spot on the floor and taking a quick smell, exclaimed, "It's blood."

Emily had moved beyond the broken down truck and began working her way back towards Evan. Walking past a work bench, she noticed the dust was not so prevalent, even missing in many spots. As she worked her way in Evan's direction, she passed a stool beside another workbench. Looking down she saw a large dark red stain. "I've got more blood over here!"

With growing dread, Emily moved to where Evan was standing. "Nothing good happened here." She shuddered. "Over there are workbenches that have obviously been used recently. There are soldering guns, tools and spare parts. If they were building the machine, I would have to say they were here."

"Look there," Evan pointed at the cement floor towards the roll up door. "See those tire tracks? And you can make out footprints in the dust. And look, there are two different sizes. Somebody was walking back and forth, possibly loading a truck? And there was more than one. And see over there? Another set of prints with a different pattern off to the side. I bet he was watching over them."

"It seems pretty obvious they were here working on the machine," Emily said out loud, "and there was more than one. Who else could they have had?"

"Well, whoever it was, they're gone now. And from the amount of blood we are seeing, they haven't gone willingly.

THIRTY THREE

They drove slowly by the dark gothic mansion. The late afternoon sun was fading behind the trees and the dark shadows left behind only made the ugly monstrosity even more ominous. Evan, slouched down in the passenger seat, looked over the window sill as they slid slowly past.

"That is one ugly house, No wonder Pensor is such a sour puss. If I lived inside that depressive pile of rock every day, I would be a grump too." The car continued up the street. Not finding anyone at the warehouse, they had decided their only choice was to brace William Pensor and get some answers.

"I'll turn around at the next block." Emily guided the car up the tree lined street. Despite the seriousness of their mission, she couldn't help but be impressed by the other houses on the block. This was a very toney part of town.

She made a U-turn at the next block. They were heading back down the street when suddenly a large black town car nosed up out of the driveway belonging to William Pensor and turned left away from them. As they were only a couple houses away, they could see Pensor himself was driving.

"Oh shit." Emily quickly turned to the curb in an empty spot. They watched as the car moved down the hill.

"Do you think he saw us?" Evan was watching intently as the car went down around the bend. "Com'n, let's go, we have to follow him."

Emily pulled the car back out onto the street and sped up to try and not lose their quarry. "I don't think so, he seemed pretty focused on his driving."

As they rounded the bend, the big black car was visible a couple of blocks ahead. "Don't get to close. We don't want him to know we're back here."

Emily gave Evan a dark look, as if to say, "Duh!"

It was obvious Pensor didn't think anyone was following him as he made no evasive maneuvers. It was also obvious he didn't drive much as he was constantly being honked at by other drivers who thought he was sloppy or down right rude in his actions.

They followed a block behind for thirty minutes as he made his way south. They wound their way through downtown LA and continued into an abandoned part of south Los Angeles. They were soon in another seemingly forgotten industrial area. If a building looked occupied by a working business, it was one out of ten.

Emily couldn't help but comment. "Jesus, this guy owns a lot of properties that seem worthless"

"Well, they're certainly locations where there is little activity and even fewer questions" Evan wondered what activities really went on in these desolate, remote parts, with real civilization just over the hill.

"Evan," Emily looked over to get Evan's eye. "What's going to happen here?"

Evan stared straight ahead.

"I mean, we're going in to try and rescue Tom, if he's there, and anyone else in danger. But the machine is in there, presumably working, or why else would Pensor be coming here."

Up ahead, Pensor turned right into a large parking lot overgrown with weeds and broken cement parking blocks. There was a U-haul truck backed up to a closed roll up door.

Emily made a quick right turn into another drive way, next to another forlorn building.

"You should call for back up" Evan opened his door.

Pensor climbed out of the car and looked quickly around. He was breathing fast, his thoughts of unlimited possibilities driving him into a feverish state.

There was a regular door next to the truck and he quickly walked to it, knocking loudly on the metal. After a few seconds, the door opened and Pensor stepped inside, the door clanged closed behind him.

Emily finished giving her boss the address and hung up her phone. "He wants us to wait, but they're probably twenty minutes away"

"I'm not waiting." Evan climbed out of the car. After a second, Emily followed suit. They moved to the corner of the building.

"Ok, this is going to be just like the last building." Emily said, breathing hard and fast. "He went in the back and that's where the open warehouse space will be. We can enter through the front door."

Emily swung around and past Evan, heading to the other side of the building. Evan followed. He reached down and flipped the strap off the top of his holster.

Once again, Emily knelt down next to the front door. Working her magic, they pushed in the door. Crouching in the open foyer, Evan down low and Emily standing over him, they both waved their guns back and forth, covering another empty, dusty office. They moved quickly to the only door across the room.

Evan was about to turn the knob when Emily grabbed his shirt and pulled him aside to her. She hesitated for a second and then stood on her toes and gave him a kiss. He pulled away and looked down at her flushed face. He looked deep into her bright eyes and then pulled her close and gave her a long, deep kiss.

Stepping back, he said, "Be careful"

He pushed open the door, he stepped inside the warehouse.

THIRTY FOUR

The door was surprisingly quiet and Evan stepped in behind a large pallet of boxes wrapped in clear plastic. He sensed Emily coming in behind him and moving off to his left. Voices could be heard coming from the far side of the room in front of him. Evan peered around the pallet and silently moved toward the voices, shifting from pallet to pallet which were scattered randomly about.

As he reached the last pallet to hide behind, he snuck a quick glance around the edge. He could see three people. Tom Davidson was facing away from Evan, bent over, putting into place the final operating parts of the work station adjacent to the upside down horseshoe machine that was familiar to Evan. An obviously agitated Peter was standing to Tom's right, a nervous sweat leaving a bright slick sheen on his forehead. There was a lot of blood caked to the side of his head, and because of the sweat was causing red rivulets to run down his neck, giving him a boogie man look.

William Pensor was standing behind Tom on the left looking intently over a piece of paper in his hand. He was reading out loud from what seemed to be a list. Next to him on the floor was a soft satchel.

"1929 Market Crash....1986 Microsoft....Rockefeller Oil..." Looking up from his murmurings, he spoke to Davidson. "Ok, *Tom*, let's start with something easy. Set up for January 1969," He glanced down to the bag at his feet. "I'll just put a little wager down on the underdog Jets to win the Super Bowl."

Evan looked cautiously about; Wendell Pensor was not in view. He glanced to his left and saw Emily working her way up to a large, rusty pile of metal on the left, trying to get a good angle on the scene.

He looked back at Pensor giving orders to move forward with a plan to make him richer, more powerful. Longview's mind flashed to another rich, arrogant monster, the memory of a man gloating over his prowess. The heat of his blood began to rise when another burning memory of a man standing over his beloved Mary, torn, bleeding and dead pushed its way into his thoughts.

Evan stepped out from behind the pallet and walking towards Pensor said, "Not so fast Tom. I don't think this piece of shit is going anywhere."

Everyone whirled to look at Evan and time seemed to stand still.

William crouched suddenly and pulling a gun from the satchel, aimed it at Tom. "Make the settings."

With no hesitation, Evan shot Pensor in the head and he collapsed to the floor.

"Evan!" Emily yelled as she stepped out of concealment. Her gun pointed across the room.

Two shots rang out almost simultaneously.

Wendell Pensor had moved into sight from behind a case on the right. He was screaming, but as he turned to shoot Evan, Emily's bullet tore into his body, throwing off his shot.

Wendell spun around and fell to the warehouse floor as did Peter, as he had caught Wendell's wild shot square in the head and was dead before he hit the cement.

For a full ten seconds the only sounds were the fading echo of gun shots reverberating from the warehouse walls and Emily's heavy breathing.

Evan casually looked at the bodies lying about and holstered his pistol.

Davidson looked down at his dead friend and coming out of his shock a little knelt on the floor beside the body. With shaking hands, he reached down and touched Peter's face. "Ah, Peter....I'm so sorry."

Emily rushed over to Evan, throwing her arms around him and laying her head on his chest, "Are you okay?" Which she immediately realized was a silly question; he was the calmest person in the room.

Evan was staring straight at the machine standing tall and ominous, overlooking the whole scene.

"Tom....Tom!" Davidson slowly looked up at Evan. The sadness and pain evident by the tracks of tears running down his dirt smudged cheeks.

"Tom, can you program the machine back to 1888?"

Emily pulled back, looking up, "Evan?"

"I should just tear it down. It's brought nothing but pain and death." A still shaking Tom rose to his feet.

"No Tom," Evan pushed Emily aside and stepped to Tom. "I *need* it one time."

Tom looked at Evan and saw in his eyes the hurt and pain. He looked down at Peter. He looked back at Evan. "Ok, you rescued me and have been

351

through more than anyone else can imagine. I will set the machine for you."

"Evan?" Emily took Longview's hand. "Evan, remember the conversation we had about changing the past. We don't know what effect you going back with have, or the results of your actions when you get there."

"That's why I asked to go back to 1888. That's the year I came here. I'm not going back to be with Mary. Time has dulled the pain. And like I said, I have discovered new things, different ideas, "he looked down into hopeful eyes, "new friends. But I *am* going back to get the snake that killed her and changed *our* future. I'm going to change his future, and I don't care what the *effect* will be!"

"Then I'm going with you," The deep, dark eyes turned from hopeful to forceful and then to playful, "you can deputize me."

"No. Remember how we also talked about how hard life was for woman back then." Evan looked into the stubborn face for a second. He turned to see the prone body of Wendell Pensor and then back to Emily. He gave her hand a tight squeeze and bending down, a quick kiss on the lips, "Ok, but bring the gun."

Together they faced Tom, "Let's do this."

Tom stared at the two determined people in front of him. Thinking quickly, he looked around the warehouse. "Ok, after you go through, I'll throw some tarps over the machine and spread some junk around. It should be okay here for a couple weeks. In two weeks, what do you need, two weeks? In three weeks from today, I will turn the machine back on in reverse." He looked at his wrist, but there was no watch. "What time is it? it doesn't matter. At three o'clock in the afternoon. If I can, I will sit as long as it takes, but if you don't come back through here within a couple hours, I will assume you decided to stay or," Davidson looked down at Peter, "or you couldn't make it."

Evan reached out and gripped Tom's shoulder, "Three weeks should be fine. Thank you Tom." He looked down at Peter, dead at their feet. "I am *also* sorry for all the death and pain. But remember, it's not the machine that did the damage. It is the greed and lust for power that lives inside man. It's not your fault for having dreams."

Tom looked at Evan. He nodded and turned to program the machine. When it began to hum and make noise like it was warming up, he turned to Emily and Evan. "Alright, this is it. You guys be careful out there. I haven't had time to research exactly what will be on the other side, but pretty sure at the time, Los

Angeles wasn't such a sprawl and you'll probably end up in the middle of the desert. You may have to hike a bit to find civilization, but it won't be too far away."

Evan reached out and shook Tom's hand. "Thank you, Tom." He looked like he wanted to say more, but just nodded his head and stepped close to the gateway.

Emily moved in and gave Tom a huge hug. "I'm so glad we found you. I'm so sorry about Peter." Tears began to leak from her eyes. "When we get back, we'll talk about all of it. Take care of yourself, and thank you." She pulled away and moved over next to Evan.

He looked down into her smiling face, "you ready?"

"Beam me up, Mr. Scott!"

Evan gave her a questioning look. He took her hand and they stepped through the portal, disappearing into thin air.

The warehouse was deathly quiet. Tom just stared at the empty portal. A thousand questions once again filled his mind as the wonder of time travel began to take over his conscious thought. For a few minutes, he just stood and let his mind go. Back to his childhood, when he thought about traveling to outer reaches of space, back to high school as he dreamed of other lands, other people and then to college when he began thinking of other times. What would it be like to live in medieval times, be a gladiator, Victorian England, or how about 2050? What would the world be like then? Or like Evan, riding his horse across lands unseen by man, to be the first to see a river, a mountain.

His dreams were interrupted by a sound in his subconscious. Getting back into focus, Tom looked around the warehouse, trying to find the source of cessation.

Not seeing anything, he shook his head. "Com'n man, let's get our beauty covered and go get some help."

He took a step towards the machine to close it down when he heard the shuffle behind him. He whirled around and found himself looking at his worst nightmare.

With a bloodied shirt and a sick grin, Wendell Pensor stepped closer, 'Hello Tom,"

He raised the gun in his hand, "No, no," was all Tom was able to get out before it smashed down on his head, and all went black.

Wendell stood looking down at Tom. When it was obvious he wasn't going to be any trouble, he turned and went to where his brother was lying, a pool of blood already thickening below his dead body.

He crouched down and turned the body over to face up. He put his hand on his lifelong and only friend and protector, a single tear escaping his blood shot eyes.

"So long my brother. Rest now, and be assured your death will not go unpunished."

Wendell reached over and picked up the revolver his brother had brought and slipped it back into the satchel on the floor. He stood up and looked around. Spotting what he was looking for, he moved over to the edge of the death scene and removed a bright red flower from the vase on a table. He moved back to his brother and crouching back down, gently, lovingly placed the flower onto his chest. He picked up the satchel and stood up. He stared at the open portal for a couple seconds, took a deep breath and with his own gun in one hand and the satchel in the other, took five steps and disappeared........

FINAL JUSTICE

ONE

The gunshot was drowned out by the Saturday night noise. Between the clanging piano, clinking glasses, poker chips shuffling, and the sea of voices rising from the saloon floor, it was just another echo, dispersed in the thick cigarette smoke that sat layered above the crowd. It did not go unnoticed however, as the trigger had barely been pulled when a large black hand circled the shooter's wrist while his arm was still in the air.

"Hey!" The gunman looked up, his eyes passing over the badge as he looked up into the dark smiling face. "Ah Deputy, I just got excited. Finally won a hand from these snakes and guess I forgot myself."

"Well Homer, seems you've had enough fun for the night. Let's just take a step outside." Deputy Sheriff Ulysses Bass Jones may have sounded jovial and friendly, but his large size and tight grip gave little room for argument, though it didn't stop one from ensuing.

"Ah com'n Deputy, I didn't mean no harm."

"Sorry Homer," the big man gently took the gun from Homer's hand and helped him to his feet. "You know the rules. No discharging of firearms within the confines of this fine establishment." He put the gun in his waistband and began to push the unhappy customer toward the back door. "We'll just go out the back so as not to disturb any of the other law abiding citizens. If you're lucky, no word of this will get back to Mr. Johnston and how you shot a hole in his ceiling."

At the mention of Johnston, Homer looked nervously back to the crowd and turned to stagger out as quickly as possible.

The whole scene was also watched by a single patron, sitting at a small table deep in the dark recess beneath the stairwell to the upper rooms. He had arrived through the back door an hour previously. He sat motionless in the shadows speaking only when a tired and worn looking waitress had taken his order for a single beer. Other than a few sips from his now warm beer, the only other movement was the watchful eyes that shifted back and forth, taking in the room and it's constantly shifting action.

As the deputy and his minor malefactor went out the back door, there was a slight commotion at the front of the saloon as Lucias Johnston pushed through the double swinging doors and strode up to the bar.

The men standing at the bar shifted nervously away, leaving a wide opening for him to occupy. Lucias was average in height, with shoulder length greasy hair. He was well dressed all in black with a pressed white shirt under his shiny vest and coat. The ugly black mole on his nose, small mean eyes and air of superiority, made him disliked. The fact he owned much of the land around town, a few businesses, including the Lucky Lady, and how he ran roughshod over everyone, made him despised and feared.

"I'll have a Whiskey, Burquoltz," he demanded, "and none of that rot gut you sell to the other customers,"

As the bartender reached under the bar and poured a glass for Johnston, Lucias turned and faced the raucous mob, "A good crowd tonight."

"Yessir, like always Mr. Johnston."

It *was* always crowded at the Lucky Lady as Lucias made sure the other two establishments in town either couldn't get enough help or enough booze to keep up with clientele. There had been a third saloon on the edge of town with a great piano and someone who could actually play it. It also had an owner who people liked and respected, but a year earlier it had mysteriously burned to the ground in the early morning hours. The fire had killed the owner who slept in an upstairs apartment and the piano player who lived in a back room. It was rumored they couldn't escape because they had been unconscious in their beds when it happened. The town doctor couldn't or wouldn't confirm anything.

In the shadows beneath the stairwell, the dark eyes seem to smolder as they took in the scene at the bar. For a brief second, the roaming eyes of Lucias Johnston hesitated and locked on before moving off to a young girl approaching from down the stairs.

Without taking his eyes off Johnston, the stranger picked up his beer and gulped down the warm liquid. It did nothing to quench the boiling hatred within. He sat for a few seconds more, trying to get control of his emotions. With a grunt, he rose and stepped to the back door and disappeared.

Outside in the darkness, the stranger stayed close to the buildings as he made his way down the back street. Coming to a door at the back of building, he knocked and waited. After a minute, the door was unlocked from within and as it swung open, he stepped inside.

Locking the door behind him, Evan Longview turned and faced Emily. "He's here."

TWO

Emily stood in the middle of the room and watched Evan. After a full minute, she moved to him and put her arms around his waist. She looked up into his eyes and saw the pain floating just below the surface anger. She laid her head on his chest and held him tightly.

"What are you going to do?" she asked nervously.

"I'm gonna kill the son of a bitch!"

He broke away from Emily and began to pace around the room. There wasn't much space as they were staying in a very small room at the back of the building. The owner of the store in front had let them use it when they had arrived that afternoon. Mrs. McLaughlin had cried out in surprise when Evan appeared in her store. She didn't really understand who Emily was, but after she settled down and began to hear that Evan was there to avenge the death of her daughter, she volunteered the back store room until they figured out what the next step would be.

It had been an extremely enlightening yet very uncomfortable few days for Emily. They had stepped through the time portal and right into a blinding sand storm. Evan took a firm grip on her arm and dragged her to the ground, where they crawled a few feet and found a large boulder. They were able to get behind it on the opposite side from which the storm was coming and get at least some protection.

After a minute, Evan said, "I'll be right back, don't move."

"Where are you going?" But he had already disappeared back in the direction they had come from.

After five minutes that seemed like twenty, she shrank back as a figure appeared next to her. Emily took a deep breath as Evan crawled in and pressed in next to her.

"What did you do?"

"I thought we should try to mark the spot so we can find it when we return. I hope it holds in this storm. I piled some rocks as best I could and scratched our initials in a couple of them....but I don't know."

They sat huddled together behind the rock for another ten minutes until the sand storm had passed and they could see as it moved away it was beginning to disperse. The sky above them was blue, but the sun was settling lower in the horizon as the afternoon began to wind down. It was still warm, though, and Emily stood to take off her jacket and shake out as much sand as possible.

"Well, that was fun. You sure know how to show a girl a good time."

Standing, Evan brushed off his own clothes with his hat. "That's nothing, wait till you realize we have to walk north for who knows how far to find another human."

Emily shaded her eyes and looked around in a circle at the open desert. There were some cactus and brush, a smattering of rocks and boulders and not much else, certainly no sign of another human or civilization.

"Well, at least I won't have to worry about another girl taking your attention." Then she remembered why they were there in the first place. "Oh God, I'm sorry Evan, I wasn't thinking…"

Evan didn't respond, he was looking at the sun and then toward the north. "Based on what little I know of this area, we should head north," he pointed to their right, "and hopefully we'll meet someone or find some shelter for the night."

Emily looked to where he was pointing. "Well hell, if the machine put us out in the same spot we went in, only in the past, we should be standing in the old industrial part of Los Angeles. Downtown proper can't be more than a couple miles away." She started off in a northwestern direction but stopped after a couple strides. "Uh, there aren't any Indians around here, are there?"

Evan took another look around to find any landmarks that would help them find the spot when they returned and then started off after Emily. Chuckling he said, "The last ones I saw were about forty miles to the east."

Ten minutes earlier, in the middle of the storm, another figure appeared out of nowhere. After hesitating, he pulled his shirt up over his face as best as possible and staggered straight ahead into the wind. After a few hundred yards, he too found a large boulder and sat down to get some relief from the billowing sand. His shoulder was throbbing with pain, but the sand had worked its way into his wound and clogged the bleeding temporarily. Wendell Pensor knew he would have to get some treatment soon, but he also knew the bullet had gone all the way through because he could feel the pain in both sides of his shoulder. He figured he would be okay for a while. Needing rest, he let his head lag down onto his chest.

A rolling sage brush bumped into his outstretched legs, startling him awake. The sand storm had subsided and the dusk was coming on. Pensor started to rise but quickly fell back in agony, his stiff shoulder sending lightning bolts of pain through his body. Gritting his teeth, he hurled himself to his feet to look around. The landscape was bare but that only made him feel confident of no impending danger. He took a quick glance at the sun, low in the sky, and trudged west in that direction, where he hoped he might pick up a trail or better yet, an easy mark.

It was almost dark and he had been walking for over an hour. His energy was draining and his steps became staggers, when he spotted a campfire up ahead. Taking a deep breath and gathering his last remaining strength, he approached the camp.

He called out, "hello there, by the campfire!" His last sight was of a couple of people standing to look his direction as he collapsed to the ground.

A sharp pain woke him and he struggled to fight off his assailant.

"Is okay, is okay….I am ges trying to clean your wound." The speaker was a Mexican woman. She dipped a rag into a small pot of water and reached back to dab at Pensor's shoulder. Grimacing, he looked at his surroundings. He was lying on a blanket next to the campfire. There was a small cart off to one side, turned on its side, probably where they hid from the storm. Next to it was a pile of goods that might have been all they had in the world. Across from the cart stood a horse tethered to a small cactus. And squatting down next to the fire, with an old rifle across his knees, was a Mexican man, his eyes warily watching his wife's patient. A quick moment of panic washed over Wendell until he spotted his satchel close by next to his side.

"How long have I been here?" Pensor managed to croak out between grunts of pain as the wife continued to dab and wipe clean his wound.

"Not long," the man answered in heavily accented English. "After you collapsed out there," he waived into the darkness, "we dragged you here and my wife has been working on you since. How did you get shot out here?"

Ignoring the question, Pensor asked one of his own. "What are you doing out here?"

The wife glanced at her husband, obvious fear and nervousness on her face.

He responded, "We are traveling from Mexico to the new Los Angeles. My brother and his family have a small home and restaurant there and we are going to join them. The storm came upon us, so we made shelter and will continue in the morning. We believe we are close and should arrive shortly after sunup."

Pensor grunted again as the wife applied some sort of salve and a cloth bandage. He relaxed back and closed his eyes. "Thank you," he murmured and passed out again.

The sun was just beginning to peek up over the eastern horizon when Pensor was awakened by movement around him. He opened his eyes to see the man and woman working to pack up the cart, which they had already pushed back onto its wheels and hooked up the horse. He held his breath as he stiffly sat up. Struggling to his feet he reached down to open his bag.

"Senor, you should stay and rest. We have left some bread and coffee there. You need more rest."

"I appreciate the help," He glanced down, "and the food, but I have to be somewhere." As he turned back to face the couple, his hand held the pistol from his bag. He raised his arm and as the man was moving to reach his rifle, Pensor shot him in the back. The woman screamed and ran to her husband's fallen body. Pensor walked over and pulled the women away, throwing her onto her back. He stood over the man who was struggling to get up and calmly shot him in the head. The wife screamed again and threw herself at Wendell. He brought the gun down on her head and she collapsed at his feet.

"I would surely love to stay and spend some *time* with you, ma'am, but I do have pressing matters elsewhere." He slowly raised the gun and with no emotion, shot her in the face.

Looking around and feeling confident that they were alone; he picked up the last remaining bag from the ground and threw it into the cart. He bent down and picked up the dead man's straw hat. Clamping in onto his head, he climbed up onto a small seat and yelled at the horse to get moving. They started off slowly to the north.

THREE

After walking with little rest most of the night, and with the sun rising on their right, Evan and Emily crested a small rise in the desert and came to the outskirts of Los Angeles. They had passed a few small huts and a larger ranch house on the way, but to Evan it was the largest town he could remember from his early life in the west. He was a little stunned to think about what this town would become in one hundred years. To Emily, it looked like an old dirty, rundown town she'd seen in books.

Trying to hide her disappointment, Emily cheerfully announced, "I can hardly wait for a hot shower and a cool bed."

Evan gave her a sideways glance and just smiled.

As they approached from the south, they came upon a road leading into the town. They walked in among a variety of people, mostly of Mexican descent, who seemed to be going in to start their work day. The conversation was lively, but not English, though Emily could pick out a word or two she recognized from a couple years of Spanish in high school.

As they reached the first main street, they stopped to get their bearings. The buildings were of varying heights, but all made of wood and stone and none taller than three stories. It was early and you could sense the town beginning to wake up. There were a couple of horse drawn carriages taking early risers to early work. Another small box carriage went by with the words, "Smile! Cold Refreshing Milk" painted on the side. There was a man across the roadway, (there was no pavement or cement) striding down the wooden sidewalk wearing a black suit with long tails and what seemed like a two foot tall top hat. He stopped in front of the tallest building on the block, pulled a watch out of his breast pocket and nodded to himself with satisfaction at what he saw. Putting the watch back, he withdrew a key from another side pocket and let himself into the front door. The sign above the door said Wells Fargo Bank.

Evan watched as another man, this one dressed less fancy in black trousers and worn black jacket approached and went into the bank.

"Com'n, follow me," Evan said without warning and stepped off the walk to cross the street. Taken by surprise, Emily hurried to catch up.

"Where are we going?"

The stepped up onto the walk in front of the bank and Evan said, "Wait here," and he went into the bank.

Emily felt very conspicuous in her blue jeans, polo shirt and light jacket. Not to mention the fact she hadn't had a shower or combed her hair in two days. Walking all night through the desert, she had been pretty comfortable in her tennis shoes, but now they seemed out of place where everyone else was wearing some sort of boot. She backed up against the wall and made herself as small as possible.

Two men on horseback went galloping down the street, kicking up clouds of dust that blew right in her direction. Trying to hold back a coughing fit, she saw a sign for a diner a couple buildings down with a woman's clothing store a little further. Across the street was a nice looking house that advertised clean rooms, *two* bathtubs and breakfast served daily. Imagining her first hot meal, a bath and clean clothes, she took a step on the sidewalk when Evan came out the door and took her by the arm.

"Let's go."

"Where are we going? Look there," Emily pointed down the street, "a restaurant, a clothing store, a bed and breakfast. We could use a little cleaning and eating."

Evan barely glanced where she was pointing. "Later, we need to get to the train station and see about a ride to Nevada City."

371

Keeping his hand on her arm, he pulled her down the walk and made a turn at the corner. "The banker said the station was down this street."

"Why did you go into the bank? Did you get money? How did you get money? Do you have ID?" Emily pulled her arm loose and stopped walking, "Evan, I'm hungry!"

Evan stopped and turned to her. She stood with her arms crossed, and her face scrunched into a pout. He began laughing.

"I'm sorry; you look ....you look like a little girl." He reached out and touched her cheek, "a very pretty little girl."

Emily grabbed his hand and held it, "Evan, I'm nervous and out of sorts. Talk to me, what is our plan?"

"We need to get to the train station and book a ride. Then I promise, we will get cleaned up and get something to eat."

They began walking again. "And how are we going to do all that. This has all happened pretty quickly. What few dollars we do have probably won't do much good around here. I mean, will it even be accepted?"

Evan squeezed her hand, "We don't need to worry about that right now. I have some money."

"You do? Like, are you rich and been holding out on me?"

Laughing again, "No, no, nothing like that. After my parents died from the virus and I became a Marshal, I sold my family ranch to the bank and put the money there till I figured out what I was going to do. Since I haven't figured anything out, it's just been sitting there, so we're good."

"Great, first class tickets, a sleeping room, waiter service, and I saw a cute little outfit in the window of that store back there."

Evan just smiled and took her hand again.

They reached a large building with a sign that read, "Western Railroad." They could see around the back where there were different types of train cars and multiple sets of tracks. This was the end and the beginning of the line. Train cars were disconnected and pushed off to side tracks to be cleaned, repaired and restocked, while other cars were attached and being readied for outgoing trips.

They went in the big front door and when their eyes had adjusted to the darkened interior, they

approached a set of windows at the end of the room.
There were a few people in line ahead of them and
while they waited they looked around at the spacious
waiting room. There were five rows of benches for
people waiting for their trains. On the far side were six
doors with glass windows leading out to the boarding
area. There were a few people milling around outside
and a few more resting on the benches inside. The
extra few people standing in line for tickets each
turned and looked at the new customers as they
approached. Their faces registered various expressions
of surprise, confusion and different levels of interest
ranging from blatant curiosity to disinterest.

When it was their turn, Evan approached the
window and purchased two tickets on the next train
leaving that would stop in Nevada City. Emily put on
a confident face and stood watching the people in the
room, trying to be oblivious to their return stars.
Sitting on the benches were a man and woman dressed
nicely in suit and dress looking straight toward her but
not actually at her. There was a cowboy sitting in the
second row next to his saddle and he was looking at
her with unabashed interest. He gave her a big gapped
tooth grin and tipped his large Stetson when their eyes
locked. Looking quickly away, she settled on a man in
the front row. He was sitting with his legs crossed and
wearing a worn, but colorful poncho. His head was

covered by a large straw hat and was tilted down, looking like he was sleeping.

Evan turned from the window. "Ok, the next train for Nevada City leaves at three o'clock this afternoon, so we have some time. Let's go get you that breakfast, out of those clothes and into a bath."

Giggling, Emily took his hand and said, "Not necessarily in that order, I hope."

It had only been a little more than an hour of travel when Wendell pulled the horse and cart off the road just outside of Los Angeles. He climbed down and pulled some of the bags from the back. Going through them, he pulled out a large, colorful poncho. Not finding much else but household wares, some woman's clothing and a few knickknacks that had zero interest to him, Wendell put the poncho on, picked up his satchel and joined a few migrants walking into town. The horse was left grazing on the side of the road.

A couple blocks into town, and Just as he was getting ready to ask directions, Wendell spotted the Western Railroad station. Going inside, he found a few people milling around. Not sensing any danger, he made his way to the front row of benches and sat down to wait. Pulling his straw hat forward he dipped his head to his chest and rested. Not sure of what to do or where to go, he figured the Marshal and his pretty lady friend would eventually wind up here. So he rested and waited. It didn't take long to be proven right.

With his head on his chest, feigning sleep, he was able to overhear the Marshal saying he had tickets to Nevada City. After the couple had exited the building, Wendell stood up, took off his hat and poncho and went to the ticket window.

"One ticket for the three o'clock train to Nevada City."

The teller pulled a ticket from a bundled stack and stamped the date on the front. "That will be three dollars please."

"Three dollars…? That's all?" Peeling a five dollar bill off of a wad from his pocket, he pushed it under the grated window.

The teller picked up the bill, "What's this?"

"What does it look like, a five dollar bill."

"Uh…sorry sir, it looks fake to me, not sure if I can accept this."

Realizing the problem, Wendell quickly said, "It's the new issue. Everyone's using them back east."

The teller, still uncertain said, "Uh..I don't know, I think I should get my boss."

Wendell didn't want to raise any alarms. "I'm telling you straight, but just to save time and show my appreciation, here is another five dollars and you can keep all the change. Just think, you'll be one of the first people in Los Angeles to have the new money." He peeled another bill from his wad and pushed it up under the window.

Looking nervously around, the teller slowly reached down and took the other bill. "Ok, what's the harm, if you're lying; it will only cost me three dollars. If you're not lying, I have more money than I make in a week." The bill quickly disappeared into a shirt pocket.

Retrieving his poncho and putting the hat back on his head, Pensor went out the door. Standing on the walk looking around, he spotted a sign over a door announcing it belonged to a doctor. Feeling the ache in his shoulder, he decided to get it cleaned up and ready for travel. He crossed the street and went in under the sign. The room held four chairs, two against each wall and a desk. There was a closed door beyond the desk. Behind the desk was a homely woman in a white dress with glasses, gray hair tied back in a bun and a not so nice disposition. There was no one else in the room.

"Yes, what can we do for you?" She asked shortly.

"I would like to see the doctor."

"I'm sorry, the doctor is busy, and he doesn't see patients without appointments. Are you new in town?"

"Yes," looking around at the empty room, "but I need to see him now."

"Well I'm sorry sir, that's just not possible." She picked up her pen, "why don't you tell me your name and we'll see if we can get you in later today."

Wendell opened his satchel, reached inside and pulled out his gun. "I want to see the doctor right now," he smiled, "Please take me to him."

Gasping, the nurse dropped her pen and put her hands up.

"This isn't a robbery you dumb bitch, just get up and lead me back to the quack."

She slowly got to her feet and looking nervously back over her shoulder, led the way into the back room. There they found the doctor snoring, with his face down on his desk, a mostly empty bottle of bourbon by his hand.

"Go stand over there," Wendell waved his gun hand toward the corner.

Moving over behind the desk, he reached down and grabbed the sleeping doctor by the back of his shirt. He lifted his head off the desk and let it drop back with a thud. The doctor woke with an exclamation that turned to surprise when he saw his crying nurse cowering in the corner.

Sensing someone behind him, he slowly began to turn around. "What's the meaning of this!" he demanded.

"I need a little help Doc and Miss Moneypenny here didn't want to disturb you. But I'm kind of in a time crunch, so we had to stop short your early morning nap."

The doctor started to argue some more until he saw the gun in Wendell's hand. "Fine, what is it you need?"

"I got a little bullet hole problem and I want you to take care of it. But first, let's tie up nursey there so I won't have to worry about her."

They found some rope in a storage closet and tied the nurse to a chair. Pensor found a small hand towel on the counter and pushed part of it into her mouth.

"There," he stood back to examine his handy work, "that should keep her for a while."

"Now," with the gun held steady on the doctor, he began to unbutton his shirt, "I'm going to sit in that chair right there and you're going to clean and stitch this hole up or whatever you need to do to make it right."

An hour later, after some grunts and groans, the doctor pushed back from Pensor. "Ok, that should keep you for a while. I wouldn't do anything too strenuous for a few days but the bullet went clean through and you obviously had some earlier help. If you come back in a week or so, I will remove the stitches and you should be good as new."

"Well Doc, not sure what my plans are for the near future, but thanks all the same. Now if you would come and trade places with me, let's get you all tied and bundled up like Ms. Crybaby over there so I can get out of here."

The doctor began to protest again, "That won't be necessary, there's been no real harm here. You just leave and we'll forget we ever saw you."

"Yes, well that's sweet of you to say Doc, but I can't take that chance."

Using a scalpel he found on a tray, Pensor cut more of the rope and tied the doctor's arms and feet to the chair. He picked up another towel and pushed it into the doctor's mouth. When he was finished, he stood back and looked around the room. A smile started to creep across his lips and he made his way behind the doctor to stand in front of the chair bound nurse. Reaching out, he made a quick swipe with the scalpel and watched as the blood gurgled out of the slice in her neck. Turning back to the doctor, he stepped up behind him.

"You know doc, I have a better idea." Pensor reached around so the doctor could see the scalpel and before he could react, sliced across his neck allowing blood to squirt out and puddle the floor.

Slipping the scalpel into his pocket, and without looking back, he walked through the reception area. Turning the sign on the window to "closed", he went out the front door, looked quickly around and started off down the street.

FOUR

They had stepped out of the small hotel and walked briskly down the walk to the train station. Emily freshly bathed and feeling like a new person, was dressed more for the times in ladies jeans, low heeled boots, a white blouse and leather vest under a short jacket with fringe. She was also wearing a nice styled cowgirl hat with a decorated band. Evan was also decked out in new jeans, new western shirt and jacket. He still had his old hat and boots, but he was now also sporting a holster with his gun tied to his leg, courtesy of the gun shop next to the hotel. He also carried a large soft satchel containing extra clothing and undergarments. They didn't know how long they would be here, but figured they could get more supplies if needed in Nevada City.

The train trip had been uneventful. Evan and Emily kept mostly to themselves in the first class car, coming out occasionally when they didn't eat in. Emily spent much of the time staring out the window at the open landscape as they sped across the state. Constantly amazed at how open the country was, so lack of civilization.

Four cars back, Wendell Pensor also sat staring out the window at the barren countryside, thinking, *and such a lack of color.* His thoughts were more focused, though, on how he was going to get even with the Marshal and his girlfriend for killing his brother. He ate his meals in the general meal car and slept sitting up in his coach seat, the uncomfortable benches and bad food only fueling his anger. He never saw Evan or Emily, but he knew they were up ahead, having watched them climb on before he himself had boarded. His time would come. He was nothing if not patient. As the train pulled out of the station, he could see a bit of activity down the street at the doctor's office. He chuckled at the memory as he slouched down and pulled his hat down over his face.

When the train finally pulled into the Nevada City station it was late afternoon. Evan and Emily were one of the first off and Evan led them straight up the street to a building with a large sign, *General Store.*

Wendell held back a little, letting most of the passengers debark while he watched out the window. When he finally did climb down, with satchel in hand, he made for the first building closest to the railway. Entering the front door of the *Last Chance Hotel*, he woke up a dozing desk clerk and booked a room. He paid using the same line as before regarding the currency but this time, the greedy clerk didn't think twice about accepting the extra-large bill.

FIVE

"You surely do make the best coffee in town, ma'am." Deputy Sheriff Jones was holding out his cup for a second helping. "Appreciate you allowing me. Most times, it's hard for someone of my…uh, stature to find good service."

Mrs. McLaughlin glanced nervously toward the back of the store. She turned to refill the deputy's mug, "Well now deputy, we are all God's creatures, even though some people can't always see straight on the matter."

The sound of a door opening and closing came from the back of the store and Evan stepped out from behind a row of dry goods.

"Good morning Mrs. Mc….. oh I'm sorry, didn't realize you had a customer."

"It's alright, Evan." Turning to face the deputy, she said, "This is Deputy Sheriff Jones. He comes in most mornings for coffee."

Evan took a step forward and put out his hand. "How do you do, I'm…."

"I know who you are sir and I know it's been a few years, but let me say how sorry I am for your loss." He reached out and shook hands, "Ulysses Bass Jones."

"Jones...Jones?" Evan looked carefully at the face of the tall deputy. "There used to be a blacksmith in town. *His* name was Jones."

"Yessir, he was my father. I used to do errands for him. Make deliveries, fetch supplies, maybe you seen me around town."

Evan smiled at a memory. "That's right, I do remember. I saw you out back of your pa's shop once; you were practicing your quick draw." Looking up into the big man's face, he said, "You've grown a little in the last few years."

"Yes sir," Jones answered shyly. "Lots of things happened since you went away. I had to grow up a lot besides in size."

Evan looked around the store and spotting a table in the back corner said, "I'd like to hear a little of what has been going on. Do you have a few minutes? Want another cup of coffee?"

Deputy Jones looked over to Mrs. McLaughlin, who nodded and said, "Ok, I got some time before I have to be home."

Just then, a sleepy Emily came out from the back door.

There was an uncomfortable silence as everyone looked at each other, then Evan spoke up. "Uh, Deputy Jones, this is a friend of mine, Emily."

The big deputy put out his hand "How do you do ma'am?"

"Fine, thank you," Emily reached out, his huge paw engulfing her hand, "Nice to meet you."

There was an awkward silence for a second that was broken by the jingling of the bell from the front door.

"I've got a customer." Mrs. Mclaughlin turned and went to greet a woman looking at dry sausages on the counter. "Hello, Mrs. Smith…."

Emily went to the counter and poured herself a cup of coffee. Turning back to the men, she said, "I'm going to get ready for the day, nice meeting you Deputy." She glanced quickly at Evan and went into the back room.

Evan gestured to the table and the men sat facing each other, Evan looking toward the front of the store.

Jones spoke first. "Well, where have you been? I know you were around here and there marshaling, but then you just disappeared."

Evan took a sip of his coffee and his eyes closed for a second. "Oh, well I went to Los Angeles to follow up a lead which didn't materialize and then got caught up with some other characters and pursuing other diversions."

"Materialize, diversions? You talk funny Marshal."

Hm, well Los Angeles is a little different. It's kind of has its own, uh, style. What about here. Tell me what's been going on here."

The big deputy looked over his shoulder and then back to Evan. "Lucias Johnston is what's happening. You know his mama died of the virus way back and last year, his daddy passed on when he got himself thrown from a horse. He hit his head on a boulder and never recovered. Lucias got everything. He's meaner than a rattle snake and sneakier than a coyote. He spends most of his time bullying ranchers in the area, trying to get them to sell. He's doing the same thing here in town. The man wants to own all of Nevada."

Evan nodded. He saw the woman customer staring down an aisle at him. When he made eye contact, she quickly turned away.

"I saw him at the Lucky Lady last night. Everyone gave him a pretty wide berth" He brought his focus back to Jones, "And you? What about you? Last I knew, the sheriff was under the Johnston thumb, so don't take this the wrong way, but how did someone of your, uh, color, get a position of authority?"

"That's a story by itself," Jones chuckled. "My daddy always wanted to get away from the forge and out into the open air, so when the word got around you had sold your ranch to the bank, my daddy hustled over and made a deal. We became the only black landowners in the area." His face turned solemn, "As you can guess, that didn't sit too well with the Johnstons."

"Daddy agreed to stay on as the blacksmith until another one could be found but one Sunday, he was down in the creek behind the house when he found a rock with sparkles. He brought it to town and the surveyor confirmed it was silver. Daddy made him promise to keep it quiet, but the man lied. A couple days later, Lucias and some of his men rode up to the house. He said he had a previous claim to the ranch and my daddy's deed was not valid. Well, you remember my daddy was bigger than me and with some help from a twelve gauge shotgun, convinced them to leave and don't come back without proof."

Evan got up to get another cup of coffee. "Do you want another?" Jones shook his head, no.

"So what happened? That still doesn't get to you becoming a deputy."

"No, that's not the end." Jones' head dropped to his chest but snapped up as Evan sat back down; there was hatred in his eyes. "No one can prove anything thing, but a couple days later, I was in town getting supplies. When I got home, daddy was lying in the dirt by the barn, dead. He'd been shot in the back." Tears were beginning to show in his eyes.

"I'm sorry, Ulysses." Evan put his hand on the big man's arm. "Let me guess, you went to town and the sheriff refused to offer any help."

"Yes and no. You see, the sheriff is a good man mostly. He's tired of the way the Johnston's have run roughshod over this town for so long, but he's just too old to do anything. So he deputized me on the spot. Said he could use the help and I could investigate on my own. Said it would probably get him killed, but it was his way of finally standing tall."

"Wow, that's quite a story." Evan sat back in his chair and took a drink of coffee. "What about the silver? I have doubts that Lucias is just sitting around with his finger up his...."

Jones gave Evan a look of curiosity. "Well, I was so damned angry about my daddy, I plum forgot about the silver for a while. When Lucias found out I was deputized, he came to town and tried to be nice and accepting and sweet talk me out of the ranch. Saying how's now that I had a steady job I should just sell to him for double what we paid and move into town to be close to work. I told him that was real generous, but that I needed time to get things together and could he give me a couple months to get everything in order?"

"And did he go for it?"

"Well, you could see in his eyes, he wasn't keen on waiting very long, but he just gave me that lizard smile and said he would be waiting for when I was ready," His eyes became black pits, "'course, I didn't say it would be a cold day in hell before I ever gave him anything but a plot of land on Boot Hill."

Deputy Jones stood up abruptly, "That was over a month ago, so I expect something will be happening soon." He nodded toward the back door. "That's a pretty new girl you got there, and I'm not sure what brought you back here, but I got a good idea. You keep your head down. You know as well as anyone, Lucias is a sick man and not to be taken lightly. Maybe we'll talk again. Thanks for the coffee." He turned and strode up the aisle to the front door. Tipping his hat to Mrs. Mclaughlin, he stepped out on the porch.

Evan looked thoughtfully after the deputy. Turning his gaze down at his third empty cup he got up and poured himself another. After another quick glance to the front of the store, he turned went into the back room.

SIX

As Deputy Jones went down the steps, he bumped shoulders with another customer coming up. The man had his head down and let out a soft grunt at contact, but continued up the stairs without stopping.

"Excuse me sir." Jones watched as the man stopped on the top step. He was wearing a long sleeve shirt and a large straw hat, but when he looked back, Jones could see his thin nose and dark eyes with seemingly no light in their depths and lips that curled up in a smirk.

Seeing the badge on the big man's shirt, the stranger said, "No, excuse me Deputy, guess my thoughts were elsewhere." The man turned and continued into the store.

Deputy Jones continued to watch thoughtfully after him until the door closed behind him. Turning away, he untied his horse, mounted and headed out of town towards home.

Pensor stepped inside the door and paused to let his eyes adjust to the darker room. The last time he had been in such open spaces with no block from the sun was when he had been a small boy growing up in Texas.

A pretty, but older woman came around from behind the counter and approached him, wiping her hands on her apron. "Good morning, sir. How may I help you?"

After a quick look around, his eyes came back look directly at her. "Well, I need some new clothes, something a little more with the times." He looked down at his own clothes and chuckled. "I'm afraid mine are a little out of date." He chuckled again.

Not seeing all that much humor in this strange man, she said, "Of course." Mrs. Mclaughlin began moving down one of the aisles. "Here are some very comfortable, durable jeans." Grabbing a pair off the shelf, she held them up. "These should fit just fine." She handed them to Wendell and continued down the aisle. "Here are a few shirts, all of which I'm sure will be to your liking. The few boots we have are on the other aisle. Mr. Gilroy's boot shop down the street has a much larger selection."

Wendell glanced quickly at the shirts and pulled one out. He followed her around the corner. "I'm sure whatever you have will be just fine. I'm not sure how long I will need them for anyway."

She gave him a curious look, not sure what he was meaning. "If you need socks and undergarments, they are down that aisle there. I will let you browse.

Just bring it all to the counter when you find what you need." Not liking the way he looked at her, she hurried back around the counter.

After only a few minutes, Wendell came to the back to the front. "This should work." He dumped his choices on the counter.

Mrs. Mclaughlin went through them, writing down all the prices. Adding them up with pencil and paper, she said, "Ok, that will be four dollars and fifty cents, please"

"Four fifty?"

"Well, I'm sorry, sir, those boots are the most expensive ones we have. Like I mentioned earlier, if you would like to try Gilroy's down the street…"

"No, no," another smile growing on his face. "Just wasn't expecting that number. It will be fine, thank you." Wendell pulled out his wad of cash and peeled off a twenty dollar bill. "Here, keep the change."

She took the bill and looked at it. "I'm sorry, I don't recognize this."

Again, he gave the story of new currency from back east.

"I'm not sure." She began to hand it back over the counter, "I'm sorry sir…" She looked up into his eyes and seeing no sign of life or compassion became afraid. She hesitated for a second and then pulled her hand back. "Ok, sir, you seem like an honest man." She put the bill into the pocket of her apron and began to bundle up his new clothes.

"That's alright; you don't have to do that. Do you have a room I can change in right now?"

She glanced nervously toward the back of the store. "I'm sorry sir. We only have a very small store room and it is a mess right now."

Pensor followed her eyes to the back. Noting her nervousness, he smiled and said, "No problem," he gathered up his purchases, "I'm staying right across the street, I'll just go back over and change." He turned and went to the front door. Turning back, he nodded his head. "Have a good day ma'am." He stepped out and closed the door behind him.

Mrs. Mclaughlin let out a loud sigh of relief and reaching into her apron, pulled out the odd looking bill. After a minute, she shrugged and put it into the cash box behind the counter.

Fifteen minutes later, Wendell emerged from the front of the hotel. Pulled his new cowboy hat down low over his eyes, locked his thumb into his belt, smiled and started up the street.

SEVEN

Nevada City was not a city by any means, and if he squinted, Wendell could almost see the end of the street a few hundred yards up. It wasn't a one street town, though, as there were a couple of other streets running parallel to the main street on either side. From his view at each corner, he could see mostly what looked like homes and an occasional smaller business. Up or down on the other streets he saw "Ben's Hats", "Polly's Pies & Diner" and there was "Gilroy's Boot Emporium." As he continued up the main street, he figured the best locations were taken by the first people to settle and supplied the most sought after services. Right next to his rundown hotel was a coffin makers' shop. Nobody wanted to be reminded of death very close to the hub of town. He passed a barber shop, a clothing store and a gunsmith. He thought back to the gun in his satchel at the hotel. He didn't have any place to carry it and didn't want to carry the bag all over. He was just exploring and getting a feel for his new environment.

There were no trees or plants on the farther out edges, but as he approached the center of town, he saw a small square with some sort of statue in the middle. It was surrounded by a few trees and a stone basin with water. A handful of benches were scattered about, mostly under the trees and a few people were sitting.

Some either eating food and some just having neighborly conversation.

The streets were all rutted dirt and the dust swirled around every time someone went by on a horse or buggy. The sun was high in the sky and the only shade was the covered, wooden walkways on both sides of the street. So, as it was, everyone walking was on the same walkway, women, children, shop keepers sweeping more dust into the air and men going from one business to another. They all looked at Wendell, sensing or knowing he was a stranger. Some acknowledging him, the women with polite smiles as they hurried past, some men with a nod and a couple cowboy types who just glared as they went by.

Up ahead, he could see the Sheriff's office past the next cross street. Looking to his right, he was standing in front of a door with a sign reading, "Ned's Place." Deciding to avoid the local sheriff for a while, he stepped inside. As usual, he had to wait a few seconds for his eyes to adjust. There was a bar running down the right side of the room. A few tables were scattered around the room to the left. There were only two people in the place, a single customer sitting on the middle stool and the bartender standing down at the far end wiping out glasses. They both turned as the door opened and watched the stranger stand for a second before moving to the stool right next to the solo customer.

"What'll it be stranger?" The bartender came down the bar.

Looking at the bottles on the back shelf, Wendell asked, "Can I get a Vodka, Orange juice."

The bartender looked confused. "I can get you some orange juice if I go around the corner to Polly's, but I don't know what, uh, what did you say, Vodka, is?" We have beer on the tap and whiskey in a bottle."

Wendell looked down at what the other customer was drinking. "I'll just have what he's having."

The bartender grabbed a small glass off the counter under the big mirror on the wall. Taking a bottle next to it, he poured out a glass and put it in front of Wendell.

"That will be two bits."

"Can I run a tab?"

The bartender now looked a little perturbed. "Sorry mister, I don't know you. Why don't we pay as we go along?"

Pensor looked at the man, his eyes boring right into his soul. He smiled his smile, "Sure, here you go."

Once again, the wad came out of his pocket and a twenty dollar bill was produced. "Will this keep us going for a while?"

The customer turned his head and his glazed eyes widened in surprise. "Say, that some stack you got there."

Taking a deep sigh, Wendell went into his spiel again. "I am traveling to California from back east. This is the new currency put out by the government." He laughed lightly, "I guess news travels a little slower out this far."

The bartender took the bill and like the storekeeper, held it up to the light. He looked around his empty bar, and held out his hand. "Ok, I'm Ned; this is my place, welcome."

"Alright Ned, tell me, what goes on in this fine town." Wendell picked up his glass and took a small sip. It took almost all of his will power not to spit it out all over Ned. It burned going down his throat, he thought he was on fire from the inside out.

Seeing his discomfort, the drunk to his left guawffed to himself, but Ned got a glass and poured a beer from the tap. He set it down on the bar. "Here, this might help as a chaser."

Pensor took a quick gulp of the semi warm beer. He almost choked *it* up also, but managed to control himself. "Thank you."

Leaning back, Wendell looked around the room. "You seem to have a nice place here, where are all the customers?"

"We're not allowed to be too busy." Ned turned and walked to the end of the bar.

"What does that mean?"

The glossy eyed customer slowly gazed up at Wendell, trying to get in focus. "It means, Mr. Johnston don't want too much business to get away from *his* bar. In fact, he don't want too much of anything to get away from him, and that's all I'm saying."

Pensor looked down the bar at Ned, who had his back to them and was furiously wiping out another glass. He looked down at the soused customer next to him. He looked at his drink, started to reach up and hesitated. "Fuck this." He got off his stool and made his way outside. Leaving the din and depressing funk behind him.

Turning right, he continued his journey up town. Quickly past the sheriff's office, where through the window, he could see an old man leaning back in his chair with his feet on the desk. He moved past the post office and then the bank. He thought about going in and trying to exchange some of his cash. He was getting tired of telling his story. But then he figured, if it was supposed to be new money, why would he want to exchange it. He cut through the park and looked at the statue. It was a moderately bad version of Abraham Lincoln. Continuing on he passed a sign that said "Bath and Barber." There was a crude wooden sign of a man in a bathtub with another man standing behind him cutting his hair. As he got closer to the end of the street, he came to a large barn with a corral behind it. The sign said "Horse Inn." The big door was open and he could see stalls lined up on both walls. There was a young man brushing a horse in front of one of the stall doors, and through the open back door, Pensor could see an older man leading a horse in from the back corral.

Crossing to the other side, Pensor made his way back down the same street. Still nodding and smiling to all whom past. This side had a much larger, nicer hotel than the one he was staying in and he made a mental note to move over here soon. There was another bar that looked as empty as Ned's and Wendell went on by, the burning indigestion from his last drink still burning inside him. Passing in front of the "Johnston's Silver Corral Buffet", the alluring fragrance of cooking food reminded Pensor that he had not had any food today. He pushed open the glass topped door and stepped inside. The restaurant was half full in the early afternoon and he was waived to a table on the back wall. A heavy woman with a huge bosom came over and asked what he'd like.

"What's good?" he asked, his eyes never leaving the round, swell of her upper breasts and the long line of cleavage that disappeared into her shirt.

"Nothing down *there* for you sweetie, but today's special is meatloaf and potatoes, only two bits." She tapped her pencil on his head in a friendly way and waited for him to order.

Like lightning, Pensor reached out and grabbed her hand with the pencil. Squeezing tight until she dropped it, he hissed through clenched teeth, "Don't touch me!"

"Hey, that hurts! I was only teasing." She backed away a couple feet and looked around the room. Nobody seemed to notice anything and she turned back to Pensor.

He instantly gave his smirky smile, "Fine, I'll have the meatloaf and potatoes. Do you have anything to drink besides warm piss and gasoline?"

The waitress was noticeably shaking as she said, "We have sarsaparilla or water."

Again with the smile, "Not sure what that first one is, so just some water, thank you."

She hurried off but looked back to see a wolfish grin on his face.

The meatloaf was dry and overcooked and the potatoes were overcooked and mushy, but with a fair amount of ketchup and butter, he was able to get them down. He ate slowly and by the time he got up to leave, the room was almost empty. He took out some money and before anyone could question him again, he left a bill on the table and headed for the door. He did take one last look back to see the waitress watching him nervously from the kitchen door. He ran his tongue down the length of his hand and turned it to wave good bye.

Turning right, he headed back to his hotel, thinking he would pack up his few things and move to the nice place at the other end of town. As the walkway ended at the next corner, he came to a big double door on the nicest building on the street. It was midafternoon and The Lucky Lady was already gearing up for the evening. He could hear the sound of music and more than a few people laughing. He was thinking this must be Mr. Johnston's place, which meant, this is where the action would be. He hurried down the street to his hotel.

He decided to get off the main drag and crossed the street to go down one of the back streets. A couple coming up the walkway stopped in stunned silence as they watched him turn the corner and disappear. Emily gripped Evan's arm so hard she drew blood.

EIGHT

The horse galloped into the big open yard and pulled up in front of the long, white house. Hopping off and throwing his reins over the rail, the cowboy ran up the stairs and knocked on the screen door. After a minute the inside door was opened by a homely young lady. Her eyes were too close together over a small pug nose to give her any chance of being pretty. She was a little overweight, though you could see she might have had a good figure earlier in life.

"Yes Earl, what can I do for you?"

"Is he in, I need to see him."

"Yes, come in, I'll go see if he's available."

She pushed open the screen door to let him pass. "Wait here and I'll check."

She glanced up at his head as she passed and he said, "Oh yeah." He quickly reached up and took off his hat, nervously holding it in his hands.

After a couple minutes, she returned, "Go on in, he's in his study."

Earl walked nervously down the hall, passing by the living area where a small boy was playing with toys on the rug. He stopped at a slightly open door and tapped lightly.

"Come in."

Earl pushed open the door and stepped a couple feet into the room. It was decorated by a sitting area to the left in front of a large plate glass window. To the right was a single chair in front of wall of books. The layer of dust a giveaway that the books were never touched. Centered in the room and set near the back wall was a large desk. There was a lamp with a burning candle and an odd shaped rock with a cigar resting on the edge. Covering most of the desk was a large map unrolled with the corners held down with what looked like checkers. Standing behind the desk and leaning down on both hands was Lucias Johnston. He was wearing a long sleeved white shirt with a vest and no jacket.

Without looking up, Lucias said, "The month is almost up. In a couple days, we're going to have to have a final talk with that nigger about his land." He tapped hard with his finger on an area on the map that was circled in black.

"Uh, yes sir, but there's something else I come to tell you."

Sensing the nervousness in the man, Lucias looked up and stood straight.

"Well, what is it?"

"Well sir, um, well…. "

"Goddamn it man, spit it out!"

"He's back sir. Evan Longview, he's back."

Johnston stared at the sweating cowboy for a long five seconds before sitting down in the large overstuffed chair behind him.

He picked up his cigar and took a couple puffs to get it going again. He stared out the window for an uncomfortable amount of time and then slowly a smile came across his face.

"Anything else?"

"Well yes sir, it seems he has a woman with him. A real looker according to Josh, he saw them come out of Mclaughlin's store and go up the street together."

"And he's sure it's Longview?"

"Yessir, I grilled him good, but he swore on his life."

"Hmmm....guess we'll have to think of a real nice welcome back gift for him. Ok, you can go, but tell the boys to stay away. Just make sure we know what he's up to."

Earl nodded and hurried out the door.

Lucias sat at his desk staring out the window until he realized his cigar had gone out. He glanced down at the map again.

"Damn!"

NINE

Ulysses Jones was walking from the barn to the house when he saw the cloud of dust coming down the road toward him. A large grin grew on his face as the beautiful face of Chvonne Sanders came into focus. She trotted into the yard and pulled up next to the big man, the dust following her and blowing past him. She threw a leg over the horse and slid down, landing gently beside him. They looked at each other for a second, then she leaped into his arms and they kissed wildly for a full minute. Stepping back to catch her breath, she smiled up at him. She looked around at the yard. The big barn was behind him. Where it used to house tools for shearing and butchering sheep, it was now under construction with the addition of horse stalls. Behind her was the small but sturdy home nestled close to base of the mountain behind it with a small creek running between. Barb wired five acres of grass stretching out and running parallel to the road she had come down.

"You've done a lot, Ulysses. The place looks nice."

"It needs a woman's touch."

She looked at him sadly. "You know I have one more year on my contract with Lucias."

Chvonne and her brother had come out west with a large group of people looking to start a new life. They both worked for a nice family of moderate wealth, not as slaves but as employees. They had an agreement to move on and get their own place when they reached California. When they had passed through town, Lucias Johnston had spotted her in the group and tried to get her to stay. She refused and the party moved on. A day past Nevada City, the family was moving a little behind the rest of the group when they were attacked and killed. Everyone except Chvonne and her brother, they were blamed for the deaths. Brought back to town and imprisoned, her brother was killed in his cell by a supposed drifting cowpoke, who disappeared shortly after. Facing a similar fate, Chvonne agreed to work for Lucias in his saloon for two years in exchange for him getting her set free. She had worked serving drinks to local patrons, singing occasionally with the off key piano and enduring drunk cowboys upstairs for those who wanted to try something a little "darker."

She had fallen for Deputy Sheriff Jones the first time he had come into the Lucky Lady. Having both suffered the loss of loved ones; they quickly formed a bond that grew beyond grief.

"Look, he wants my land and the silver that's probably on it. I could trade it to him for your last year."

"Ulysses, no! This is your land. You've paid for it with blood, most likely spilled by him. Don't give in to him."

"I know, but I'm going crazy every time I know you're working at that place"

"Me too, baby. But you've got to hang on. Time will pass and then we can be together."

Jones looked down at the beautiful woman, moisture beginning to well up in his eyes. "You know he's never going to let that happen, Chvonne. He's going to find a way to keep you under his thumb forever and he's going to try to kill me and get my land."

She reached up and put her hand on his cheek, a tear coming down her own cheek. "We'll think of something, I know we will." She took his hand and began to lead him toward the house.

"In the meantime, I have to go to work soon, so let's go make a memory I can keep in my head tonight."

He tried to smile but let her lead him. Thinking back to his morning conversation he said, "We may have surprise up our sleeve anyway."

TEN

"I feel like I'm on a movie set." Emily and Evan were coming down the front steps of the store. He looked up the street.

"It just looks bigger to me. I don't remember so many buildings," he pointed up the street in the direction of the statue, "and what is that up there?"

Emily took his arm, "Let's do some reconnaissance." She led him across the street and they started up the right side.

There was a continuous smattering of people on the walkway. The men had on long pants, boots and the occasional jacket, even though it was very warm. The women were all covered completely in long dresses with layers underneath. Most had on some sort of bonnet or hat. None of them had on any makeup. He didn't recognize many of them, and the ones he did just stared at him, like they'd seen a ghost or a monster.

Emily noticed it and said, "I thought you lived here? Why is everyone averting eye contact when they obviously recognize you?"

They continued to walk, "Well, maybe because after Mary died, I wasn't a very pleasant person to be around. Actually, I was pretty much the biggest jerk in the area, including Lucias, and that's saying something."

"You? Not my teddy bear," Emily hugged his arm, "though I have seen you when you're very serious and bent on some mission or other."

"Yeah, well, think *that* times one hundred and then add a bottle of whiskey. Hey…. and speaking of whiskey, good to see some things haven't changed too much. Let's step in here."

Emily looked up at the sign, "Ned's Place." They pushed inside and after adjusting to the darkness, Evan approached the bar. Again, the only customer sat in the middle of the bar and the bartender was standing away from him, polishing something.

"Hello Ned"

Ned came down the bar to get a closer look at the stranger. His eyes flew open in surprise when recognition set in. "Marshal, well damn!" then he saw the other person was a woman, "sorry ma'am, excuse my mouth." Ned suddenly got nervous, "Uh Marshal, should she be in here?"

"I'm pretty sure I'm old enough to drink." Emily stepped up to the bar, "In fact, I'll have a Vodka Tonic."

Ned looked over at the other customer, who was watching everything through glassy, semi closed eyes. "Uh, we don't have that here ma'am, just beer and whiskey." He looked back to Evan, "you're the second person today to ask for that."

Evan moved up and sat down on a stool one over from the other customer, his odor not much to be around. Emily sat down on his right. Evan said, "Whiskey then, and a beer for my friend here."

"What, I can't handle whiskey? Give me the same as him." She elbowed Evan in the ribs and giggled "maybe bring him the chaser."

Nat set two glasses on the bar and poured a shot of whiskey into each. Then he grabbed a mug and poured a beer from the tap and set it down between them. Emily reached out and picked up the glasses and handed one to Evan.

She tapped his glass and took her shot all in one action. This time, Ned's shirt wasn't so lucky, as Emily immediately spit out the drink all over the bar and him. She grabbed quickly for the beer and gulped down half the glass before setting it down, out of breath.

"Jesus, no wonder you were always in a bad mood. That stuff tastes like kerosene."

Ned stepped back, a little in shock, but Evan was laughing out loud. He tossed his whiskey back in one gulp and wiped his mouth with satisfaction. He pointed to his glass to signal for another.

"As you know, I've been gone a while, so why don't you catch me up, starting with the other customer who ordered a vodka."

Ned refilled his shot glass and put the bottle on the bar. "Well, he was an odd man. I mean, he was dressed ok, but his clothes looked brand new. He was slim with a very thin nose. His eyes...his eyes looked like they were dead. I mean, there was nothing behind them. He came in and ordered vodka with orange juice. When I told him we didn't have that, whatever it is, he also ordered the whiskey and beer and had pretty much the same reaction as this young lady." He eyed her nervously.

"Yeah, and he had a pretty good wad of money." The lump on the other stool decided to join the conversation.

"That's right," Ned turned to the back of the bar and opened the cigar box under the counter. "He gave me this, said it was the new currency coming out of Washington." He put the twenty dollar bill on the counter in front of Evan and Emily. They both just looked at it, not bothering to pick it up, and then looked at each other.

Evan was the first to move. He stood up quickly, "What do we owe you?"

A startled Ned said, "No charge, Marshal, a free round for my last best customer. Besides, this here bill will cover it."

Evan took Emily's arm and they hurried out the front door and stopped, looking up and down the street.

"Shit," Emily was the first to speak, "how is that possible? I mean, who could it be? There was no one standing when we went through except Tom."

"You heard Ned, the description. It was Wendell Pensor, the guy you shot in the warehouse. He probably did the dirty work. William was older and seemed...uh above it. He was the brains. This guy was the weapon. He probably kidnapped Tom. We saw him shoot Peter and there were other bodies in the warehouse. Maybe your shot didn't kill him."

"But how would he have followed us. That would mean…..Tom?"

Evan grabbed her shoulders and made her face him. "We don't know that. We don't know anything and we can't think about that now. We just have to keep our eyes open and try to find out what he's doing here and what he wants, though I have a pretty good idea."

Emily looked up into Evan's eyes. She put her arms around him and drew him close. "Did you really drink that stuff? It's making my stomach turn."

"You need to put something else in there. Let's go find some food."

They turned and headed up the street. They got past one more building when they both stopped and stared. Wendell Pensor was coming down the street on the other side a couple blocks up. Before they could move, he crossed to their side and disappeared down a side street.

For a second they didn't move, and then Evan took off toward the corner. When he got there, he stopped and cautiously looked around the edge of the building. There was no one in sight. Emily caught up with him and looked down the empty street.

421

"Shit."

Emily started down walk around the corner. Evan reached out and grabbed her arm.

"Stop, we probably won't find him. There're only two of us and too many places to look. Besides, we don't know anything about this guy except that he's probably a kidnapper and a killer. Let's don't just run into him around a blind corner. We know he's here now, so let's keep our eyes open and go eat. We can think about our next move while we do that."

Emily stood staring down the empty street. The FBI in her wanted to tear off after this guy, but she realized she was in an unfamiliar place and even stranger environment. She turned back to Evan, "Ok, but I'm worried about Tom. We need to find that guy and put the screws to him."

They crossed the street and stepped up on the walkway. The sheriff's office was the first building on their right, and as they approached, the door opened and a man stepped out. When he turned toward Evan and Emily, he stopped still.

"Hello Longview, longtime no see."

ELEVEN

When Evan saw Lucias Johnston facing him, he froze for a second and then took a step forward, his hand going to the gun at his side. Emily put a restraining hand on his arm. "Evan, we're right in front of the sheriff's office."

Lucias had a big grin on his face. "Yeah, Longview, we're right in front of the sheriff's office. You of all people should know what that means." He turned his gaze to Emily. "I heard you were back in town, and I heard you had a new girl, but the description didn't do her justice." He tipped his hat toward Emily, "Why, you are fine looking woman, ma'am." He reached out his hand, "Lucias Johnston, at your service."

Emily recoiled and made no effort to shake hands. Lucias put on an exaggerated sad face and pulled his hand back. "Well, you've obviously been getting your impression of me from an unreliable source," he smirked, nodding at Evan. "I must say, Longview, at least your consistent with your type of women. Like me, we both like them a little feisty."

Evan took two steps, got right in Johnston's face and hissed, "You're a fucking, lowdown murderer and I'm going to make you pay."

"Evan, is that you?" The old sheriff stepped out of his office. "My goodness son, where have you been?" He stepped around Lucias and seeing Emily said, "And who is this lovely lass?"

He put his hand to his hat, "Sheriff Bosco Garfield, ma'am, at your service. My friends just call me Boz"

Emily just nodded and turned to Evan. "I'm famished, let's go get that lunch." She took his hand and started up the walk. She didn't look at Lucias but nodded to the sheriff.

Evan stopped and turned back, "I'm coming for you Johnston, and real soon."

Lucias smiled and pretended shivering. "Ooo, I'll guess I'll watch my back."

"You won't need to watch your back, you piece of shit, 'cause I'll be coming straight at you." He turned and walked off with Emily.

"Did you say hungry? I know of a great little buffet up the street," Lucias laughed after them, but as he turned to go across the street his face contorted into a scowl.

TWELVE

Wendell Pensor sat in his room staring out the small window that overlooked the train tracks coming into town. He'd been sitting for a longtime, letting his mind wander. He had spotted Longview and the girl as he turned down the side street. Hoping they wouldn't notice him, he nonetheless starting running to the next corner. Turning right, he had gone half a block and then hid behind a large stack of hay in an empty lot. After twenty minutes, he figured they weren't following and in the hazy dusk, he made his way back to his hotel. Now he was just sitting on the floor next to his bed, staring out the window. As the day became night he decided to stick with his plan and head over to the Lucky Lady. There had to be more to this town. All he'd seen so far was dirt, dirty wood and dirty people. If the Lucky Lady was the hub of this hole, as he figured, then that's probably where Longview and his whore would show up. It was time to take care of them and blow this dust bowl. He picked up his satchel and checked to make sure he had everything. He didn't think he was coming back.

After eating an early dinner in a small bar-b-que restaurant at the end of town, Evan and Emily had wandered back through town, keeping a wary eye out for Pensor.

"This is nuts Evan, first we came back from the future to kill the arch enemy of your past. And now we have some psycho from the future roaming around this past, probably hunting us for killing his brother. Sound about right?"

"Yep, just about sums it up." Evan's eyes were sliding back and forth, taking in the whole town before them. "Let's stop in at Ned's for a nightcap. I want to get back to the room. Have to think about tomorrow. We are running out of time and need a plan."

Emily took his arm and looked up into his face. Her young girlish giggle bubbling out. "Do we have to spend all night thinking?"

THIRTEEN

Pensor pushed through the swinging doors of the Lucky Lady. It was early evening and dark outside, but the main floor of the Lucky Lady was lit brightly by a huge chandelier hanging from the ceiling and already half full of the evening's usual congregation. He slid onto a bar stool on the short side of the bar with his back to the wall and put his satchel on the floor by his feet. Not wanting to stand out, when the bartender moved down to him, he ordered a cold beer and hoped it would be better than earlier. When he'd been served, he held his breath and took a sip. This beer was much colder which helped hide the bitter flavor and he figured he could keep it down.

He sat and watched people for about an hour come in and find seats at card tables or just drink. In his mind's eye, it was just like an old western. The patrons were all men, some dressed nicer in long coats and white shirts, but the majority was dirty cowboys, dressed in buckskin pants, flannel shirts and bandanas around their necks. Some had vests, and all of them wore hats. They were White, Mexican, and one man who looked Indian. They all needed a shave. The exceptions were the few waitresses who seemed to double as whores and every once in a while, one would move up the long stairwell to his left with some dirty cowboy in pursuit.

As he ordered his third beer, there was a slight wave of commotion at the far end of the bar and a beautiful black girl came from out of the back putting the finishing touches on her hair. She was dressed like the other women, but her face was smooth and there was still a youthful energy to her walk. She smiled at the men and made her way over to the piano player who had been banging away for the last hour. He stopped whatever he was playing and started in on a version of "The Pecos Queen." She had a soft voice and sang with passion, but soon the hum in the room returned to normal and she finished the song with almost no one paying much attention. When she finished, there was a small smattering of applause only she could hear. She smiled at the men nearest and began walking down the bar. She stopped for an occasional word with some of the regulars and even accepted a quick drink from the bartender.

As she came closer to his end of the bar, and not seeing Longview anywhere, Wendell began to think he might have some time to enjoy the offerings. This whore was by far the prettiest thing he had seen in this town since he got here. Just as he stood up from his seat, a hand reached out and grabbed the girl by the wrist.

"Good evening Miss Chvonne." The cowboy had obviously been here a long while as he stumbled up out of his chair. "How's 'bout you and I go upstairs and kick this night off with a bang?"

She tried to free her wrist, "Why Rufus, I don't know if you could get upstairs."

There was a little laugh from the table he had been seated at, "and besides, you never have enough money, so why don't you let go of me and let me buy you another drink."

Rufus gave her a wolfish grin and said, "Well, I got a surprise for you." He reached into a front vest pocket and produced a gold coin. "Finally got lucky and I been waiting here half the day for you, so let's go." He turned and pulled her to the stairs. Chvonne went along, though not looking too happy.

Wendell stood and watched the scene with a mixture of surprise and envy. As they reached the top of the stairs his mind made a decision, so he reached down for his satchel and followed them up the stairs.

As he reached the top of the stairs, the sheriff pushed through the front doors and went to the bar. "Good evening Jon, let me have a shot of that good whiskey." The sheriff often made a last round of the town before getting off shift. He usually made the Lucky Lady his last stop and the deputy knew to find him here if he wasn't in the office.

As he threw down the shot, the burning liquid helping to clear the dust from the day, he turned at the sound of a loud voice upstairs.

"Hey, you can't do that! Who the hell you think you are?" Rufus was pounding on the door and trying the handle to push his way back inside but something or someone was blocking it. "I paid for that!"

The sheriff sighed and turned back to the bar. Holding up the glass for another, he looked longingly around the room, hoping his big deputy was here to take over. The bartender refilled his glass and as he lifted it to drink, there was a loud scream from upstairs. Specifically from the room Rufus was struggling to get into.

Wendell turned the knob and entered the room. The drunken cowboy was standing with his back to him; the pretty lady was sitting on the bed. A look of surprise blossomed on her face as she watched the stranger grab Rufus by the back of his shirt and hurl him out the door, kicking it closed behind him. He quickly grabbed a chair sitting against the wall and propped it up under the handle.

Turning back to Chvonne, he said, "I don't want sloppy seconds."

Chvonne stood up and over the pounding and yelling from outside said, "I don't know who you think you are, but you can't just barge in here and throw out a good paying customer."

Wendell reached down and opened his satchel. "I have good money, and I didn't want to go after some disgusting, drunk cowboy." He stood up and reaching out, he flicked his wrist and sliced a three inch gash into her cheek with the scalpel in his hand.

Chvonne put her hand to her cheek and when she looked down and saw all the blood, she screamed. She backed away around the bed and screamed again.

Pensor was having trouble thinking straight with all the noise. The yelling from outside and the screaming from inside was making him confused and his thoughts blurry.

The handle of the door shook and a voice yelled, "What's going on in there? Chvonne, are you alright?"

Chvonne kept her hand on her face and stood cowering in the corner, too scared of the wild man waving the knife to say anything.

The voice called out, "I'm coming in." There was a loud crash and the door smashed open, cracking the back of the chair.

Pensor quickly moved to the side of the door and as the sheriff came stumbling in, he stepped up and swiped again with the scalpel. The sheriff's neck began spewing out blood and Chvonne screamed again. Wendell looked at Chvonne and then down at the sheriff who had fallen to his knees desperately trying to stop the gushing blood. He quickly bent down and picked up his satchel and ran out the door. He rushed past a bewildered Rufus and down the stairs. It had all happened so fast, no one reacted as he flew out the front door. He grabbed at the first horse he found at the rail, fighting to get into the stirrup with his satchel still in his hand. Finally getting control, he kicked the horse and began galloping down the street. He almost ran over Deputy Jones, who had heard the screams and was running toward the saloon. Jones dove to the right as Pensor yanked the horse to *his* right and headed down a side street.

At the sound of a running horse, Evan got up and peaked out the curtain on the back wall. It was dark and all he could make out was a horse and rider galloping out the back of town toward the mountains.

FOURTEEN

The smell of fresh coffee wafted into room, stirring Emily from her pleasant dream of a green forest, clear water stream and a naked Evan swimming slowly toward her. "Wake up sleepy head, time to get going."

Evan pushed the door closed behind him and handed her a cup of hot coffee, as she sat up in their small cot sized bed. "This is really *swell*," she said looking around, "but I can hardly wait to get to a real bed in a real room, in a real house or hotel."

Evan smiled down at her with understanding, and then the smile quickly disappeared. "I know, and I appreciate your understanding. Soon, though, maybe we'll just be able to stay in the biggest house in the valley."

It dawned on Emily what he meant and she said, "I understand Evan, but do you have to do this? I mean, it's not going to bring her back and from what I've read; revenge does not make you feel better. It's just another layer of emotion you have to put somewhere in your memory."

Evan thought back to another woman who had tried to talk him out of his actions. He gave Emily the short version. "I have to because I can, because someone has to. If those that can don't, the Lucias Johnstons of the world just keep running over everyone. And usually, those people get hurt." He sat on the bed next to her. "Why did you become an FBI agent? Wasn't it to catch bad guys, to right wrongs? What did it say on the side of the police cars back in LA, "to protect and serve? It's not different in these times. Law enforcement all has the same ideals, the same responsibilities." He looked at her.

"Ok, ok, I get it. I just don't want you to go off all half-crazy and do something stupid, like get killed. What the hell would I do, I mean, I can't even get a good cappuccino, geez."

Evan smiled again, leaned over and gave her a kiss on the lips. It started to linger when he broke it off. "Speaking of law enforcement, Mrs. Mclaughlin told me there was quite a ruckus going on last night. I'm going to find that big 'ole deputy and see what's going on. You get up and get ready; I want to do a little checking on my "arch enemy."" He leaned over and gave her a quick kiss, stood up and went out the door into the store.

Evan went out the store front and down the stairs. Turning to his left he started up the street. As he approached the Sheriff's office, he saw Deputy Sheriff Jones tying a roll to a horse on the rail.

"What's up Ulysses? Going somewhere?"

"What's it to you," looking over the top of his horse, Ulysses glared at Evan, taking a second to realize who it was. "Oh hello, yes, I gotta go out of town for a little bit."

"I heard there was some goings on last night. What happened?"

Jones pulled the last strap down tight and stepped around the horse next to Evan. With a quiet intense voice he said, "Someone killed the sheriff last night. Cut his throat like it was butter, bled out in a minute."

"Oh shit, I'm sorry. Who was it?" Evan asked but he was sure he already knew.

"Some stranger, nobody knew who he was. Witnesses say he was just sitting at the bar for a while and then went upstairs to be with one of the girls. Actually threw a customer out of the room trying to cut in." The deputy looked down, but not before Evan could see the sadness in his eyes.

"How about the girl, what happened to her?"

Jones slowly lifted his head and Evan could see the hate in his eyes, had felt it himself. "He cut her, real bad." He reached up to check the rifle in the side loop. "He stole a horse and took off out of town. I'm going after him, and I seriously doubt he's coming back."

Evan remembered the galloping horseman from last night. "I'll go with you."

"No, don't need no help. I gotta do this."

"Look, I know those hills, been running around in them my whole life. Besides, two is better than one. I know something about this guy, he's a killer."

Deputy Jones looked at Evan for a minute. "Ok, go down to the stable and tell Jonas you want the Sheriff's horse, *he* won't be needing it."

Evan grabbed the big man's shoulder. "OK, I got to go tell Emily I'll be gone, grab some gear and then I'll meet you here in twenty minutes."

FIFTEEN

Through the open back door of the small storeroom, Emily watched Evan and the Deputy Sheriff as they rode out of town toward the mountains. After fifteen minutes of heated discussion, while Evan packed a bed roll and Emily tried to talk him out of going, they hugged hard for a few seconds; he kissed her on the lips, turned and walked out the front door. She watched them ride for another minute until they were small specs lost in the brush and then letting out a deep breath, stepped back in and closed the door.

She quickly finished getting ready for the day. She hadn't brought any makeup with her but was getting used to not wearing any. It certainly shortened her prep time. She slipped into her new boots and went out the door to get another cup of coffee.

As she was pouring a mug from the seemingly never ending pot, Emily could see Mrs. Mclaughlin through the glass on the front door, sweeping the front porch. She took her mug and went to sit at the small table in the back. Mrs. Mclaughlin came in the door and saw Emily sitting down in the back. She put the broom away behind the counter and came down to pour herself some coffee. She picked up a plate with some cookies and brought them over to the table. "Mind if I sit?"

Emily, who had been watching her, said, "not at all, please."

Mrs. Mclaughlin gathered her skirt and slid onto the other chair. She sat for second looking at her coffee mug.

Trying to break the uncomfortable silence, Emily asked, "Did you make these?" She reached out, took a cookie and bit off a small piece. "Yum, these are good."

"Yes, last night. I like to have them for the customers. I always wanted this place to be a place where they felt comfortable, kind of a social place." She looked toward the front of the store, perhaps willing a customer to come in. "My husband died in the virus attack six years ago. That virus took half the town it seemed, including both of Evan's parents.

My daughter," moisture began to appear in her eyes, "my daughter Mary, though I expect you know who she is....was, came back from the east to help me." She stopped talking for a couple seconds and took a deep breath.

Emily reached out and put her hand on the emotional woman's hand.

"After she was killed, it was just me. I've tried to keep myself busy for these past years. The store gives me something to take my mind off of the past most of the time. I think the town's people spend more time here than necessary out of pity, but to be honest, I don't mind the company.

"Tell me about Evan." Emily reached down for another cookie. "We've only known each other for a year or so, but he doesn't talk much about his past."

"Evan," a small smile came to Mrs. Mclaughlin's face. "Evan was an angel, at least before...before."

"I know," Emily assured her, "it's okay."

"They knew each other since they were little children. They went to school together for a few years. He was kind of her guardian angel. Mary was a little feisty and wasn't afraid to say what was on her mind. Sometimes that didn't always sit well with the older children, especially Lucias Johnston. He was the bully, still is, but he never seemed to want to face up to Evan. I think Evan used to make up a reason to come to town for supplies. He would just hang around the store waiting for Mary to show up. When we sent Mary back east to stay with my sister, Evan was crushed. You hardly ever saw him after that, and when we did, he was very serious, business like. Just got what he needed and then left." She paused to sip her coffee. "I'm sure he held some resentment for us, but we did what we thought best for our little girl."

"What happened after his parents died?"

"Well, for a month or so, we almost never saw him. He was so sad…the whole town was sad. Everyone had lost someone." She pointed out the window, "that cemetery out there is filled with family and friends." She turned her gaze back to Emily, "On the day Mary arrived from back east, she ran into Evan on that front porch right out there," she nodded toward the front door, "and they were almost inseparable from then on." She gave Emily a pointed look, "Of course, they went to their own beds at night."

A flush began to creep up Emily's neck. She quickly took a sip of coffee, "What happened after the…uh, tragedy?"

After a slight pause and deep breath, Mrs. Mclaughlin said, "Evan went crazy. He tore around town, yelling at the sheriff, who God rest his soul, wouldn't do anything if it meant upsetting the Johnstons. There was no proof of anything, but Evan was convinced it was Lucias Johnston and he went out to their ranch to kill him. Instead, Lucias's father had him beat near to death and thrown into the desert outside of town."

Emily's eyes widened in horror.

"The deputy sheriff, though he wasn't a deputy back then, found him and brought him here. He stayed in the same room back there for a week while I cleaned his wounds and fed him soup. When he was able to, he got up and rode straight to Carson City where he joined the U.S. Marshals. After that, it's a lot of rumors and stories, though, here in town; we got to witness his anger occasionally. He was very bitter, determined to prove that Lucias was Mary's killer. For three years he roamed the country side, tracking down every outlaw, rustler or bank robber he could find, bringing them in battered or even dead. Then a little over a year ago, he just disappeared. We heard he rode off to California, but we hadn't heard or seen him since, until you arrived couple days ago."

Emily started to say something and then stopped. She wasn't sure how the poor woman would handle the news. After a full minute of silence, she decided, the obviously still mourning mother deserved to know. "He found it, Mrs. Mclaughlin, Evan found proof of who raped and killed your daughter."

Mrs. Mclaughlin's hand flew to her mouth. Just then the bell rang as someone came through the front door. Both women looked down the aisle and saw Lucias Johnston standing there smiling back at them.

SIXTEEN

Evan had forgotten how magnificent the mountains were. The tall buildings in Los Angeles and the dusty dreary western town were no match for the majestic beauty of the wild, with its towering trees, lush undergrowth, diversified wildlife and the sounds of a natural, living wilderness.

They'd been able to easily follow the fresh tracks and crushed grass to the base of the mountain. They had ridden at a gallop across the plain so no conversation was possible, but now they began to climb the hillside and their pace slowed as they warily looked around.

"So Evan, you mentioned you knew this "killer", how so?" Ulysses ducked to go under a low hanging branch.

Evan thought about how to answer the question. The path they followed was just as easy on the hill as down on the plain. Pensor was obviously not a frontiersman and his trail was marked by broken branches, fresh hoof prints and all the signs of a man trying to go fast but not careful. He decided that some of the truth would be okay.

"His name is William Pensor. He and his older brother were causing some problems for Emily and her friends. It's a long story, but I believe he kidnapped one friend and killed a couple others. Emily and I rescued the friend, but I killed his brother and she wounded *him*. I think he followed us here to get revenge."

"Jesus, man, it's just an adventure to be around you." They were silent for couple minutes. "That Emily girl seems like a nice person. What's her story?" He chuckled, "How did she get mixed up with the likes of you?"

"Well," Evan smiled as he thought back, "During one of my "adventures," I literally landed in the dirt at her feet. Maye she has a thing for dust covered cowboys. Her friends and I have been tangled up with the Pensor brothers for some time. I guess we kind of grew on each other."

Changing the subject, Evan looked over to the big man, "That girl that got cut, she means something to you." It was a statement, not a question.

Ulysses continued to watch the trail ahead. "Yeah, she does. We're going to get married. Settle down on that ranch of yours. Raise some horses, mine some silver, have a passle of kids and grow old together. She thinks she owes Lucias Johnston another year of service for something bad *he* done in the first place."

"That sounds like Lucias. Well, you're not going to have to wait that year. Not if I have anything to say about it."

Ulysses looked over at the taught face and was about to say something when Evan suddenly pointed up the hill.

"Look, there's something moving up there!"

They pulled up and dismounted. Splitting apart they continued up the hill, pulling their horses behind them. Zigzagging behind trees, they came close enough to see a horse lying on its side. It was weakly pawing in the air but didn't seem able to get up.

Ulysses looked around and said, "Watch out for me, I'm going to take a look."

Evan pulled his gun and began searching the surrounding hill for any signs of other life. Ulysses bent at the waist, scuttled up the hill next to the horse. After a quick look and feel, he whispered back, "Broken leg, must have stepped into a hole. The damn fool was just pushing too fast without paying attention."

Evan joined him, looking down at the wounded animal and then back up the mountain. "He's on foot now, can't be more than a few hours ahead of us."

Looking at the brand on the horse's rump, Ulysses pulled his pistol and said, "Old man Wilson ain't going to be too happy about losing a horse like this." He pulled the trigger and the echo of the gunshot resounded through the trees.

SEVENTEEN

"Morning ladies," Lucias tipped his hat and touched his fingers to the brim, "must be my lucky day, the two most beautiful ladies in this town and both in one place."

The two ladies stood motionless for a couple seconds and then Mrs. Mclaughlin went behind the counter, to put a barrier between herself and Johnston. Emily watched her go and then turned back to Lucias.

"You should try a different line, Mr. Johnston, flattery doesn't look good on you."

The fake smile dropped from his face. "You should be careful how you talk to me miss. I don't take too much to sass from little girls." He turned his gaze to where Mrs. Mclaughlin was standing, "do I?"

The blood drained from Mrs. Mclaughlin's face but her eyes filled with blood red hatred.

The smile returned, "Now what I came by for was to see if you had thought any more about my offer."

Visibly trying to control the shaking in her body, and with clenched fists, Mrs. Mclaughlin responded, "As a matter of fact, I haven't *thought* about your offer for a single second."

"Well that genuinely hurts my feelings. I believe it was very generous. Possibly double what this place is worth. Why, you could retire in comfort and spend the rest of your days knitting on your front porch, or, oh this would be good. You could come down to the Lucky Lady and I could give you a job as the house mother. You're a little long in the tooth to actually be a working girl."

His superior laugh was cut off when he had to duck from a flying jar of peach preserves. It flew passed his head to where it shattered and oozed down the wall.

Mrs. Mclaughlin picked up another jar, "I have no intention of selling to you now or ever, so you can bully these townsfolk with cheap product and high pricing. " She took a deep breath, "Now I'm going to ask you to leave. And if you ever get any ideas of *burning* me out, there are plenty of good people left in this town who know of your activities. People are getting fed up with your tactics of intimidation and persecution."

For a second, Lucias lost his air of superiority, but it quickly returned. He looked over at Emily with a smirk, tipped his hat, took a quick glance to make sure no other jars were coming his way and went out the front door.

Emily looked to Mrs. Mclaughlin who was breathing heavily as she put the jar of peaches back on the shelf behind her. "I'll be right back." And before the older lady could say anything, she slipped out the front door.

Standing on the porch, she spotted Lucias striding up the street toward the Lucky Lady. "Hey, Dickweed," She called out to him.

Johnston stopped in his tracks and slowly turned around, the snake smile growing on his face as he saw Emily approaching him.

The people walking on both sides of the street stopped to see what was happening.

Emily walked right up to him and before he could say a word, she wound up and clocked him with a right cross to his face. He immediately collapsed into the dusty road.

She stood right over him while he rubbed his face. She talked out loud for everyone to hear, "You're a thieving, bully piece of shit, and if you ever threaten or come near that poor old lady again, I will personally make it my life's mission to track you down and kick the living crap out of you." She stood for a second longer, glaring down at him, and then stepped away and went back into the store.

Lucias watched her walk away and then slowly got up from the ground. He dusted himself off, stood up straight, and continued on to the Lucky Lady, ignoring the smiling faces around him.

EIGHTEEN

The afternoon sun was drifting over the mountain top. The temperature had dropped considerably as they climbed higher. Evan and Ulysses had alternated riding and walking their horses. There wasn't much conversation. Each man keeping his own thoughts while watching the terrain around and above.

Ulysses was thinking about Chvonne, hoping she was feeling better while at the same time, planning his actions once they found Pensor.

Evan's thoughts surrounded the passing time line and trying to understand his emotions. There was a time when he desperately wanted to kill Lucias Johnston, he still did. But time and life have a way of smoothing over the rough spots, dulling the pain. He had allowed Emily to seep into his being and make him feel hunger again, and not just for vengeance. And then there was the upcoming decision. Their time in this present was getting short, or was it? This was *his* time. Did he *want* to go back to the future? Would Emily want to stay in this time? He chuckled to himself; the beds in the future were way more comfortable.

The gun shot echoed down the hillside, passing right through them. Both men quickly dismounted. They were spaced thirty yards apart and with guns drawn moved warily up the hillside. After ten minutes of slow moving, they approached a crest. They tied their horses off to branches and moved slowly up the last one hundred feet. They took their hats off and lying on their stomachs, they inched up to peek over the edge.

In front of them was a small meadow of short grass. It was fifty yards wide and about twenty five yards deep. There were only a few trees, mostly on the right side, so they could easily see the whole scene in front of them.

Wendell Pensor was backed up against the far wall as the hill resumed its upward climb. He was yelling and waving his pistol back and forth. The target of his attention was three large wolves, who sensing weakness in their prey, were dancing about, looking for an opportunity to attack.

With a quick look at each other, Evan and Ulysses climbed up and stood at the edge of the meadow. The wolves, smelling a change in the air, turned and snarled at the new combatants. When their attention diverted outward, Wendell took a quick shot at the nearest beast, kicking up dust at its feet. Almost immediately, a second shot rang out and Wendell screamed in agony as his gun went flying from his hand, blood spouting from a hole in his arm. Sensing this might be more than they bargained for, the wolves turned and ran to the trees and disappeared.

"My, you have been practicing." An appreciative Evan nodded at Ulysses, "though from here, I would have expected a little closer to the heart."

"I wasn't aiming at his heart."

Wendell stood holding his arm while the two men approached. He thought about reaching for his gun, but had barely made a move when another bullet thudded into the dirt behind his head. He froze and looked coldly at his enemies.

Evan and Ulysses walked closer to Pensor. Evan stopped five feet away but Ulysses walked right up to him and punched him in the stomach. Wendell started to bend over as the air exploded from his lungs but the angry deputy quickly followed with a sharp uppercut to his chin. Wendell flew over onto his back, where he turned onto his side and curled up in a fetal position. One hand was holding his stomach while his other hand was holding his bloody arm. He began to moan and cry.

Ulysses looked down in disgust. "This man is a killer? Coward is more like it?" He spat on Wendell and turned away. "Watch him, I'll be right back."

Evan didn't say a word as Ulysses walked back to the edge and went down the hill. He turned back to Wendell, who had stopped crying and was trying to sit up.

"Well, looks like you're in it now asshole. It was bad enough you killed our friends, but then you had to follow us here. What happened to Tom? Did you kill him also? And then you went and picked on the girl of the biggest guy in the territory. Tsk, tsk, not very bright."

Wendell looked up and smirked, "We'll see. You're the law; you have to take me back for trial. All this talk of time travel and murderers with no proof, hell, the sheriff was self-defense. The jury is going to have a confusing time believing anything."

Ulysses came up over the edge of the meadow, leading both horses. When he got near, he threw the reins of Evan's horse around a bush. "Get him up"

Evan reached down and yanked Pensor to his feet. "Aaaah, my arm."

Ulysses threw Evan a short length of rope. "Here, tie his arms behind his back."

Evan looked at Ulysses for second, shrugged and went to work on Pensor.

"Hey, that really hurts, I've been shot you know."

Evan cinched the knot tight, "Not going to bother you for long."

When he was finished, Ulysses helped Evan lift Pensor and put him on the back of Evan's horse.

Ulysses climbed up onto his horse and pointed to the trees, "I saw a good spot right down over yonder. Let's go."

Pensor was becoming unsure of things when Ulysses started off toward the tree line and Evan grabbed the reins of his horse and followed.

"Hey, what's going on, town is back that way," a nervous Pensor said, pointing off to his right.

"We're not going back to town, as least not yet." Ulysses threw the words back over his shoulder as he move out.

They reached the end of the meadow and began to move down in the trees. After only twenty yards, they came upon an old, very large tree with strong looking branches starting fifteen feet from the ground. Thrown around one of these branches and hanging down was a rope, tied into a noose.

"Hey," Wendell kicked the horse to break free, but Evan just held tight to the reins and spoke quietly to the horse. He led the horse over next to where Ulysses was sitting. Ulysses grabbed the rope and put the noose around Wendell's head.

Stepping back, Evan looked up at Ulysses, who looked at Pensor for a second and then nodded his head.

"William Pensor, you are being charged with the murder of the sheriff of Nevada City and other such unnamed victims. You have been a kidnapper and a cutter of woman. As dutiful officers of the law, we condemn you to hang for your sins. Any last words?"

"You can't do this, I get a trial...." His words were cut off as Ulysses reached over and slapped the horse on the rump. It jolted off, leaving Wendell Pensor to swing from the tree. Unfortunately for Wendell, his neck did not break, and so his death was one of slow and painful asphyxiation.

"Welcome to my world."

NINETEEN

"Com'n you lug. Get up. I'm bored." Emily sat on the edge of the cot and poked at Evan.

He had shown up very early in the morning while it was still dark outside. He said he and Ulysses had ridden all night wanting to get back to town. The trip had been successful in that they had tracked down and finished Pensor and that's all he had said. Ulysses had gone off to check on Chvonne and Evan had come straight back to the small storeroom, needing to sleep, if even for a few hours.

Evan pulled the blanket up to cover his head. "What time is it?"

"Oh, I don't know, let me check the clock, oh yeah, we don't have one. I'll just run outside and check the sundial…. Hell, I don't know. It's day time. Get up." She stood up and wacked the pillow where she assumed his head was.

Ok, ok… leave me alone." Evan peeked out of the covers. Seeing the coast clear, he sat up and rubbed his eyes. Emily opened the back door and stood staring out at the mountains in the distance. "What did you do while I was gone?"

Turning back to face Evan, she said, "Oh well, let's see. I had a nice chat with Mrs. Mclaughlin , mostly about you. We had a little run in with your friend Lucias Johnston. Did you know he is trying to buy her out, even offered to put her to work in his brothel? And then what, oh yeah, I followed him out the door and knocked him on his ass, right in the middle of the street. If the town folk weren't so afraid of him, I think I would have gotten a standing ovation. Other than that, a pretty peaceful day." She crossed her arms and looked defiantly at him.

"That was probably a big mistake," Evan held back a laugh and tried to say seriously. "Most people don't cross Lucias and get away with it."

"Well, I'm not most people."

"You're certainly right about that." Scratching his head he said, "Tell you what, since we both had pretty exciting days yesterday, how's 'bout we do something nice together today?"

"Do we have the time? I'm sure we're running against the clock to get back"

"Well, that's what we can talk about," Evan said mysteriously getting up and getting dressed. "Why don't you meet me out front of the store in fifteen minutes, I'll be right there."

"Ok, what should I wear, these jeans and boots or these jeans and boot? I could throw on this ole hat I've had for a week."

A sly smile lit up his face, "That will be just fine." He bent down and pecked her on the cheek and went out the door.

Twenty minutes later, Emily came out the front door to find Evan sitting in a small open wagon being drawn by a single horse. He had a sappy smile on his face as he jumped down to help her up on the single bench seat.

"Your chariot my love, sorry, best I could do in so short a time."

Emily sat on the hard wood bench and looked into the back of the wagon. There was a large basket covered with a cloth, but she could see a bottle of something sticking out of one corner.

"My you've been a quick, busy beaver."

Evan jumped up on his side of the bench, "Oh that, just a little something. Ned lent me his wagon here and helped whip up some vittles from his kitchen. Thought we might enjoy a picnic, just you and me. I know a pretty little place."

"Now you're talking my language you big stud." She put her arm through his and her head on his shoulder. "Lead on, my love." She smiled as they pulled away down the street.

They headed northwest out of town and after a little while Evan turned right down a dirt road. It was paralleled by a green pasture that ran for a few acres. Eventually they came to an open yard with a small but neat house on the left and a large barn on the right. A creek ran twinkling behind the house at the base of the mountain sitting like a behemoth guard.

Evan pulled the horse to a stop between the house and the barn. "This was my home."

"Oh Evan, it's beautiful. Why did you ever sell it?"

He thought about it. "Things were pretty confusing back then. The town had been devastated by the virus, including my parents." He hesitated, "This is where Mary was murdered. I guess there just seemed to be too many bad memories. I kind of went off half crazy. I was drinking heavily and trying to burn memories." He turned to Emily, "Eventually, I landed at your feet and the rest is history." He leaned in and kissed her.

"Com'n, we're almost there." He snapped the horse into motion and headed back to the creek. He turned right and headed up a grown over pathway just wide enough for the wagon. They followed the track along the base of the mountain until they came to a little bridge crossing the creek. "We'll have to walk from here."

He helped her down, and reached in the back of the wagon to get the basket. They crossed the bridge and turned right onto a foot path that ran alongside the creek. They walked a couple hundred yards, the path starting to rise as it wound its way up the mountain. They came to a small grassy area on the right where the creek came around a turn from above. It was surrounded by trees that formed nice shade. "Here we are."

Emily stood and looked all around, the mountain, the trees, and the creek. "It's beautiful, Evan"

"Great, let's eat, I'm starving." He moved over to the far edge where they would be right above the creek. He took the cloth off the basket and spread it out on the grass. He laid out a couple of beef sandwiches that had been quickly thrown together, two pickle spears and a pouch of chips. He pulled out the bottle of wine that had already been corked and poured some into a couple glasses he had taken from the bar.

Handing one to Emily, he said, "Here's to you."

Emily took the glass and tapped his, "Here's to us."

They sat down and quickly ate the food. There was no conversation as they were both content to be with each other and listen to the sounds of the mountain. When all the food was gone, Emily reached out a poured another glass of wine for each of them. She picked up Evan's glass to hand it to him, but he was on his feet, awkwardly trying to get his boots off. If she was giggling watching him dance around, she was laughing out loud as he hopped about getting his pants off.

"What are you doing?'

"Going swimming, what does it look like I'm doing?"

"It looks like you're doing a war dance. Besides, I don't have a bathing suit."

"Neither do I," he said. He stepped out of his underwear and stood there before her in nothing but his cowboy hat.

"Look," he pointed across the creek. "Where the creek hits that wall and makes its turn, the water is fairly deep, deep enough anyway." He bent down and picked up his gun. He walked over to the edge of the water and hung the holster from a low hanging branch.

"Deep enough for what?"

He gave her a big smile and dove into the water. He came up spluttering and wiping his eyes. "Com'n."

Emily looked around and then rose and walked over to the nearest tree. Stepping behind it, she undressed, holding out each piece of clothing for show as a tease. When she had held up her last piece of undergarment, she stepped out from behind the tree. She smiled shyly and made a half- hearted effort to cover herself. Stepping down to the water's edge, she daintily put out her leg and dipped her toe into the water.

"Ooh, that's cold!"

"Not from where I'm standing," Evan panted.

Emily giggled, "are you sure the cold water isn't having even a *small* effect on you?"

"Why don't you come over here and find out."

And she did.

After a while they separated. They floated in bliss for a couple minutes until Emily said, "I getting cold. I'm going back to the blanket."

She swam until she could touch the bottom and then stood up and walked out of the water. She stepped up the small embankment when a clapping came from across the small space. Standing on the edge of the trees stood Lucias Johnston.

"Well done, well done."

TWENTY

Stepping away from the tree he had been leaning on, Lucias moved toward Emily. There was a welt on his left cheek where Emily had hit him. It was starting to turn an ugly yellow.

"I have to say, seeing you like this is almost enough to make me forget yesterday."

"You stay back asshole or I'll do it again."

Evan was moving slowly, keeping Emily between him and Lucias. He figured if he couldn't see Lucias clearly, then he couldn't be seen for the same reason.

"Now that's not going to happen." Lucias pulled back his jacket and took out his pistol, aiming it at Emily. "Why don't you come over here and give me some of that loving, darling, you seem quite good at it. I'm sure your boyfriend won't mind. It won't be the first time we shared a woman."

Then everything happened at once. Evan roared and dove the last few feet to the branch and grabbed his gun. Emily screamed and ran toward Lucias. Johnston took a panicked step back and fired at her. The bullet went under her arm and burned along her rib cage, knocking her sideways. Evan came out of the water as Emily fell, and started blasting at Lucias. The first bullet, shot in rushed anger, missed and hit the tree next to Johnston's face. Lucias ran back to the cover of the trees. The next two bullets also missed and he ran, zigzagging behind trees, back to the trail and his horse. Evan kept pulling the trigger but the gun had jammed and nothing else happened.

He stumbled out of the water and ran to Emily. She was lying on her back across the blanket looking at her side. She started to laugh as he knelt next to her.

"What's funny, are you hurt?"

She lifted her arm and he could see the crease where the bullet had broken the skin as it passed on by. He pulled her to him and hugged as tight as he could.

TWENTY ONE

The moon was glowing bright, but the long house was just a block shape in the deep darkness outside its circle of light. There were no lights on inside as a rustling sound came from the side. A black shadow moved under the railing and moved along the around the full length porch that wrapped around the house. The shadow stopped, facing the front door. The dark intruder stood motionless for a full minute. It seemed to shift up and down like a deep breath and then an arm extended and rapped quickly on the wood frame.

A full three minutes went by and finally a dim light came on in an upstairs window. After another minute, the light disappeared from the upstairs and a couple minutes later appeared through the front door glass.

A figure appeared through the glass door. The curtain covering the window was drawn aside slowly and a candle was held up to the glass. After a couple seconds, the latch on the door was turned and the inner door was pulled open.

Lucias Johnston stood looking out at the visitor, a questioning look on his face. "It seems a little late…I thought you made it clear…."

His words were cut off by a knife that sliced through the air and buried itself in his belly. It took a quick upper motion and was then withdrawn. Johnston's breath went out of him and he collapsed backward onto the floor. The candle flew from his hand and landed on the floor under the curtains next to the door, immediately catching them on fire.

The shadow on the porch stood for a second, watching Johnston squirm on the floor. Gathering itself, it spit on Johnston and then moved quickly to the left and disappeared around the corner.

A cowpoke in the bunkhouse across the yard came out to relieve himself when he saw the flames growing inside the main house.

TWENTY TWO

"The train should be here in a few minutes." Ned looked at his watch and then put it back in his pocket.

There were seven people on the platform waiting for the three o'clock afternoon west to Los Angeles. One was a salesman going to find new markets and four were there to see off Evan and Emily.

"You know Marshal, you could stay. This territory could always use a man with your...uh talents." Ulysses put out his big paw and shook hands with Evan.

"Oh, I think this territory will be in good hands, *Sheriff*," he turned to Chvonne, "you take care of this man. He's a good one. By the way, he wants a passel of kids." Evan smiled as he leaned in and gave her a kiss above the scar running down her cheek.

Emily gave a huge hug to Mrs. Mclaughlin. "You stay strong, now. Fight for what is yours."

Ned piped in, "Oh I think that will be easier now. Lucias Johnston is said to be on his death bed. They say he is fighting for his life, but maybe only has only a few more days. Pretty mysterious... someone snuck up and stabbed him. With his house burning up, they only just barely got his family out."

Evan stepped over to Mrs. Mclaughlin. For a second he just looked into her face, and then he stepped forward and gave her a hug. He whispered, "We'll always have Mary, thank you."

The train pulled up and with an exhale of smoke and steam came to a stop at the platform.

Evan picked up their one satchel and putting a hand on Emily's back they entered the open door. Turning on the top step, he nodded and touched his fingers to the brim of his hat. He turned away and went down the aisle to sit with Emily, facing west.

After another minute, the train blew its whistle and pulled out from the station. A few seconds later the small group on the platform watched it disappear into the failing sun as it headed west.

The End

There was silence for three seconds and then the whole room erupted in applause, everyone rising to their feet. The lights came on as the curtain went